Review Quotes for *Beneath the Mask*
Uncommon Lords and Ladies, Book One

By V—

… This tale has many twists and turns that ramp up the tension in believable ways. A regency romance to remember.

By J—

… Even if you're not sure if this is your kind of book, if you read the description and feel called to read more, do so. You won't regret it.

By D—

Awesome Regency Romance! … was pleasantly surprised to be sucked into the story and taken for a wild romping good time!

A Country Masquerade

UNCOMMON LORDS AND LADIES

BOOK TWO

Margaret McGaffey Fisk

An ACOA Publication

A Country Masquerade

ISBN-13: 978-1-63139-008-1

Cover created by Patrick Lynn Smith

First Print Edition

Chapter One

ady Barbara Whitfeld stood still as Sarah helped her out of the simple, but elegant, white gown she'd worn to the poetry reading.

She hardly noticed Sarah's efforts, her mind still caught up in the rich tones and lovely words Aubrey St. Vincent had offered in his reading. He'd put the rest of the gentlemen to shame.

"Your mother should not be having you out so late every night," Sarah scolded. "You'll have to sleep well past noon to keep from getting dark circles beneath your eyes, and what then will the young gentlemen say."

Barbara laughed as cloth pooled about her feet. "Sarah, you sound like a woman twice your age. You know full well you'd have been happy at my side. You're just jealous." She stepped free and sat at the dressing table.

Her best friend and maid softened enough to smile. "Jealous of what? Listening to conceited men talking about lines on paper? I think you're mistaken."

"Ah, but what lines. To hear them read aloud makes such a difference. Resonate tones, elocution … it makes the poems come alive, I tell you."

Sarah released the last of the pins holding back Barbara's riot of dark brown curls and ran her fingers through to loosen them further. "He was there, then, was he?"

Barbara raised both hands to cover her cheeks, but from Sarah's knowing glance reflected in the mirror, she knew she'd failed to hide her response. She shrugged as though it were of no consequence, then a grin burst out across her lips. "Aubrey St. Vincent. A better specimen of the male breed I've yet to see. Handsome, reasoned, and kind. The perfect gentleman."

"You'd have me believe him a paragon of virtues. The only man to meet such a standard is one still in the cradle, and even then they're all about demanding attention." Sarah laid a heavy stroke through Barbara's hair, and it caught on a tangle.

"Not so rough," Barbara cried. "And he is all that and more." She raised a hand to count off on her fingers. "He escorts his youngest sister to all manner of gatherings when other young men are off seeking their own pleasures. He doesn't retire to the card room the moment they arrive at an event. He's willing to participate when asked like tonight, though he had no plans to read. One of the readers fell ill and could not attend. Then there's how he considers education in philosophy something even women should be able to strive for."

"Enough, enough," Sarah wailed, both hands pressed to her ears though the twinkle in her eyes belied her protests. "You've made quite a study of the man, but I've heard it all before. You marked him as your interest at the very start of the season. So tell me, did you speak with him this time?"

All confidence drained from Barbara as she stared at her twisting fingers, no longer raised to count his worth. She'd encountered Aubrey on her first outing when, sitting against the wall unnoticed, she'd overheard him discussing how unsettled the Continent was. His conversation attracted her attention when the other young men spoke only of fashion and horses.

Since then, his presence acted like a beacon, calling out to her. She did what she could to be within earshot, and if she succeeded, almost every time she learned something new or had a thought to ponder. Still, she'd never spoken a single word to the man.

Sarah tucked a curl back behind Barbara's ear. "Your mother would be happy to arrange an introduction, I'm sure. He's a man of good standing, from a good family, and with a title of his own free and clear since he has only sisters. An earl, he'll be."

Barbara pulled away and rose, though what she intended once upright, she had no idea. "I've seen the way mothers bring their daughters up to meet him. He's surrounded by them too often for me to miss. I can't come to him as just another young lady in white and expect him to notice."

"Don't you think that way," Sarah said, rushing to catch her arm. "You meet with him proper, Barbara, or you'll do nothing but make yourself out to be a fool, especially when the man in question shows no sign of returning your regard. But then, how could he share your interest when you've avoided the chance for an introduction. You want to stand out from the rest. That's how to do it. Get your introduction and show Lord Aubrey you can put more than two sentences together without dissolving into cloying giggles."

They shared a significant look, remembering the afternoon party Lady Whitfeld had arranged shortly after Barbara's presentation. Sarah had assisted the staff and so suffered the same babble and attempts to preen Barbara had. A bunch of ninnies with nothing of consequence between their ears, and her mother wanted her to find bosom friends among them.

Barbara had Sarah for her companion. None of them had offered an adequate substitute.

Her mirth faded as she addressed the flaw in her approach. "But what if I do? What if, when faced with none other than the most perfect Aubrey St. Vincent, my tongue curls up in my mouth and my mind vanishes into the clouds. Sarah, how can I be sure of the impression I'll give. You've heard my mother often enough. She says first impressions are the most important as they form the foundation of everything going forward. I cannot chance this going astray."

Sarah shook her head, but when she met Barbara's gaze, her own held sympathy. "Better to take that risk than never to chance at all. Trust yourself enough. You've certainly studied his habits, read whatever you heard him mention, and even plagued your father about the questions you didn't understand. You've prepared for this moment better than most gentleman study for their examinations. Besides, how could he not be taken in by your combination of beauty and thought? If he isn't, then he's not the paragon you seem to think him either."

Barbara laughed at Sarah's stout support, but knew she'd be hard pressed to put her friend's advice into effect when faced with the gentleman in question.

"Just promise me you'll try nothing foolish. Tradition has set these ways for presentation to society, and it's because they prove worthwhile. Hatching some crazy plan will only bring you trouble."

Barbara turned away more to hide her smile than because she disagreed. "You're sounding old enough to be my mother again, Sarah. Not so long ago, you were happy to join me in whatever adventures I could concoct."

She climbed into bed, pulling the covers up under her chin so she could peek out at her friend.

Sarah paused in collecting the discarded clothing. "Fair enough," she said, her gaze on a distance place, "But that was when you were at your father's country estate, or your uncle's farm, not here in London. You're not to run wild. It will do you a disservice and break your mother's heart. If sounding old is how I must be to keep you from trouble, then I'll turn the hag rather than see you receive a reputation you cannot recover from."

Barbara sank lower, no longer playing as she accepted the somber warning. London did have its own standards, and gossip ran rampant. She'd taken many months to adjust when brought up from the country a few years ago, and even now found its strictures confining.

"Besides," Sarah added with a rich chuckle, "If you fail to catch in your season, you'll be left to live out your days under your mother's thumb, which means I will too. That's a sorry end neither of us would prefer."

Though her mother little deserved such a slight, and well Sarah knew it, Barbara appreciated the effort to lighten her mood. She waved her friend off with a smile. "Then I'd best catch some sleep or those black circles will come whether you will them or not."

Arms full with soiled clothing, Sarah paused in the doorway. "I'll bring you a cup of chamomile tea. That will send you into a deep, soothing rest."

Her friend didn't wait for Barbara to answer, and from the yawn that split Barbara's face, she suspected sleep would overtake her long before Sarah returned. At least the tea would not go to waste, and Sarah needed the rest as much as any what with having to manage Barbara's complicated wardrobe now that she'd been presented.

Thoughts full of balls, readings, and theater, Barbara sank into oblivion. At least in her dreams, she could amaze Aubrey with her wit and wisdom.

Chapter Two

Aubrey took a sip of punch from the cup in his hand and let the drink soothe his throat. A pity it couldn't quiet the cacophony around him.

"You've done me quite the favor," Jasper said with a lopsided grin as he waved toward his mother's ballroom floor and the bevy of young ladies vying for attention. "I thought myself beyond all this now that I'm a happily married man."

"And to think you once believed your mother and wife could split the confines of London with you and none would suffer for it."

His friend gave a deep laugh that yet held a level of content Aubrey would never have expected to hear from him.

"How is the Lady Pendleton faring at your country estate, anyhow? I've seen so little of you since your wedding, I half thought to run out there myself and make sure she hadn't confined you to the cellars."

"Counting the minutes until I return to her side, or so I hope she is based on my own preoccupation. A better match I could not have found had I searched the length and breadth of England for a score of years." He clapped Aubrey on the shoulder. "We used to mutter about the trap of marriage, but those were the words of ignorance, I promise you."

Aubrey brushed Jasper's hand from his shoulder. "Speak for yourself, old man. I was never one to mourn it."

"True enough. And how goes your search for the perfect mate? Should you tire of the effort, you're welcome to take a rest at my home. Daphne and I would be glad to see you."

"Growing weary of each other's company so soon? Why, there's not a year gone by since you bound your lives together." He glanced out at the gathering as he spoke, a longing fierce as a stab in the gut overtaking him. Since his friend confessed the truth of their love, with Daphne's permission, he saw Jasper's transformation into the happy groom in a different light, and one he envied. He'd been seeking the woman created just for him for more than a year now, but his best friend tripped over Daphne without any effort while Aubrey was left searching.

From the expression on Jasper's face, his friend had made some comment requiring an answer but Aubrey had not the faintest idea what it might be.

"Just look at them," he muttered, revealing the cause of his distraction. "There's not a level head or a serious thought among them. I have no idea why your mother would seek them out when she has no daughter to cast among them. She always was one for parties, though."

"And matchmaking. Don't forget how she likes to keep her hand in even now. She was considering who might serve for you just this morning. My mother knows the bloodline, habits, and secrets of every single soul who graces that floor out there, and many more as well. You'd do worse than let her give you a hand. She says Whitfeld's daughter has shown some potential."

That drew Aubrey's attention from the dancers and his own morose thoughts. "Your mother wouldn't know a good match if it lit a fire beneath her skirts. You forget in your wedded bliss that had your mother had her way, you'd have been tied to a wife who thought of piety more than convention and spent her time among the poor. Had fate not intervened, you'd be crying for me to give you a good excuse to avoid services every day of the week when Sunday proved too little worship for her liking." He nodded toward where the Dowager Lady Pendleton held court. "Your mother lines up lists in her head that hold only titles and wealth as well you know."

Jasper lifted both hands, almost spilling his drink in the process. "Enough, enough. I surrender the point. She might not understand the workings of a young man's heart, but at least she knows more than you can have gathered standing here in the shadows. She talks to the girls, and to their mothers. Can you say the same?"

"You never had to ride the horse to know its value," Aubrey said with more force than he'd intended. "I've been chaperoning Isabella for weeks now as my mother recovers from being ill, though I'm starting to think she malingers just to avoid the clash of so many trying to speak inanities in rooms with more echoes than a mountain range. If not for the music, I'd swear I'd woken to find myself trapped in a flock of geese. If there's an intelligent mind out there, it's growing duller by the moment, beaten into submission by talk of weather and fashion."

Jasper sent Aubrey a raised eyebrow at that, and Aubrey softened enough to laugh, his outfit a match to any on the dance floor.

"True enough," he said in answer to the unspoken criticism. "But just because I keep to the fashion doesn't mean I need to discuss it every waking moment."

Aubrey heaved a great sigh. "It's been a sorry London without you in it, my friend. I'd had hopes at first you'd leave your wife and return to keep me company, but you thoroughly dashed them when you told me the truth. I'm left adrift with no one to spar against unless you count greybeards. Any younger who are mature enough to consider more than how many folds it takes to form the latest cravat are busy with wives and children."

With a shake of his head, Jasper murmured, "You poor, bedeviled man. Surrounded by young, fertile, beautiful women all eager to accept a dance, and you find no conversation to be had."

The mischief in his eyes undercut his attempt at sympathy. Instead, he punched Aubrey on the shoulder. "You should be out there dancing, not lingering here with the married men and older women. You'll not find the lady to match you without taking a step toward them. One might think you afraid the way you cling to the shadows. They're just girls. Nothing to fear."

Aubrey rubbed his arm and gave Jasper a frown with more weight than his friend's expression had held. "If I fear for anything, it's for my sanity. You think I came to this position by chance? Point me out this Whitfeld girl your mother thinks would make a good match. I dare you to mark her in this crowd. If she has anything to distinguish her, let that guide you. But once you realize they're all cut from the same cloth with no distinguishing feature beyond who is bold and frivolous, or shy and frivolous, can you please let it rest. I hear enough of this from my mother and sisters to hold me in good stead. With you, I expect more, though maybe Daphne has drawn the wit from your tongue as much as the cynic from your heart. My coin rests on this girl being the worst of the lot if your mother's past ventures are any measure of her understanding."

This time the serious expression on his friend's visage held nothing of mockery as he laid a heavy hand on Aubrey's shoulder. "You're right. I have no cause to challenge you in your search. You know how little my own efforts had to do with my success better than most. I'm only in London for a short while, and here I've dragged you to a debutante party just so I didn't have to suffer it on my own. What say we head down to White's instead? There we'll find your greybeards and likely a conversation or two with more meaning than the words exchanged between movements."

"You forget I'd have been here whether you needed the company or not. I can't very well abandon my sister, and this late in the day, the conversations will be dulled by the spirits already consumed."

"Better that than here among the geese as you so carefully described them. Come with me. My mother will be delighted to take over as chaperone, and can send your sister home in state when the last dance has come to a close. I'll even divert any attempt to introduce you to the Whitfeld girl as my penance. As of this moment, I swear to provide you an environment free of debutantes, especially those who want to bend your ear about fashion and weather."

Remembering just how easily Jasper could talk him into trouble, still Aubrey found himself agreeing. Surely The Dowager Lady Pendleton would make a suitable substitute, and if she could steer Isabella toward some compatible gentlemen, maybe the endless round of events would cease. With his other two sisters already married, she remained the last to secure her future.

The thought held less joy than might have been expected from his sour words earlier, but his mood had little to do with the goal of these events and much to do with his own failure to find a young lady he'd be willing to spend an afternoon with, much less his whole life. Should Isabella choose a suitor, his mother's full attention would turn to his unhappy bachelor state.

arbara struggled to restrain herself as she fought the need to leap up and tell Aubrey just what she thought of him now.

Sarah had spoken truly when she called out Barbara's description of him as fantasy.

She'd grown tired of the constant rounds and dances, and settled here only moments before when she noticed Aubrey in deep discussion. Never had she imagined they'd be discussing her very own self.

All this time, Barbara had been so worried she'd come across as tongue-tied when introduced and spoil that delicate first impression. She shouldn't have worried at all. He didn't even need to meet her to judge her unworthy.

Fuming, she glared as two men made their way across the room to speak with their hostess, and the woman who'd birthed this stranger from what Barbara had overheard. She remembered her mother mentioning some manner of upset regarding the man and his marriage bed, but he seemed well enough set up now, unlike her Aubrey.

No, Barbara thought, *not her Aubrey*. She had no intention of tying herself to such an arrogant bore. All his talk of the female spirit, and this was how he truly viewed them. His every virtue proved to be little more than a show, and he called her frivolous.

The glare she sent to his back should have melted the fine-cut jacket if there were any justice in the world. But for that to happen, he had to care for her opinions. He clearly did not. He saw her as nothing more than a goose among a flock of same, with — what had he said? — nothing to distinguish her.

Rage welled up enough to make the room uncomfortably warm,

and she sprang to her feet, unable to sit a moment longer. She scanned the room until she caught the eye of a young viscount she'd been introduced to earlier.

He flushed at her bold gaze, but it did not deter him from coming over to claim her hand.

Barbara barely noticed him though, as she saw Aubrey headed for the door. She laughed aloud, though whether the viscount said a word that could have been entertaining, she hadn't a clue. No, she only wanted Aubrey to see her, to distinguish her from the rest as the most frivolous of all. So he'd judged her, so she would prove to be.

Though the target of her anger left with barely a glance in the direction of the dancers, anger fueled Barbara through the rest of the night. She smiled, laughed, and danced until her feet ached almost more than her tattered heart.

How could she have missed the truth in her careful study of the man? How could she not have seen how arrogance overcame wit, how rather than being helpful, he sought only to raise his own importance?

She had no more answers when her mother called for their carriage than she'd possessed upon her discovery, but the seeds of her anger had blossomed into what could only be hatred.

"Barbara, my dear, I'd never have thought it of you, but tonight you were the belle of the ball. Take care not to crowd out all the other girls, but it warms my heart to see you taking a true interest in your coming out. Here I thought you scornful of the whole event. Beyond the readings, you seemed more interested in talking politics with your father." She gave a delicate shudder. "And yet you proved me wrong. Lady Pendleton knows how to provide a ball for the society papers, and you're sure to have a mention or two. Why, I wouldn't be surprised if the Viscount Charleston doesn't send round for permission, and he's not the only one."

Pressing a hand to her temples, Barbara stared into the inky darkness beyond the carriage window. She couldn't remember which of the many gentlemen to share her dance card had been Charleston, but it didn't matter much. None of them had distinguished themselves any more than Aubrey saw among the young ladies.

"Just remember you promised the choice would be mine to make," Barbara said, cutting through another enthusiastic accounting.

"Yes, yes. Though why we agreed still baffles me. Your father ought to know well enough by now the risks of giving you your head. Still, with your beauty to counter how you overthink every blessed thing, perhaps it's best to hold out for the most promising offer. It's not as though you'll be limited to the one, what with how engaging you were this night."

She reached out to stroke a hand down one of the curls Sarah had left free when tending to Barbara's hair, as though beauty held more value than any other feature. And perhaps in this lifetime, she had the right of it, for surely no one judged Barbara for her words.

Just yesterday evening, this conversation would have amused Barbara to no end, having already chosen the one offer she'd accept no matter who else came calling. Now she had little reason to hold her parents to their word, a promise extracted after she'd heard Aubrey speak out against the dismissal of all female persons.

He'd been mocked by his fellows as having been raised in a female-infested environment, but he'd held firm. She could only wonder at his purpose now that she knew his true nature. Had he known she sat listening? And if he had, it seemed brutally clear he'd seen only the curls her mother loved so much and not the person hidden beneath them.

Barbara straightened her spine and forced her gaze to where her mother sat at her side. "I suspect I've begun anew, Mother. No more will I seek after those who show false wit and modesty. Why confine myself when there are so many willing to court my pleasant features? The season has just begun for me, though it's already half over."

Her mother had the foresight to look a little perturbed at Barbara's announcement, but then how could she protest when this had been what she'd wanted from the start? She had no need to know what motivated Barbara's change, nor would she ever find out. Not a single person would know of the burning ache having taken up residence in Barbara's chest, an ache born not of action but of lost chances and false appearances. The man she'd thought Aubrey to be had clearly never existed anywhere beyond her very own head.

She would neither settle for someone of lesser stature, nor sit on the sidelines as she waited for this paragon to appear. Sarah had been right all along. Had she studied less and procured an introduction sooner, she would have learned his true nature before he weaseled his way into her heart. She would not make that mistake again. Perhaps the gentlemen she'd danced with this night had little to distinguish themselves, but unlike Aubrey, she had no intention of judging them unfairly. She would make a point of speaking to every single one of them before she decided who would have the pleasure — nay, privilege — of joining his life to her own.

Chapter Three

Barbara let her gaze wander around the room, trying not to look for the one man she hoped never to see again.

The drawing room had been made over into a small theater, rows of chairs facing a dais where select members would read poetry and perhaps the hostess would convince her daughter to play a tune on the pianoforte.

Just a few days earlier, Barbara would have looked forward to such an event, hoping to learn of a poet she had yet to encounter, yes, but also on the off chance she could let Aubrey's deep tones pull her into the world of imagination.

Now, though she would not admit this to anyone — not even Sarah — she grew tired of the round of parties, balls, poetry readings, and the like. Everyone seemed too lively, and her the worst of all as she played for an audience that had yet to make an appearance.

"It's so easy for you," the girl seated to her right said, placing a hand on Barbara's arm. "With such rich curls and smooth skin, why you have every gentleman in London at your feet without even trying."

Barbara gave the girl a faint smile, knowing any attempt to explain how her beauty offered more obstacle than support would fail. She wracked her memory for the girl's name along with a topic her mother would consider appropriate.

As much as she hated to admit it, she'd had the same disparaging thoughts about the other debutantes as Aubrey proclaimed, but having felt the pain of them, she was determined never to fall into such a trap again. She would not put herself above these poor girls who most likely had no chance to learn better. Not every father allowed his female children into the library, and often even then, they'd be steered to books of less consequence as their mothers were sure to command what would be acceptable for their young minds.

She forgot herself enough to let out a sigh, recognizing the offense too late to repair it.

Hannah — Barbara finally remembered — visibly withdrew into herself, her pasty complexion blooming with a red that would have been attractive had it not grown in unsightly patches.

"I didn't mean to presume," Hannah muttered, turning away and twisting her hands together.

"Oh, please, it's I who must apologize. I fear I've had too little sleep of late to be much company. My mother is determined to make the most of the season, and I find it wearying."

Hannah turned back with a shy smile. "Don't let anyone else hear you say that or people will start to question your stamina, though how they could with the way you take command of the dance floor, I know not. Some of the girls thought a duel would break out over the last spot on your card the other night."

Barbara ducked her head even as she remembered the contest of words that almost had her hand the card over for them to share so she could just go home.

She laughed; she danced; she made pretty conversation.

Her mother had been nothing but encouraging and delighted to see Barbara making an effort at last. Talk around the table tossed out titles as though they were nothing less than diamonds. Word had it a duke had expressed interest even. That information made her ever more grateful for the promise she'd extracted. He was sixty if a day, and gout kept him from the dance floor or any other activity beyond gossiping about his fellows, but apparently she'd caught his eye from the sidelines.

There'd been a time when the attention might have lightened her spirits, though better if she felt any of them saw beyond the pretty wrapping to the person below. But the marriage mart offered little chance for a true meeting of minds. The lucky girls were able to present their accomplishments in gatherings such as these, but accomplishments had little to do with thought. Stitching, music, dance. These were the signs of a proper upbringing, not reading or considerations of politics and law.

She barely managed to suppress another offending sigh when Hannah grabbed her arm with a grip strong enough to bruise.

"Look. There he is. I do so hope he'll be reading tonight. His voice makes a shiver run down my spine."

Barbara knew in her gut just whom she'd see when she turned, but no matter how much she told herself not to look, her gaze fell on none other than Aubrey St. Vincent, resplendent in his coat and trousers. Her heart gave a jump before she remembered just how little the man thought of her, or rather that he thought her to be so little.

She shifted in her seat so he would not be within her vision and sought another topic of conversation, but Hannah would not be persuaded to turn aside.

"There goes young Emily. She's much too precocious by half. She pretends to like his sister, Isabella, but she hardly gave the girl a nod when her mother was escorting her about. We're not fooled, are we, Barbara? She's set her cap for Lord Aubrey St. Vincent and will do whatever she can to catch his attention. It's deplorable."

Barbara needed neither to agree nor disagree. The words were clearly quoted from someone, most likely Hannah's mother, or perhaps her older sister with the lack of the title. The young girl's expression held more of longing than contempt.

"He's not worth your consideration."

That got Hannah's attention if only for a quick glance. "How can you say that? To claim he's kind on the eyes is understating the truth, his voice is a dream, and I've heard tell he even spoke on letting women into Oxford. Imagine that. Not something I would ever aspire to, but it certainly offers proof of his preferential gaze on the female sort, don't you think? Not to mention he's heir to the Earl."

Not wanting to explain how she'd come by her reluctance, Barbara gave a slight shrug. "It would appear so. It's not always the case that appearances are truth is all I meant. And you want to be cautious."

Hannah turned to her then with a frown. "Not all of us have so many vying for our least attention that we can afford to be cautious as you say. Besides, it does no harm at all to dream. I have as little chance as Lady Emily even were I to mirror her actions and throw myself at his feet."

The fierce words gave Barbara pause, showing as they did a much deeper consideration than any conversation they'd exchanged so far. "Don't be so quick to measure yourself wanting, Hannah. There is someone out there for you who will look askance at all others only to settle his gaze upon you and never turn away."

As though the serious moment had never occurred, Hannah colored once again. "You truly think so?"

Ignoring her own predicament, Barbara gave a firm nod. "I truly think so."

And thinking so had gotten her into this trouble in the first place. She'd been so sure Aubrey held that place only to discover him a wolf in sheep's clothing. He'd seemed so serious and constrained, but he had only been so for lack of a companion. Married or not, Lord Pendleton seemed just as happy to spend his time wasting coin at the card tables and drinking himself into a stupor with Aubrey at his side. He'd said so himself.

"What is it? You look so cross."

Barbara hadn't realized how easily her gaze sought out the source of her thoughts. Not Lord Pendleton rather, but Aubrey St. Vincent. The man had taught her how little she could trust the male half of the species to be what it seemed. She should be grateful for the education, but her aching heart left little room for gratitude.

"It's nothing. Something I remembered from earlier." She dismissed the moment with a wave of her hand, but could not wipe it from her mind as easily as she had from Hannah's.

The others gathered round and settled into chairs, a hush falling over the room as the first reader stepped to the front.

Despite herself, Barbara couldn't help comparing his stance to that of Aubrey, how his shoulders seemed less broad, his leg less toned, but worst of all was the nasal quality to his voice that made the most eloquent of lines seem overdone. The man who followed him had a deep enough voice, but the wind whistled through his teeth with every fourth word, turning the poem into a hissing contest between snakes until she wanted to beg him to choose something less ridden with any letter sending his tongue to curl against his side teeth.

Her head started to ache before the third reader, and though she knew herself to be less than fair to any of them, she could not stop how her thoughts measured each against the one performance she had grown to look forward to. The situation only worsened when Aubrey himself took the raised step with a bound and gave the gathered members of the ton a smile sure to melt the hearts of any woman old enough to care and not yet in her grave.

Barbara squinted to make him seem less appealing and scowled at him from her seat, fully aware he would not have acknowledged her even had she been sitting in the very front. Admiring or embittered, she was beneath his notice and so might as well have not existed at all.

"Our hostess has graciously asked me to stand in a round. How could I object when she has provided this lovely event for us?"

His deep tones threatened to melt her heart as well until she remembered his own words belittling and dismissing these events. How he'd longed for his mother to regain her strength and take these chores off his hands. He presented a pretty demeanor to match his handsome visage, but both were no more than varnish over chipped and cracked porcelain.

She slumped down in her seat as far as the rigid piece in her corset would allow and prayed for the sky to fall so she could leave this company and suffer his presence no more.

God had bigger things on his mind, though, and despite her head pounding so hard she wondered if she'd fallen ill, the evening dragged on even once Aubrey stepped down, though not for long. Lady Emily was the next to beg his favor, asking him to turn her music as she entertained them all from the pianoforte.

Once again, courtesy demanded Barbara give her full attention to a vision including the one man she wished would drop off the Dover cliffs and so she suffered it. Even had she wanted to beg off, she had no intention of explaining the situation to her mother. Enduring soothing words and avoiding attempts to procure a proper introduction so she could prove her worth when his had been the one found wanting would do little to ease her head or the aching of her heart.

"Ah, there you are," Jasper declared as Aubrey's butler ushered him into the study. "I half expected you to be at an afternoon tea or perhaps squiring your sister around the gardens."

Aubrey pushed back from his desk and rubbed a hand down his face as he looked on his friend. "And here I thought you came into town because you had business to conduct. Feeling neglected?"

Jasper sank into the plump chair to one side of the desk. "I'll admit I'd hoped to claim more of your time myself, but you're right. I did come on business. I'm engaging an engineer to repair the mill. Well, that and to help a local gentleman farmer spread word about his new breeding stock."

"Sheep?"

"Horses. He's been dabbling in horse breeding for years now, with a few moderate successes, but the latest two-year-olds are remarkable. Enough to make a name for himself if word gets around."

Aubrey slapped his hands to his knees and laughed. "Who would have imagined the two of us would turn respectable. You worrying about breeding stock, and I've taken over much of the estate management so my father can focus on politics. We've come a bit away from betting on carriage races through the streets of London, not that either of us had so little on our minds even then."

Jasper straightened from his slouch to say, "Love of a good woman will ground a man, though I'm not sure I can credit my Daphne with anything but a need to move to the country until the rumors died down. I wasn't expecting to find it so appealing, to be honest, but there's something bracing about the fresh air, and I have good relations with my neighbors. Much less parading about, that's for sure."

"How is Daphne finding it?"

Jasper barked a laugh. "She was made for the country. Her father had only brought the two girls to town a year or two before I crossed paths with Daphne. My lady love has a bit of the wild in her. Much better suited for the country for all she'd find more young ladies for her dance school here than there."

Aubrey rose to pour the two of them a light sherry. "So she is teaching?" he asked as he handed over one glass and returned to his seat.

"She's canvasing the local area for suitable young ladies and training the staff while she's waiting for the right moment to make the offer. You have a fondness for elevated events. You should see our dinners. Often as not, the serving platters are delivered with a flourish or a spin."

"I can just imagine, but I suppose she must keep herself busy somehow. If you think your life has changed, take a moment to consider hers. At least you perform many of the same tasks. London is still talking about her, wondering where the masked dancer went and when she'll be back."

Jasper stiffened at the mention. "Never."

Aubrey waved a hand as though to dispel the sudden tension. "Of course. I didn't mean to say she would. I doubt she'd return to that life now even if you chose to step out of her way. She did it when she thought she had nothing to lose. Your reputation and hers are in the balance. The woman loves you more deeply than any other I've seen." He stifled a sigh, thoughts drawn to his own fruitless search for such a match.

"You were always the confident one, Aubrey. Don't let your faith be shaken now. If I can find a match, surely you can, especially with all the events you're attending."

Aubrey let the sherry swirl around on his tongue for a moment before answering. "I haven't the chance to find a true match what with pushy females and their mothers trying to catch my eye. I don't so much mind the events as you know, though last night I was called upon to attend one young woman who has been nothing but persistent in her pursuit. You know as well as I do they have tallies to measure a man's worth, tallies that mark only titles, the heft of the purse, and pleasant features, with the last holding the least weight."

Jasper leaned forward, his eyes twinkling with mirth. "And you want to be considered for your good looks alone? Why I haven't been gone a year and you've turned vain."

With a shake of his head that didn't quite mask the slight smile his friend's words provoked, Aubrey dismissed the charge. "I'd rather be measured for who I am than for any of the items in their considerations. The readings are fine, and you know I favor theater, but the balls are nothing but disappointments. The purpose there is to see and be seen, as though a glimpse is all it would take to see through to a person's soul."

"You could always take them riding in your carriage. There'd be time to delve into their thoughts then."

Aubrey could not prevent the shudder that overtook him. "Thank you but no. That long in the company of some gentle lady whose thoughts are filled with fashion and the latest gossip. Better you had me scheduled for a stay in Bedlam. Or is it that you plan to drive me there yourself."

Jasper rose to clap Aubrey on the shoulder. "Buck up, my friend. It can't be as bad as all that. And if it is, the offer to come for an extended stay is always open. My manor is large enough to keep you in peace and quiet, though I can't guarantee none of the local gentry will bring their daughters round for a meeting."

"I may just have to take you up on that kind offer once my mother's feeling better. You can show me this piece of horseflesh you seem to find so dashing as an excuse should my mother protest."

"Surely she wouldn't, not after how you've stepped in to keep your sister's season as active as it could possibly be. Your mother must be feeling up to the task now if you're here and not running about after Isabella."

Aubrey brushed the papers scattered across the polished surface before him. "I had some work to catch up on what with maintaining Isabella's heavy social schedule, but you're not far off. The household, my mother included, is resting up for a night out at the theater. You're welcome to join us. I can't promise an act to approach that of your lady wife, but there's a play I've yet to see that's been receiving good word. And at least there I'll be safe from the attempts to secure my fortune, my title, and even my person."

"But not your heart. I do understand now, Aubrey. I needed to find my match to see you as anything less than a hopeless romantic. There's nothing for it but to keep looking. The journey might be arduous, but the reward is worth every step."

Aubrey stared at his friend for a long while, assessing the happiness mixed in with Jasper's ever-present confidence, or rather the confidence he'd seen slip only rarely. "I never thought to hear you say such a thing."

"Nor I, but I'd like to think I always had it in me to learn, and now I have the best of teachers."

"Daphne?"

"Her, and my own heart. It's a wondrous organ I'd much neglected in my early years."

Aubrey shrugged. "It's not like you had much of an example to base upon. My parents want nothing less than a joyful match for each of their children, one to rival their own. I just wish they wouldn't try quite so hard to bring it about."

Jasper laughed as he ran a finger along Aubrey's book collection before pulling forth a volume of poems that caught his eye. "So what you're saying is your mother's illness, though requiring so much of you, came at an opportune time?"

The thought had not occurred before, busy as he'd been rushing around after his youngest sister, but now Aubrey froze as it struck him. "You see the truth for what it is, my friend, whether it's measuring a horse race or my own predicament. At least she returns to society through a dramatic event. I'll have one day's rest before the parade of possibles begins once again."

Jasper thrust the volume back in place and turned with a sour look. "You weigh your mother's determination too light. Even with theater, there's the intermission to consider, and I wouldn't put it past her to have seeded the box with a prospect or two."

Aubrey groaned, wishing he could deny what Jasper had brought to mind and knowing he could not. "I beg of you. Come with me. I'll sit in the farthest corner with you between me and any other. You're a happily married man and so beneath their notice."

"Only if you promise to come for a visit. Daphne and I miss the company, though it seems your need outweighs ours. Still, you might try conversing with them. You never know what there is to discover hidden under their masks of propriety."

Aubrey shook his head with a smile. "I doubt London is big enough for two like your Daphne, and I fear she's solidly taken. If you promise to discourage any attempt at inane converse so I can simply enjoy the play, I will agree to come for that visit as soon as my mother is able to resume her duties."

"Is visiting such a hardship that you must bargain for terms?" Jasper shook his head to deny the need for an answer. "Your dedication to your sister is admirable."

If any understood the pressures of family and responsibility, it would be Jasper, though his story came to a satisfactory conclusion while Aubrey had no such hope for his own.

"It's exhausting, but your company will help make it less so."

"Then for your sake, I'll agree to this outing. I came to tell you I planned to head back to the manor come morning. A night at the theater seems a proper sending off."

Aubrey laughed. "I doubt you'll be leaving before afternoon with how late the night will run. You'll suffer an adjustment back to country hours once you reach home.

"An early bedtime is quite welcome with Daphne to share the space." Jasper grinned. "Someday you'll understand that truth as well."

Clapping his friend on the shoulder, Aubrey said, "It doesn't seem to have had that effect on my parents. Late nights and later mornings is as much the rule among the married as those Londoners still in their wilder years."

Jasper only shook his head, a country man now for all he'd been the toast of the town a bare year earlier.

Chapter Four

Barbara entered the ballroom only half watching where she put her feet as she scanned for the man she dreaded seeing, and yet every event seemed somehow flat when he failed to put in an appearance.

Two weeks had passed since she'd learned his true nature, and for one of those, his friend, Lord Pendleton, had been absent.

Though she no longer sought him out, Barbara had watched Aubrey smile and pass the time with women of all ages. She'd caught the edge of some of his conversations, and even had the twisted pleasure of hearing him read from a new play the other night.

How easy it would be to fall under his spell again, to accept the smiles and quiet conversation as a sign of his true measure.

Her gaze brushed his firm shoulders as she found him standing over to one side.

She turned away abruptly, missing the servant offering a tray of delicate nibbles to the guests by a sliver of air. One more charge to lay at his feet, and once more he remained ignorant of his tampering in her life.

No amount of pretty curls would save her the mockery to follow if she upset a food tray all over her white muslin with half the ton watching.

Lady Emily had already gone to him, ignoring poor Isabella as usual.

Barbara suffered a rush of sympathy for the poor girl always in her brother's shadow, but no matter how much she might want to intervene, she would not, could not, make polite conversation with

Isabella's devil of a brother and keep her composure. They might all be fooled, taken in by a handsome face and good manners, but she'd seen what hid beneath. It held more brimstone than roses.

"My mother says not to frown as it makes you age all the faster."

Barbara turned to greet Hannah, trying to wipe the scowl from her face. She'd planned to show him just how lively she could be. Her efforts would come to naught if she wasted time glaring at the one who'd yet to encounter her directly.

She had barons, viscounts like her father, and even a duke asking after her. Aubrey St. Vincent was no more than another face in the crowd and one of little consequence.

Forcing her mind away from the object of her ire, Barbara gave her new friend a glittering smile. Not that they were real friends or anything. They'd spoken only of appropriate topics and had yet to visit beyond crossing paths at events such as these. Still, the thought of someone hoping she would make an appearance, someone other than the vapid suitors who barely stirred her emotions, gave her something to look forward to. The endless events were otherwise wearing. She saw no end in sight, and no answer for those who threatened to come to her door and speak with her father.

Barbara laughed aloud at that thought, enough so she had to wave her hand in dismissal to avoid explaining her thoughts to Hannah who would be unlikely to understand. As she'd chastised that first night at the poetry reading, there were many who would swoon in delight at the suggestion of making a call on one's father. Barbara might swoon, but only if Sarah had tied her corset too tight, something that had begun to be considered a fashion, though not broadly enough to require Barbara adopt the practice.

A marquess who'd attempted to claim a second dance just the night before caught her eye and headed toward them.

She'd barely made her way to the side of their hostess and already the men descended, not a one of them seeing beyond her well-brushed curls.

"Lady Barbara."

She accepted the greeting with a nod, but before he could ask for her dance card, she turned to Hannah and pulled the other girl forward. "Have you had the pleasure of meeting Miss Hannah? She's a wonderful dancer by all accounts. I hear the musicians tuning up to begin the next set. You should take this occasion to enjoy each other's company."

Hannah blossomed with that unfortunate blush of hers, and the marquess looked put out, but Barbara had observed him well enough through her own encounter to know he would avoid appearing the boor.

Sure enough, he offered his hand and led Hannah toward the area set aside for dancing. He made it all of three steps before he paused to call back a request she hold a spot on her card for him.

Barbara gave no response, annoyed he threatened what just might be the high point in Hannah's evening.

Still, the encounter warned her not to dawdle on her way over to the matron presiding over this ball. Her mother had failed to notice when the sight of Aubrey slowed her steps, and then Hannah had intercepted her, leaving Lady Whitfeld to stand near their hostess with a pained expression visible even across the room.

She expected a careful lecture on the importance of following the proper conventions, and then a suggestion that she might, should this unfortunate happenstance occur another time, have invited the marquess along with her rather than foisting him off on another young woman. Barbara felt sure her sharp-eyed mother had missed nothing of the encounter, yet another reason why she must learn to control her features whenever Aubrey came into view.

It would not be wise to give her parents reason to speculate, nor had she any interest in their attempts to rectify what they were sure to see as an unhappy mistake.

Barbara stepped over to her mother's side with a determined walk. They might think her unlucky to have caught the edge of an unflattering conversation, but she saw things quite differently. Had she not been present on that day, when Aubrey had his friend at his side and so could relax the mask he wore over his true self, she would have continued to be as deluded as was Lady Emily. The only difference being that Lady Emily deserved what she found in his company for how she used his sister as an excuse then excluded the poor girl.

Once again, Barbara's attention wandered to where they had been standing last she'd seen them, to check on Isabella of course and for no other reason, but they had moved away. She had no interest in searching the dance floor, or worse, the side chambers to find them.

The gentleman who approached as soon as she'd made her formal greeting introduced himself with her mother's permission as a French aristocrat of late from Paris. She accepted his hand for her first dance, hoping he'd have something more to say in his heavily accented French than most of the gentlemen could offer in their native English.

The conversation should have served as a distraction, but he showed little willingness to dwell on the difficult times facing his country, asking instead after her dressmaker in a unique approach, but one that offered nothing of interest. The time when she'd overheard Aubrey discussing the French Revolution drifted into her mind. He'd considered both the horrors and just how they'd come about rather than condemning the peasantry out of hand as many did. She'd never quite considered the situation in that way before.

Barbara saw no irony in how her attempt to broaden her suitors only brought her firmly back to thoughts of Aubrey St. Vincent. The cursed man never seemed far from her thoughts.

He'd been too much a part of her existence through the beginning of the season and seemed determined to impress himself on the remainder just as heavily.

At least she knew he suffered alongside her, if not for the same reasons. With his friend gone, he had no one with whom he could reveal his true nature. The tension must have been plaguing him.

She only hoped it soon became unbearable and he fled London for quieter climes. Barbara saw little chance of finding someone to warm her heart and tease her mind elsewise with her unable to concentrate on a single word they exchanged with her.

The music ended, but before she could safely ensconce herself at her mother's side, another came to claim her hand. The gentlemen to follow seemed neither to mind nor notice her distraction. If anything, it made her more appealing, a fact that soured her against them each and every one.

Surely London held one man who would not be so swayed by pretty looks that he never saw the person caged within them.

Aubrey listened with half an ear as Lady Emily recounted yet another of her father's stories about his merchant fleet. He'd been intrigued when first introduced some weeks earlier to find a young lady of quality willing to speak of the trade her father plied when his knighthood failed to bring in enough to support his family. Her opinions on the shipping itself made her stand out among the other debutantes.

He'd soon learned what had appeared to be thought had been nothing more than parroting whatever her father spoke of across the table, a predilection that became clear when Aubrey chanced to share a game with the man at White's.

If anything, it showed her to be a dutiful, attentive daughter because she repeated her father's tales almost word for word, qualities some might find more appealing than an economic bent to her mind. The man himself tended to restate the same events more than once if they held any glimmer of interest. Aubrey had soon heard the full round of tales, and as such, could not rely on the entertainment of a new gem coming from the girl's lips either.

He nodded, even offered a smile, as she told of a silk trade gone well, an account that might have brought suitors with pockets to let that closer to point but he managed his father's affairs well enough for the St. Vincents to be quite comfortable. Not that he'd had to dig them out of a disaster as Jasper had done when he took over the full title. Aubrey only kept successful estates doing what they did best.

"And if not for that fortunate storm, the crates of silk would have arrived too late for her ladyship's wedding. Wouldn't that have been a disaster?"

"I doubt the seamen considered a storm to be fortunate. Damage to the ship is costly enough, but lives could have been lost, and most likely were."

The girl pouted, an unsubtle reminder that he was not to question a word of her tales, nor expect her to think beyond the confines of her father's telling. For all she knew, half the crew were swept overboard before the vessel limped the rest of the way into port three days early.

Isabella put a hand on his arm, a reminder of just why he suffered this girl and all the rest. "I'm sure Lady Emily didn't mean to be insensitive, Aubrey. It's just that seamen expect such storms."

The lady in question barely gave Isabella a glance despite the support, further irritating Aubrey.

"Is there anyone you'd like me to introduce you to, Isabella? Mother will call me remiss if she learns you stood to the side all night with nothing but talk of silks to show for your attendance."

His sister cast her gaze on the floor and mutely shook her head, the wasted effort to defend having used up the last of her confidence.

"Come," he said, tucking Isabella's arm through his and offering a nod to Lady Emily in lieu of a farewell. "We'll take a turn around the room and see if we can't find you a gentleman after all who would give you the chance to put your dance instructor's training to good use." Not that she'd had the luck to secure an instructor as talented as Daphne's. Maybe then his sister would be less retiring around those of the masculine gender.

Isabella clung to his arm a little too tightly, but he tried not to let it worry him. If only his mother would be well enough to take over this task. Not that he planned to abandon his youngest sister at the first opportunity. He'd stand steadfast at her side as long as needed. But he felt ill-equipped for navigating the complexities of the marriage mart on the part of a young lady, not that he'd been any more successful on his own behalf. Surely she'd do better under another's tutelage.

They had come to a halt, ostensibly to admire a decorative tree, when Aubrey realized his sister's attention had wandered from the chance of shelter behind the greenery.

Isabella gazed upon the dance floor.

Cursing his inattention, Aubrey followed her look to discover which of the many young men had caught her eye at last, perhaps well enough to ease Isabella's crippling shyness so she could have a successful season after all.

He grunted in annoyance as the path of her gaze led not to a man but to the dark-haired beauty he'd seen holding court at many of these events. The girl never had one man around her but she had four, and he'd heard rumors her admirers almost came to blows on the dance floor over her some weeks past.

The Whitfeld daughter.

They'd never been introduced, nor had he seen her close enough to make her out from the crowd, but she stood in his head as an example of all that was wrong with the seasons and coming out.

Here his sweet, good-natured sister stood against the wall with only her brother for company while men flocked around one woman, dancing attendance in the hopes of being graced with a tale of how she'd purchased the ribbons he could see laced through her curls.

He caught Isabella's arm and turned her away. "Don't trouble yourself. She can only marry one of them, leaving the rest to seek again."

That startled a laugh from Isabella, though she brought up both hands to smother it. Her eyes danced with merriment above her fingers. "As though we weren't all hoping for her cast offs already," she said in a faint voice. "But no, I wasn't looking among her suitors. It's Lady Barbara's confidence and her ability to navigate this arena that draws my gaze. How I wish I were like her."

"Don't," he said with a bit more force than intended. "She's nothing more than a feather hat, all pretty colors and fierce activity. But when you look beneath, it's an old biddy, sour-faced with nothing to say for herself and no care for how those broad feathers poke anyone foolish enough to venture near."

Isabella tapped his arm, her eyes wide with speculation as she studied him. "One might think you hold a grudge against the young lady, brother. Or an inclination. Perhaps we should make our way over to her and get you an introduction."

Aubrey deliberately turned his back on the sight and held up a hand to dissuade his sister. "I have little interest in fighting off her entourage or in encouraging gossip about my affairs. She's proven to be a favorite of the rumor mill already. Besides, it's not this lady so much as those of her ilk. They're much the same. Nothing to say for themselves of any importance and counting on their fine looks to make a good catch while girls with more value than could be found in a single ribbon on that dark head are left unnoticed."

His sister gave him a sad smile. "Don't lay my weakness at her feet, Aubrey. From all I've heard, she'd be as likely to toss one of her flock in my direction as to leave the bunch to attend me. Why, Hannah can speak no wrong of her, and I would have sworn I saw Lady Barbara give over a gentleman to her care earlier this very night."

He shrugged. "It's not as though she cost herself anything. She could give away half her suitors and still have a dozen more than society and Church would allow." Aubrey forced his thoughts to his sister, unwilling to let his opinions sour her for this event. "Who is this Hannah you speak of? Surely you haven't managed to make a new acquaintance with me standing chaperone. I think I would have noticed."

Isabella only shook her head, but let him change the direction of their conversation all the same. "I met her at the tea party Mother held last week. She's getting stronger, don't you think?"

"All too eager to have done with me?" Aubrey asked, grateful to leave Lady Barbara behind when, with every word, Isabella found herself lacking in comparison. "And here I thought I'd acquitted myself well."

Again his sister shook her head side to side, but the sparkle in her eyes showed humor held sway over concern. If only one of the gentlemen had the chance to see her like this. When facing a man outside of her family, she turned to pale stone. Even Jasper, safely married and not part of this infernal contest, drove her behind her fan and twisted her eloquent tongue into incoherent whispers.

"You know full well I'm just happy to see her recovering after such a nasty illness. Be careful or I'll have Mother keep you on through the rest of the season. I know how much you adore parading me around for those few not already partial to another. Or is it all a mask for the truth, which is you standing judgment on those young ladies present as you search for your own to claim? You mock Lady Barbara, but if more of the female kind were like Lady Emily, you'd have your own flock, leaving me pushed to the outside and neglected."

Her teasing comments struck a little too close for comfort. Still, Aubrey had no intention of turning this from her season to his.

Lady Emily might be the bolder, but he'd observed the sideways glances and been introduced by enough eager mothers to confirm his placement in the ranking. He had only to give them the slightest encouragement, and he'd be overwhelmed by those vying for the position of his wife. And not a one among them had the least interest in the man within his fine suit.

"Enough of this talk, or I'll do what Mother has told me to and take you over to the nearest gentleman to force an introduction. She does not hold to letting you control your own way."

Though she recovered quickly, Aubrey had not missed the look of horror on her face even as Isabella quipped, "And that, my dear brother, is why I'm happy to let her gather her strength and keep you at my side instead."

Chapter Five

"Barbara, wake yourself quickly."

She groaned and batted at the hand shaking her shoulder, but Sarah had never been one to give up and this morning proved no different.

"Come, Barbara. Your father has sent for you."

That drove away the last of her weary state, and she pushed herself upright, her covers spilling over one side in a cascade of cloth. "My father?"

She glanced toward the window, expecting to find the sun already sinking past its apex. They'd been to a theatrical extravaganza the previous night that ran far into the wee hours of the morning, but still she hadn't expected to oversleep so grossly.

A faint grey sky greeted her beyond the lace curtains, the product of overcast that masked all but the hint of a globe still at its height.

Sarah, looking all too alert for having stayed up to see Barbara safely into bed, gave a soothing smile. "There's nothing out of place nor reason to worry. Your father just finished with a most promising visitation, and the young gentleman wishes to speak to you."

Bemused, Barbara could only stare at her friend as she tried to gather her thoughts.

Sarah laughed and turned to the wardrobe to choose an appropriate gown for visitors when none of the morning gowns would suit with their unadorned, reclaimed fabric.

The glimpse of a cheeky smile before Sarah turned away offered the telling clue, and Barbara's sleep-addled mind finally caught up with the events at hand. "Who is this caller?" For just one fraction of a moment, her thoughts swung to Aubrey before she dismissed it as an impossibility, and an unwanted one as well.

"How am I to know? I don't wander about among the peerage. You've hardly had time for any activity one such as myself could chaperone of late. He's a handsome one, though, and well-mannered from what I could tell."

Barbara swung her legs free and crossed to give her friend a hug. "You know your company would be as welcome as any had I a choice in the matter. I wish we had more time to spend together."

Sarah shrugged with one shoulder, but the blush tainting her cheek told Barbara she'd read the situation correctly.

"Just you wait until you make your match. Soon you'll have plenty others to keep you busy, that is if your mother even lets me come with you."

A full laugh wiped away any lingering sleepiness despite the short rest.

Suddenly, Barbara felt ready to take on the challenge of the day and her caller who had arrived close to unfashionably early. "As if Mother would try to separate us now. It's not like she succeeded when we were younger, and she'd not risk a falling out with her only daughter."

"It's your father who most threatens me at the moment, Barbara. If I don't get you tidy and down to the morning room quickly, he'll ship me off to the country estate, never to see London again."

Remembering the freedom of the country and pleasures won on childhood visits to her uncle's holdings, Barbara could hardly consider that a punishment. But she could see the thought had her friend flustered. "I'm up, and you're an old hand at making me more than presentable. There's nothing to fear except the purpose for this visit."

Sarah shook her head even as she pulled the underdress over Barbara's shoulders. "As if you had any doubt to his purpose. He might have come earlier than the other two, but he'll have gotten the same speech from your father and now seeks to ply his case with you. Don't wait too long to decide among them, or there will be lines out the front door and down the street."

Barbara helped smooth the next layer of fabric down, annoyed she'd missed the chance to linger in her lighter garments. "There's not a thing to distinguish them beyond land and title. I have well enough of both. My father's estate will go to my children, unlike some entitled only to the male line, and what care I for a shift in my standing."

Threading a ribbon through to tame Barbara's curls in place of a long brushing, Sarah said only, "You'd care if your station lowered through all this."

"At least then I wouldn't be put on show, commanded to parade about for all comers."

The image broke what tension had started to gather, and they laughed together, much too jolly for the hour.

"At least they haven't checked your teeth the way your uncle assesses horses to add to his breeding program."

Barbara snapped her teeth at Sarah and let loose a high whinny even as her friend ushered her out the door, a bright blush painted on both their cheeks. Their lips held smiles to match the sparkle in their eyes.

They passed a mirror and Barbara thought they could be mistaken for sisters out seeking fun as much as mistress and maid.

When they reached the morning room, though, all frivolous thought vanished with the realization of what awaited her.

She may have been misguided in her first choice, but she refused to settle for less than a true match in heart and mind when she had her whole life ahead of her.

Some girls might be willing to marry an old goat knowing he'd soon die off and leave them free to live a life less strangled by convention, but not her.

Barbara might not always agree with her parents, and they'd been known to give each other icy glares on occasion, but with everything that counted, they stood together. She wanted nothing less for her own pairing, though she had little hope of finding it any time soon if the events so far this season proved any indication.

Sarah swung the door wide after a quick rap on the wood in warning, unaware of the turn in Barbara's mood.

The gap revealed a baron with whom she'd danced a few nights previous. He stood out from the others because he had taken a turn around the room with her while the musicians rested. They'd conversed on nothing significant, but some of his observations had amused her.

It could have been a worse selection to begin her day, but she wanted to demand just how he thought he knew her well enough to offer a future between them of companionship much less more.

She restrained her tongue and sat prettily in the chair while her father stood just outside, allowing the baron privacy to make his case, but not enough to compromise her.

Her thoughts wandered as he spoke of his holdings and the connections he'd made at court.

Perhaps those girls seeking an older man had something to their thinking. Convention held her bound in this uncomfortable situation. She could not reject his offer without cause, and the only cause they'd understand would be accepting another. She could only delay the choice.

None of the gentlemen, those who had spoken with her father, or those she'd engaged in conversation or shared a dance with, offered hope of a true bond as far as she could tell.

He caught her hand, and Barbara started at the touch, struggling to draw his name from her memory. She found only a faint impression of their time together, one that failed to give her anything but his title, something he made sure to emphasize at the least occasion, though it were not so high as to be remarkable among her suitors.

"Will you but agree?"

Whatever answer she might have given, Barbara had nothing but supposition to lead her to the question.

Surely he would not press her so quickly on the matter of marriage. He must have proposed some lesser engagement.

Grasping at straws, she chose her answer more from Sarah's loneliness than any hope of it being a direct response to his query. "I'd love a carriage turn through the gardens. I've been so engaged of late some fresh air and a touch of sun will do me good."

His grin confirmed she'd read the situation correctly. "My phaeton is quite elegant and swift. I've a matched pair most envy."

Visions of a ride with Sarah along for company vanished at this description. She could not imagine what they'd find to converse about, nor had Barbara any interest in watching him handle what most likely were a skittish pair through the busy lanes of the garden, but she'd said too much to withdraw with any measure of grace.

"I'll not have my daughter going about in some racing equipment, young man," her father said, leaning in the door. "You will return tomorrow at a reasonable hour and in a sturdy vehicle with space enough for my daughter's maid. For now, I think our repast is ready and have no interest in a meal gone off warm."

The baron apologized all the way to the front door, and Barbara barely restrained the need to hug her father for his rescue.

"A racing phaeton. Just imagine," Lord Whitfeld muttered to himself as he escorted her to the breakfast room, clearly having his own reasons for denying the baron his wish.

For just a heartbeat, she wondered how it would be to have the wind rushing through her hair as they sped down the lane. Convention constrained her from ever finding out, but she'd prefer her own hand on the reins, something so far beyond the pale as to be unimaginable, or should have been.

"Another offer was it?" her mother asked as they joined her for the meal. "And so eager. He must not have been as late at the theater the previous night as we were."

Barbara let her father explain the early engagement as she gathered a selection from the side table. At least she had a carriage ride to look forward to. She had not been dissembling when she said she'd do better for some fresh air.

"That's an impressive list you've gathered, my dear," Lady Whitfeld announced at last, drawing Barbara into the conversation. "A duke, a marquess, a viscount, and a baron or two. Even better, all but one of them is in good standing with the banks."

Facing her mother's eager expression across the table soured what remained of Barbara's cheer. "And what's so impressive about them?"

Her question startled both parents, her mother going so far as to drop the knife she'd been holding. It clattered to the table as she stared at Barbara.

"Impressive are their titles and social standing. Why, any of the group would ensure your place in society, and that of your children," her mother said with a pointed look to her own progeny. Having been raised in a tradesman's house, wealthy or not, Lady Whitfeld's elevation had been marked, her husband a prime catch.

"And that they have avoided the layers of debt sinking so many of the peerage is a measure of their acumen, especially at so young an age."

"More likely that of their parents or men of business." Barbara glanced from one parent to the next. "Is it so wrong to want what you have? To measure my life partner by more than the blunt in his pocket and his crest?"

Her parents exchanged a concerned look, but it was her mother who answered, "We did not come to this marriage with the understanding we have reached. It grew in the course of our lives. You see the result of much hard work and compromise. It's not something that can be measured in the courting."

A laugh came from her lips before she could smother it. "Are you saying Father chose you for practical concerns? I, for one, don't believe that for a moment. He's only happy to see those with good management because he'd been one of them and could marry for reasons other than to rescue his own inheritance."

"Really, Barbara. Is that any way to speak to your mother?" Lord Whitfeld clearly could not deny the words so chose to question her tone instead.

She did not understand why they were so determined for her to settle when her father had not.

"It's different for the girls," Lady Whitfeld said as though Barbara had spoken her question aloud, "And where your father weighs in your favor, my own background is much more humble."

Barbara lowered her fork to the table, taking a moment to settle it against the fine linen before asking, "Are you saying we cannot secure a second season or even a third?"

From the flush that rose to color her father's neck, the question hit too close to the mark, or so she thought until he marshalled a response.

"I won't have you spreading rumors about my pockets. We are as well set up as any, and better than most. It's not a matter of suffering your indecision. It's how long you have to find a match before you start to look as though you are on the shelf compared to the fresh flowers, or you get a reputation for dangling hope when there is none."

Lady Whitfeld leaned across the table to brush Barbara's hand. "Right now you're the belle of the ball, my dear. Gentlemen hope to claim a spot on your card while the young ladies look to you for someone to emulate. Such a state cannot last. Soon enough, the gentlemen will sour at being set against each other, and the girls will start to wonder at how you diminish their hopes by collecting all the eligible suitors for yourself. Some might even come to question your breeding, or think you vindictive."

Her thoughts flashed to Aubrey, but her parents could not know the cause for her change in state.

Lord Whitfeld clasped his wife's hand, smiling at her even as he spoke. "Though you have the right of my feelings, I was not the only one to notice such a beauty. The reasons her parents supported my offer out of the many made had little to do with how well we would suit so many years later."

Barbara leaned forward to watch her parents, feeling in awe and much the intruder as she often did. How could they deny her desire for the same connection with her life mate?

Her mother turned then and met her gaze. "Unlike you, my father had no intention of letting a flighty young girl, in his own words, make so important a decision as to choose her husband, especially not when he hoped to gain a place in society as a result." She glanced at her husband before continuing, "And I had no way of knowing his interest would deepen from an infatuation to something much stronger. Why, we barely knew each other back then. No more than you know any of those now vying for your hand."

The rattle of teacups against their saucers gave voice to the force with which Barbara propelled herself up from the table. "So your grand advice is what? Go down to White's and toss a few cards to choose among them? Or maybe head to the docks and roll dice? If there's no way to judge my future from what I can see, where's the point in a choice at all?"

"Now, Barbara, don't agitate yourself." Her father half rose to stop her. "We're not saying there's no choice to be made, just that you do not have the ability to see into the future. The aspects you might consider important now could prove to be so much less so. This is why parents judge based on title and wealth. If you suit at all, there's a chance you'll grow to have more of a connection as you face life together."

"A chance. A hope. These are not words to measure my future against. None of these gentlemen give me the least expectation of their regard deepening, nor do I have even a passing fancy for them."

This time both her parents thrust to their feet, albeit with more grace so the table didn't shift.

"Barbara, if you are incapable of taking this task, then we will have to choose for you," her father announced even as her mother said, "No need to be so frivolous."

The last struck harder, measuring as it did against Aubrey's plain speaking where he thought he would not be overheard, but Barbara ignored the twinge to glare at her father. "You promised I could make the choice, and you'll not be changing that. I will make a decision, but I will not be hasty, and it will not be now. Now, I'm going for a ride to clear my head."

As she left the room, she heard her mother exclaim, "I knew no good would come of giving our daughter her way in this."

She did not hear her father's reply, but didn't need to. She had enough to fuel her angry march through the house in how her father tried to go back on his word and her mother saw frivolity in a diminishing hope for happiness.

"Sarah," she called out as soon as she reached her rooms, knowing her friend would be busy arranging the next of her outfits. "Where are you, Sarah? I'm going for a ride, and you'll be my chaperone."

Her friend glanced up from the outfit she'd been repairing. "Now?"

"Yes, right now."

Whether picking up on her tone, or just as eager to leave the confines of their town house, Barbara could not complain about the maid's speed. Still, it seemed an age before they quit the residence.

If only she had a field to bolt across like she had when visiting her uncle as a child. Here she had only tidy streets and a garden where any hint of wildness would set the gossips spinning.

Chapter Six

Barbara handled her palfrey with ease, Sarah having no difficulty either. They'd both ridden many a more challenging beast at Uncle Ferrier's stables, and on more difficult terrain, but there they could flaunt convention, hitch up their skirts, and sit astride. In Hyde Park, though, where they could encounter all manner of elegant members of society, Barbara had to keep her disposition, and position, within the bounds of convention.

"It's so unfair, Sarah," she burst out as they ambled along the bridle path. "For every moment there is a rule, or a half dozen, and horrors if you slip up even once. The gossips will dine on your story until nothing is left of your reputation to salvage. Look at us, competent and able, yet confined to perch on unstable equipage, while if our horses dare stretch their legs, we must rein them in tight enough to put a permanent curl in their necks."

Sarah glanced at the path quickly filling with others enjoying the cool breezes in early summer. "Would you rather give them their heads and trample all those before you? Sometimes convention serves the people as in this case."

The image rose before Barbara's eyes and she stifled a laugh at the thought. "You understand me well enough. I have the need to run, but there's no place I can do so, on horseback or on foot, without bringing the eyes of the ton onto my head and provoking my mother to wrath."

"Your mother could manage at best an icy tone, as well you know. She indulges you almost as much as your father does, much to their current regret."

Barbara twisted in her saddle at that, threatening to loosen the whole and send her flying to the ground. "You are on their side then? You think I should be grateful for my offers, and choose one among them with the hope affection might grow?"

"It is how most find their way to a comfortable existence. Another effective convention with the years behind it as proof."

Barbara's fidgeting set the horse to sidle, and she barely managed not to crash into a young man passing them.

"Good day, ladies," he said, touching the brim of his rather impressive top hat.

"Good day," they murmured in response, Sarah making no attempt to correct the impression she belonged with Barbara by station as well as affection. Dressed in one of Barbara's cast-off riding habits, she had the mark of a lady if not the bloodline.

Barbara held her tongue long enough for him to move out of earshot before returning to their conversation. "Take that young gentleman. He sees the two of us following all the strict rules governing a ride in London from our dresses to the sideways perch. He judges us based on those same rules, just as all the gentlemen who sought after me have done. They see not the person but how well the person conforms to the rules. If I were to demand they see me as I am, I'd break the rules enough that none would want to be seen in my vicinity, much less to tie their lives to mine."

"The way you go on about them, sometimes I wonder if you wouldn't find value in such an event." The sparkle in her eyes gave away Sarah's teasing more than her words, but to a degree, they properly described the situation.

"Would a spinster's life be so bad? You would no longer have to worry about fitting into a new household. We could stay with the familiar. My father's estate will pass into my charge so we'd not want for money, and my mother may encourage me to find a match, but you know she dreads the loss of female companionship."

Sarah shook her head, the picture clearly too daunting to imagine. "You do not have it in you to become the retiring spinster, and you'd lack widowhood to bestow a cloak of respectability. Besides, with as many suitors as you have collected already, should you try to withdraw from the field, I'm sure one amongst them would take it upon himself to throw you over his horse and race you up to Gretna Green before you could settle into a spinster state. I suspect your father wouldn't contest the action either." She laughed at the thought before continuing, "It's not the life for you, nor would you be happy to fall to it. You've always been one for choices, and you're lucky in this to have many."

Barbara waited for a woman with three young children to cross their path then said with as much force as the patience had created, "A choice between nothings is still nothing. Not a one of them has any idea who I am. How am I to trust that they are choosing me and not some image built up from layer upon layer of convention?"

Her voice having risen louder than she'd intended, Barbara gave a quick glance ahead to see whether she could have been overheard.

Had she been walking, she would have stumbled.

As it was, a blush heated her cheeks at the sight of just who approached on the cross path. She would suffer a hundred deaths if she were to learn he'd overheard her pained exclamation.

Out of the corner of her eye, she saw Sarah give her an odd look, but she couldn't shift her gaze from the man coming ever closer, propelled by his own horse and hers, both keeping to the steady gait prescribed by the very convention she'd scorned.

A quickly indrawn breath showed her friend had just noticed what captured Barbara's attention, but it made no difference. Barbara had no time to relax her features before Aubrey glanced toward her, his look of concentration fading as he became aware of their presence.

His face transformed with a smile that set Barbara's heart to pounding, a response induced by the reminder of his cutting comments, or so she told herself.

"Good da—"

Barbara didn't give him the chance to finish his greeting.

She pressed her spur into the side of her palfrey with a little more force than intended.

The horse leapt forward, almost making her humiliation complete, but she managed to throw her weight to the right enough to keep her saddle in place, an effort that denied her more than a blurred impression of his smile turning to confusion before she'd gone far enough to lose him behind her. Had she fallen, he'd be obliged to come to her aid, another way convention would serve to harm her, but as it was, for him to charge after in hopes of an explanation would violate those very conventions she had broken.

Sarah came up on her side, a frown gracing her features. "That was not kind," she chided. "You claim you want people to know your true nature, but if this is what you meant, perhaps your hopes of a future are better served by staying within the rules."

Barbara said nothing, waiting for her pulse to settle from the strain of the chance meeting with one she'd hoped to avoid. It seemed God sought to punish her for every last transgression by taunting her with her mistakes. Had Aubrey but been the man she'd thought him, she'd have delighted in the chance to join her way to his and share insights.

As it was, she could not stand a moment in his presence without his cutting words resounding in her ears and making her aware every thought he conveyed served only to mask the rot that formed his center. No matter how pretty the dressing, if the meat beneath had spoiled, the illness to follow made any enjoyment lose its value.

A ubrey reined in his gelding and stared after the two ladies, his muddled thoughts unable to absorb what had just occurred.

He could not fathom what the dark-haired beauty had against him, the same woman Isabella held in such high regard if he had not been mistaken, but neither could he imagine the charge from his presence an accident, not when she'd shown such skill in righting herself.

Having grown up surrounded by girls, he'd once tried his seat on one of the saddles meant for women. He could safely state they required either miracle or great skill to manage at anything faster than a sedate walk.

She'd mastered the ungainly object without even a yelp of fear, a trait unexpected in one of the young ladies in London. She must have spent some time in the country to have such a talented seat.

The observation struck him as funny, but he had no one with which to share it since Jasper had returned to the country, leaving London that much more barren a place.

Aubrey gave a half salute to the rapidly departing ladies, the Whitfeld daughter having won him one favor at least.

He'd set out on this ride firmly aware of the solitude, and not having sought it out. While he appreciated the fresh air and activity, he felt much more conscious of the slim company he now kept.

In one quick encounter, she'd wiped the sorry state from his mind for long enough to get a glimpse of a lovely countenance despite the shade of her bonnet.

However, instead of discovering if more lay behind her pleasant features than a vapid emptiness as Isabella had promised, she'd offered up a curiosity, a mystery even, and one he might just have to solve at the next chance.

Aubrey shook his head with a laugh. Her response most likely was rooted in his failure to join the crowd around her at every event. Yet despite that realization, he continued on his way in a much lighter mood. Perhaps he'd been a little too hasty in her case, missing the quarry in the blur of sameness offered by the other debutantes.

He'd planned to beg off the night's dance since his mother felt well enough to attend, but something told him better sport would be found on the dance floor than at White's.

If nothing else, he could ensure Isabella had the opportunity to engage in conversation with the one she considered worth emulating. Far better that than let his mother take hand in the situation and push Isabella too fast and too far until she had been reduced to a shadow of her lively self and all potential suitors overlooked her value.

Decided, he kneed his gelding around and returned the way he'd come in a faster gait, though not so quick as to raise attention. Aubrey had neither the need nor the intention of running after the Whitfeld girl, not when he knew with reasonable certainty exactly where she would be that very evening. If she had more between her ears than fluff, she'd be happy to engage in conversation of the like not often found on the dance floor. And if she should not, he could dismiss her with confidence such that no one, neither Jasper nor Isabella, could question his efforts.

Chapter Seven

Their return to the Whitfeld town house passed in an uncomfortable silence. Barbara knew her impulsive action had been as rude as Sarah claimed, but she refused to say so aloud. Aubrey St. Vincent deserved what she'd done and worse. He deserved to be revealed as the snake he truly was for the protection of all young ladies taken in by his apparent demeanor.

He had spoiled her ride like he spoiled every event at which he made an appearance, and even brought conflict with her friend. Barbara would have been happy never to encounter him again in any forum, ballroom dance, or bridle path, though she had little hope of such a happening coming to be.

Her outfit reeked of horse, and her visage held none of the delight a horseback ride should have offered as she mounted the short steps to the house with Sarah trailing after. And now, instead of continuing their conversations of the ride, she had to look forward to changing and a quick wash in uncomfortable silence.

Their butler Mr. Simmons swung the door wide the moment she let the knocker meet its rest, as though he'd been waiting for them.

Barbara gave him a nod and swept toward the stairs, not waiting to let Sarah catch up.

The butler coughed once. "Lady Barbara."

He paused until she turned, startled.

"Your father commands your presence in his study."

Raising the thick skirt of her riding habit with both hands, she said, "Tell him I'll be down as soon as I've changed. I'm not fit company."

Sarah muttered something Barbara chose not to hear as she brushed past.

Barbara let her go, knowing Sarah needed to arrange a tub, but when she turned to follow, Simmons caught hold of her arm.

"He said immediately, my lady. I'm sure he can suffer your current state."

Barbara stared at him, shocked both by the touch and his determination that she stand before her father in a dirty dress with the stench of a ride surrounding her.

He raised both hands and took a step back as though repelled by her gaze, an apology in his eyes. "He said for me to catch you the moment you returned, my lady, and gave no mention of letting you prepare yourself in advance of the meeting."

Barbara let loose a long sigh. "Well then, I suppose I must go." She once again gathered her skirts and marched toward her father's study, head held high despite knowing she was not at her best. Perhaps he had yet another suitor awaiting her pleasure. At least this gentleman would see her exactly as she was and convention be damned.

Simmons reached the door before her only by breaking into an undignified stride and ducking in front of her. Barbara felt a momentary flash of pleasure followed with embarrassment. He'd only been following her father's command and had not set out to make her unsettled.

The door swung wide before she could do more than regret her disheveled appearance. She might not appreciate how gentlemen seemed incapable of looking beyond the package, but that didn't mean she wanted them to recoil from her with fingers pinched over their noses.

The sight that greeted her, though, held only one of the male persuasion: her father. Her mother graced the stately room with her presence as well, and from the Lady Whitfeld's expression, she had not shared in her husband's urgency.

"Come in," Lord Whitfeld said with a measured tone reminding Barbara of when she'd been called to task as a young girl for her latest escapade.

She entered the space reluctantly and stood before his desk without attempting to take a seat until told to do so, a directive her father pointedly neglected as he stared at her in silence.

"Oh do let the girl sit down," her mother burst out all of a sudden. "There's no reason to make this any less pleasant than it already is."

Barbara waited for her father to nod in silent agreement before taking her mother's words for permission. Still, when she sat, it was to perch on the very edge of the chair, her back as rigid as the busk tucked into her corsets. Tension swept her every muscle until she ached from head to toe, but she kept her expression neutral. Her behavior at the morning meal had left much to be desired, but surely her mother would have taken on that scolding.

He continued to frown at her for a moment longer until even her mother fought the need to fidget. Then, with so little warning Barbara jumped in surprise, he said, "Your mother and I have discussed your behavior toward those come seeking your hand. You've become nothing less than a frivolous chit trifling with the hearts and lives of the men who seek you out. Not only that, but you seem to have little consideration for the others in this year's marriage mart who suffer from having so many pulled from the scene as they hold out for your answer."

Barbara's face heated at this evidence she'd succeeded so well in her wish to meet with Aubrey's unkind assessment. She had attempted to turn some of her suitors to other girls, though with little success, but it measured poorly against her harsh words in quitting the breakfast table just this morning. "I'm sorry to have disappointed you," she said, her tone soft.

Her father raised one hand. If anything, his frown cut deeper into his serious visage. "It is too late for pretty words, Barbara. I never expected you'd so abuse our trust and that of your suitors when I agreed to let you choose your own match. I hold to my word despite my statement at breakfast, but I'll not be the master of your willful torment."

She half rose to protest then fell back on the seat, aware nothing she could offer would improve the situation. When she'd extracted that promise, she'd had her sights firmly set on Aubrey, and every intention of concocting the necessary plan to claim him for her own. How many times had they told her to mend her unruly ways, to act within the constraints of society? Sarah had said as much only recently.

Barbara had brought their condemnation on her head, and nothing would change the past. She could only meekly accept their chastising now and show with her actions how she'd learned from the experience.

"Would that you'd shown such restraint earlier," her mother murmured.

Something in her mother's tone brought Barbara's attention to fix on her father rather than her own shortcomings. Again, he gave her only silence in return, a silence heavy with disappointment, but holding more.

Lady Whitfeld launched to her feet. "Just tell her. I fear my heart can take this tension no longer."

He spared his wife a glance, grimaced, then rested his face on steepled fingers for a moment. "Your mother and I have decided you lack the maturity for coming out, though we'd had high hopes at the beginning of your season. Your maid has been set about the task of packing up your things. You will be sent to the country to live at the Ferrier holdings until such time as reports of your behavior show you've grown up enough to return."

Barbara stared at her father in shock. Whatever she'd expected, this had never entered her thoughts.

"You're sending me away?" For all she'd struggled with the conventions, and had her heart crushed by unthinking words, she'd kept away from scandal. Just what would the gossips make of her vanishing without warning? Her reputation would suffer worse than if she cantered through Hyde Park, knocking pedestrians left and right.

Her mother came to her side and caught hold of one of Barbara's hands. "It's not forever, my dear. And you'll be able to finish out your season should my brother's reports please."

She jerked her hand free. "And what of those suitors you hold in such regard?" Her question was directed not at her mother but at the man surely behind this decision.

Lord Whitfeld had the grace to look uncomfortable, but when he spoke, not a hint of it showed in the sonorous tones. "They'll turn their attention elsewhere, I suspect. Especially when I will be unable to give them a day upon which you'll return. Should any hold steadfast, maybe that will offer you the distinction you seem to find so lacking."

Barbara turned to her mother. "They'll think me compromised. You know they will."

Where she'd expected support from the woman who had always counseled her to stay within expectations, Lady Whitfeld offered only a sad smile and quick shake of her head. "That you'd think to the gossips first, and not the suffering of those partial to you, shows this action — though dramatic — the right and only course. I've made mistakes before in managing a season, but I'll not let you ruin both your future and that of those you trifle with. Your cousins, Charlotte especially, are more than capable of teaching you the value of hard work and life itself, something you seem to have forgotten in the flash and glitter of the town existence. It's not all pretty dresses and flowery words. There are people behind each conversation, a fact you neglect when you dangle hope so broadly only to laugh as they come to blows."

"I never laughed." The sour mutter offered little to support her case when she could not protest the majority. She'd done as she had to condemn a man who had never bothered to speak with her. But what of those who had sought her attention, time, and even her hand? Them she'd seen as little more than pawns in her game to show Aubrey just how she would appear had she been the girl he'd thought her to be.

"Go on with you now," her mother said. "Sarah will need your help if you are to begin your journey before nightfall. You've enjoyed your time in the country in the past. It will not be so horrible."

"Do not soften this for her, my dear. She earned her punishment and must suffer it if she's to learn the error of her ways." He turned his sharp gaze on Barbara. "The carriage will leave when I say it will, and if you have nothing to wear once you get to your uncle's holdings, I'm sure your cousins can dress you in their cast-offs. It would serve you well. You are our only daughter, and it would seem we've pandered to your wishes too often for you to learn the value of those around you. Now get from my sight. I have nothing more to say to you."

Her father's condemnation weighed heavier than any other as Barbara obeyed his command. He'd been the one to encourage her in unconventional pursuits, to answer her questions when she sought to explore unwomanly concepts, and to give her books from the shelves where more than light novels rested. She'd given no thought to how her behavior would reflect on her parents when reacting to Aubrey's assessment. Nor had she considered how her actions would affect the suitors she dismissed as shallow. In pretending frivolity, she'd discovered the true depths of her own character.

Barbara returned to her room deep in thought to find it overrun with the chaos of packing.

Sarah came to her then, their argument forgotten as she put her arms around Barbara for comfort. "It's not as bad as it seems," she said. "You'll see. This will all turn out for the best."

Though Barbara doubted that statement, she had nothing better to offer. At least time in the country meant freedom from the ever-confining rules of London society, though she suspected she'd be taking them along with her, measured in her father's harsh tones.

Chapter Eight

Aubrey arrived at the ball in a strange state of anticipation. Whether he'd been too hasty in his dismissal of Lady Barbara, or had grown desperate for something to break the monotony, the encounter in the park had forced itself to the front of his thoughts all day.

"You're in a jolly mood this evening, brother," Isabella said as they stepped from the carriage. "I thought the moment Mother could stay on her feet you'd be off on gentlemanly pursuits. Could it be you've finally found one to pique your interest?"

"Oh, do not tease him so," their mother said as Aubrey took the place of the footman to hand her down. "You wouldn't want to chance scaring the boy off. I'd half despaired of him ever settling his interest on one of the female persuasion for all his love of poetry and talk of the ideal mate."

Aubrey looked from one to the other of them and lifted both arms to their service. "So it's tease or speak not at all? These are the choices you consider?"

Isabella pinched his arm where hers lay entwined. "Don't you try to distract me. I'll ferret out who brought the spark into your eyes, just you wait."

He clicked his tongue. "Should you put half that much energy into finding a match of your own, I'd no longer have to take you to assemblies such as these."

She jerked her arm free, but when he sought to apologize, she said, "You had every opportunity to cry off this night." Her tone showed she had not taken offense. "I ask only why the change."

"Perhaps your pretty words the other night have swayed me. I intend to introduce you to the lady who has caught your favor."

Her brow furrowed as she sought his meaning, then Isabella shook her head. "You can't mean to vie with the crowd for Lady Barbara."

Aubrey swept an awkward bow, his other arm still secured by his mother. "I seek only to please my sister and make the introduction." She had no need to know the lady in question had made her feelings clear, nor how he intended to find the source for such a strong response.

Experience gained through observing his friend Jasper had revealed marked aversion often enough a sign of strong feelings in the other direction. Whether he wanted to pursue such interests or not, his curiosity, and good manners, demanded some resolution to his apparent crime. Surely neither Jasper nor Isabella had spread his comments, and he'd had no direct contact with Lady Barbara before that moment in the park.

If he found the source of her disdain as frivolous as he'd once considered the woman, he wished well to whichever of her suitors she chose. He only hoped the gentleman in question was ready to suffer a shrew in his bed, as a woman who held such inconsequential grudges must turn out to be one.

If, on the other hand, her cause seemed just, he'd seek to repair the insult and hope to find his efforts rewarded by an acquaintance less bland than the rest of those introduced with the season.

His mother slapped him with her fan. "You look besotted already so don't think to trick your mother with words of how good a brother you are. Let us sally forth and meet the original who managed to shake your convictions about every debutante on offer."

Aubrey would have trailed in their wake if not for the firm grips on each of his arms. How could he hope to deduce the truth of his offence when they were in full matchmaking mode?

His fears, though, proved unfounded. He didn't know whether to be relieved or regretful when, despite all three of their efforts to discover her, it seemed the Lady Barbara had chosen not to attend.

The only good came in the many male glances sent Isabella's way. Caught up in her sisterly mission, Isabella had overcome her shyness. Her eyes twinkled with suppressed delight at his uncomfortable state, and a blush painted red prettily across each cheek.

"I fear she has not made an appearance, Aubrey," Isabella said at last, when they had made sure to go through every room opened for the event at least twice.

Aubrey reached that conclusion some time before, but had kept silent to ensure the gentlemen of the ton got to see this side of Isabella. "Perhaps you should take a turn on the dance floor before we try once again? There is many a young man trying to catch your eye."

She froze and glanced around, ducking her head as she met the first gaze only to peep from beneath the tendrils of hair come loose in her determined search.

Though he'd thought to curse at his ill-considered words, he swallowed the response at the sight of a smile twitching on her lips.

His mother raised an eyebrow at the gentleman in question and gave an imperious wave to draw him over. With Lady St. Vincent taking a hand, Isabella would have little choice but to concede at least one turn around the dance floor.

Aubrey stepped back, no longer necessary and having failed at his own purpose. He tried to see her absence as a sign he should dismiss the encounter, but the Lady Barbara's mystery lingered.

When Isabella returned from her dance, her face flushed, he reached for her arm to continue the search as promised, but his mother waved him off.

"Her dance card is full, Aubrey, or will be the moment she makes it available. Take yourself off to the card room if you can find no other companion than your sister."

The color drained from Isabella's face, and she shot him a pleading look.

"I'm happy to wait here."

"Nonsense." Lady St. Vincent took him by the arm and pulled him one step off. "You stand sentinel over her, and the others will think their attentions unwanted. Give her a moment to flourish, and she'll forget why she ever stood back."

Aubrey looked to his sister for confirmation, but before he could catch her downturned gaze, his mother pushed him away forcibly. He had no choice but to go lest he cause a scene and worsen Isabella's state.

He chose not to go far.

His frown grew as the hours lengthened, as much from how Isabella shrank away from forced encounters with one gentleman after another as from the inability to confront his own lady. He had no more claim to her than any of these to Isabella, but he planned to pursue the possibility.

His sister never stepped onto the dance floor again, those interested turning aside either from her lack of response or from his mother's unsubtle efforts.

At last, he could tolerate neither his nor Isabella's torment any longer and strode back to their side.

"I think we've made enough of a mark for this evening, Mother. I've a mind to quit these environs."

She raised one eyebrow. "You can take the carriage. There's no need for you to stay. Just send it back once you reach White's or wherever else you plan to seek your entertainment."

A sigh of disappointment from his sister proved he'd been right to intervene, and he had no intention of giving up.

"I have reports to go over in the morning, a happening already begun from the longcase clock in the hallway. Since I'm homeward bound, it seems foolish to make the trip twice. Besides, Isabella raised some interest this night. Best let it grow in her absence."

A spark returned to Isabella at that statement when he'd despaired of her recovering any energy as wane as she appeared.

"Listen to him, Mother. Why else would he be so driven to seek out one he's never spoken to before?"

He didn't need to correct her words as they had not, indeed, spoken during the encounter in the park, but he did give her a glower in response to the teasing.

She only laced her arm through his and turned toward where their host and hostess held court to speak their goodbyes.

Lady St. Vincent let out a long-suffering sigh before engaging his other arm and giving in.

At least the return to gaiety meant no chance of questions about Isabella's stamina, something their mother needed to consider when she pressed so hard that Isabella paled in strain. Clearly his sister still needed him at her side, the presence of their mother notwithstanding. And if remaining would ensure he'd be able to confront his lady of mystery the sooner for it, he could not complain.

Chapter Nine

Despite her father's threat, by the time the carriage pulled away from the town house, night had passed into the early morning hours. Exhausted by the feverish packing on top of an emotional day, both Sarah and Barbara soon nodded off.

"We're here, my lady."

The coachman's warning call woke Barbara from a deep sleep. She blinked to clear her vision, giving Sarah a wan smile as the smooth rhythm of movement ended when the horses pulled up to a sizable farmhouse.

"Oh, but no one shall be awake," Barbara said as she realized the sun had yet to reach its full height.

"Not to worry, my lady. This here's a working farm. There'll be many about for the midday meal. Their day began long ago." The footman lowered the step and put out a hand to help her and a drowsy Sarah down.

Though it had been a handful of years since she'd had the chance to visit, Barbara now remembered they did keep country hours, and that meant up with the sun to make the most of the natural light. Balls and theatrical events running almost until the first rays of sunlight streaked the sky would be unheard of here.

Sure enough, not just her uncle but all four of her cousins came pouring out of the house, her father having sent a rider ahead the previous day.

"Barbara, welcome to my home," her uncle said, his somber expression giving evidence of more in the message than a simple announcement of intent.

Still, the girls showed no such restraint as they rushed forward to hug and greet both her and Sarah.

"Cousin Barbara, it's been too long."

"Much too long. And Sarah, we'd hoped you would accompany our cousin."

"We've been awaiting your arrival since yesterday."

"Come on in out of the sun. It must have been a tiring ride."

They spoke all at once, leaving Barbara no time to comprehend Charlotte's command until her oldest cousin finished by taking her arm and pulling her forward. She had a vague impression of Marian, the next oldest, catching Sarah, with Jane and Georgiana left to trail after.

Soon, all six of them were settled at the wood block table in the warm kitchen as Charlotte directed their cook to make tea and bring over the rolls left from the morning meal. Uncle Ferrier had taken himself off to do whatever it was he had to, freeing Barbara of his censure so she could enjoy her cousins wholeheartedly.

"You must tell us of London," Marian said, kneeling on the bench across from Barbara and leaning forward to rest her chin on crossed arms. "Charlotte never speaks of her season, and we have no other to plague. If only the Pendletons were blessed with daughters, we might have been invited up to the manor, but with a son, there were no balls, and Father didn't let us go to the other activities."

The long trip was enough to slow her mind, but Barbara came fully awake at the name. "The Pendletons have an estate nearby?"

"Oh yes," her cousin continued, unaware of the tension her comment had provoked. "Lord Pendleton took up residence with his new bride just last year, though the family visited rarely before then."

"Now, Marian, what have I told you about gossip," Charlotte said, putting an end to the font of information with Barbara in possession of only enough to vex.

She had been sent from London and thought herself finally free of reminders only to find this the very home of Aubrey's best friend.

"They've been all but hermits there, though much doings at the estate beforehand and after. And the new minister and his wife are said to be related," Jane took up where her older sister had left off.

Charlotte sent a measured gaze at the girl, and she also quieted, but Barbara took some relief in this extra bit of knowledge. If they'd been secluded, there was no reason to expect that to change now. Nor had she any reason to think Aubrey would quit London during the season either, not with his own interests and those of his sister.

The questions continued, and though Charlotte added none to the pile, neither did she categorize the doings of London folk as gossip to be quashed. Barbara told them what she could and left some questions to Sarah to answer. When she was allowed to pause, she savored the fresh baked bread and a strong cup of tea.

A smile curled her lips unbidden as the open honesty of her cousins worked its way beneath her constraints. Her attempt to keep up both the rules of convention and then the appearance of frivolity when in London had exhausted her. Not that Lord Aubrey had seemed to notice.

She pushed her renewed irritation aside.

Here, she had no need to pretend to be anything other than she was, and Uncle had been known to look the other way should she need to stretch her legs, something unheard of in London.

Despite her best efforts, a yawn broke across her face, soon mirrored by Sarah.

"Would you look at the two of you? I'm guessing you haven't seen this side of noon in an age. London hours are all about the night, are they not?" Jane gave them a wink with her question, and Barbara saw no need to take offense at the teasing.

Charlotte stood up and swept their plates away. "More likely they have been traveling all night to get here even if they made good time with the roads free of farm traffic in the late hours. Used to London hours or not, it's wearing on a body. "Marian, Georgie, finish clearing up here so Cook can ready luncheon for Father and the farm hands. Jane, let's show our dear friends to the guestroom. You'll both feel so much better after a nap. We'll have time to visit later."

Everyone, Sarah and Barbara included, recognized a command when they heard one.

arbara woke up starving to discover she'd slept the day through from the sunrise painting the sky.

"The sleepy one has woken," a voice called from the doorway, revealed to be Marian when she stepped inside. "Your season must have been exhausting from how soundly you've slept. You didn't even wake up for dinner."

"I surely feel the lack now." Her stomach rumbled as though in agreement, and she glanced around for Sarah.

"Can you not dress yourself?"

Marian's tone held a mix of wonder and contempt that sat unhappily in Barbara's ears, but she dismissed it, determined not to let her visit become corrupted as her season had. "You'd have a time of it too with fashions as they are and so many layers, but no. I just wondered where she was. She's always been the one to wake me."

Her cousin gave a pitying look. "We don't stand on such ceremony here, as you should remember. Sarah's like a member of the family. She's played with all of us a time or two, and we'll not have her thrust in a servant's role when it's not necessary."

"She'll enjoy that. In London she had duties that extended beyond my care despite being more of a friend than solely my maid."

Jane poked her head around the doorframe just in time to hear the last comment. She burst into a fit of laughter and took a moment to get under control, at which point she gasped out, "You think friends and family free from duties? It's no wonder your father thought you needed a clearer understanding of how most live. We all have chores. And you will be helping us with them."

Barbara colored at the knowledge that more than just her uncle knew why she'd been sent down from London, but as to the rest, she gave a shrug. "I don't know how much use I'll be around the farm, but I'm happy to do my share."

"That's the attitude," Charlotte said, joining them, "But words are easy, and you're still abed. I brought you an older dress of mine." She lifted one arm to indicate the clothing thrown over it. "From what

Sarah has been telling us, none of what you packed will suit. I suppose you have little need for rough clothes as you sweep from ball to ball, but it would be a pity to have them spoiled."

Not wanting to appear resistant, Barbara stepped free of her covers to take the simple dress and hold it against her light nightgown. She'd grown accustomed to just Sarah attending her in the mornings, and she had no brothers or sisters to crowd in before she'd risen.

Ever vigilant, Charlotte recognized the problem before Barbara said a word. She ushered the others out. "Just because we have visitors doesn't mean the cows are to be neglected. Barbara will join us as soon as she's ready. You can find us in the kitchen," she called over her shoulder.

Barbara took a deep breath, happy to be on her own at last, though she missed Sarah's company in the morning. It seemed her friend had taken the previous day to find her footing in this busy household while Barbara had wasted the time asleep.

Her stomach rumbled again, speeding her through the process of divesting herself of the nightgown and pulling the dress over her shoulders. The top had no corset to bind, and simple laces held it closed without the restraint of the posture board she normally suffered.

She spun in a circle, letting the soft, un-embroidered cloth swirl around her until it settled against her legs. Her cousins might be more used to this life than she was, but they most likely were unaware of the benefits to it despite chores she felt sure would stretch both her energy and her talents. Perhaps it was the deep sleep, or maybe the country air, but Barbara felt more refreshed than she'd been for a long while. She intended to enjoy every moment of the feeling.

Chapter Ten

A week passed in which Aubrey faithfully escorted his sister to every possible event, even urging them on when his mother showed signs of tiring and Isabella begged for a quiet night at home. He'd almost had a rebellion on his hands this very night, with his sister claiming blisters, but since she'd yet to dance with any of the gentlemen their mother introduced her to beyond the night he'd first sought Lady Barbara, he called her out on the lie.

With their mother gone for a powder while they stood on the sidelines of yet another dance floor, Isabella leaned over to whisper, "You could always ask after her."

He didn't bother to protest, knowing neither of the women with him would believe him any more than he'd accepted tales of blisters.

"Or just listen in to the gossip. Someone's sure to know if she's fallen ill or run off with one of her many suitors."

She laughed then, and he turned a sour look on his sister even though he recognized her animation just might gain her the attention she deserved as it had that one night.

Just then, Sir Willoughby came upon them, shooting a pointed look at Aubrey for an introduction.

"Willoughby," Aubrey said, happy to oblige. "Have you met my sister Lady Isabella?"

The young man bowed over Isabella's hand as he murmured, "I haven't had the pleasure."

Though he'd clearly expected a reply, Isabella only looked at him for a moment in uncomfortable silence before dropping her gaze to her now-twisted fingers.

Aubrey wanted to chastise her, but knew it would only make the situation worse.

After an awkward silence, Willoughby shrugged. "I believe I'm wanted in the card room." With a perfunctory bow and a murmured farewell, he took himself off to save her the embarrassment.

Isabella held up a hand to stave off Aubrey's words. "Don't. If I could be like Lady Barbara, all smiles and laughter, I would be. But anything my tongue let slip would only have condemned me further."

Though he hadn't planned to scold her, Aubrey worried she'd never have a chance with how withdrawn she became the moment someone approached, but whatever he tried had little effect except to worsen his sister's condition. If he could have changed that, he would have. Instead, he could only hope someone would see past her retiring behavior to the lively person behind.

"Ah, your most fervent admirer approaches."

Aubrey turned to look, startled out of his thoughts at the bitter tinge to his sister's words.

"Lady Isabella. Lord Aubrey. There you are. I had concerns you would not attend."

Having done the bare minimum to acknowledge his sister, Lady Emily turned ever so slightly so her side faced Isabella, and her full attention fell on Aubrey. The girl had become quite the nuisance, and he did not appreciate how she treated his sister, but he'd had as little success discouraging Lady Emily as encouraging Isabella.

Rather than shrinking away as she usually did, though, Isabella moved closer to him and raised her chin as if readying for battle. "We were just talking about how strange it is we haven't seen the Lady Barbara for a full week."

Aubrey could have groaned at the words, his fascination with the lady in question something he'd intended to keep private.

Lady Emily looked between the two then returned her gaze to him, a pout making her lower lip fuller in a way some might find attractive. To him, it only showed her petulant nature. "I had not thought you caught up in the fascination with that girl. Surely she has enough admirers to show it a waste."

He forced a relaxed shrug. "Perhaps she's accepted one of them and so no longer has to display herself on the marriage mart."

Lady Emily laughed then, a high-pitched titter that grated on his nerves. "Not that I have heard. Word is her parents sent her out to the country. Perhaps it's an indiscretion, and she'll be absent a full nine months."

"Oh, surely not," Isabella said, breaking into what had become a private conversation. "She's been nothing but proper. I won't believe it of her."

Though his encounter with Lady Barbara held little of proper behavior, he was inclined to agree with his sister. Nothing in her flashing eyes or the way she firmed her lips before charging off matched with one making dalliances on the side.

He'd examined every aspect of their one meeting at length, remembering details he had not known he'd noticed at the time.

She'd been full of indignation, of rage, though for what cause he could not imagine. And now, it seemed, he had little hope of discovering an answer. Whatever the reason for her exit from London, she had avoided his inquiries with as much success as her efforts to keep apart on the bridle path.

His mind wandered, as it often did, but now he became aware Lady Emily had continued to cast aspersions on Lady Barbara, most likely in a misguided attempt to dissuade his interest. However, Isabella had stepped into the gap with a fierce defense of this woman she knew only by reputation, and her voice had climbed high enough to draw attention.

"Lady Emily, I think you had best move on," he said, his tone coated in ice. "My sister finds malicious gossip repugnant, as do I."

She gaped at him for a moment, clearly having lost herself in the attempt to slander another. She paled, then a blush tinged her features a deep red, the transition so rapid he half-feared she'd faint dead away, leaving him to deal with the results.

But Lady Emily released a forceful, "Well, I never," spun on her heel, and marched away with military precision.

Aubrey stared after her, bemused. Had he known the direct approach would prove so effective, he would have used it long ago.

Isabella let loose a peal of laughter that again drew looks, some from young gentlemen, and not in condemnation. They were as fatigued by the bland nature of most debutantes as he had become. If only Isabella didn't wither the moment she noticed the attention, her color fading and her whole being seeming to become smaller.

A sigh dragged from Aubrey at the observation. Not that he wanted his little sister to become as forward as Lady Emily and foist herself off on those who show no interest, but she had to try at least.

As though she read his thoughts, Isabella tugged his sleeve. "You have your answer now, and more. Could we not return home early tonight? I grow weary of all this affectation."

Aubrey could not but agree with her assessment if not her wish.

In all the season, only one of the female sort had caught his attention, and she had taken herself out of the running by means of quitting London all together. The question of why she'd found him so repugnant continued to plague him, but he'd find no answers here.

"Come. Let's find Mother, make our excuses, and call for the carriage. There's no need to chance her having a relapse, nor her illness spreading to you."

A spike of fear thrust through him at the thought of Lady Barbara having retired from the field due to illness, his response all out of proportion to his interest. Surely a curiosity, some slight mystery, could not have claimed his attention quite so fiercely?

Just then, his gaze swept over a familiar face, though he didn't at first recognize it. "Isn't that the young gentleman you danced with at the Mackeley's ball?"

Isabella spun to follow his direction, her eagerness heartening. Though she ducked her head when the particular gentleman noticed her interest, Aubrey detected the hint of a smile on her lips.

"Surely we could suffer to stay for the next dance," he said, nodding toward the man even as he struggled to remember a name to go with the face.

"Lord Aubrey. Lady Isabella. A pleasure."

Before Aubrey could reveal the blunder of forgetting the man's name, Isabella sank into a curtsy, her cheeks stained red. "Mr. Ingham. A pleasure to see you again."

As though they'd exhausted the full of their conversation, the two only stared at each other, raising Aubrey's hopes for all they'd hardly spoken.

"I see the musicians are preparing for the next set," he commented in an attempt to prompt Mr. Ingham. The gentleman might not have a title, but surely their mother had to see the value in any partner for his youngest sister, if only in hopes she might grow accustomed to stepping out.

Mr. Ingham coughed once. "I suppose your dance card is all full. I'm surprised I didn't notice you out there."

Isabella dropped her gaze at that, her shoulders curled in embarrassment.

To save her the answer, Aubrey spoke for her, "I believe this dance is still open."

A quick smiled broke the young man's serious expression for a heartbeat before his hand came forward in offer. "Would you grant me the pleasure of this dance?"

Isabella didn't hesitate and Aubrey soon enjoyed the sight of his sister taking her place on the dance floor after all.

"Just how did you manage that," Lady St. Vincent said, returning to his side.

"I think I had little enough to do with it."

She raised her monocle to get a better look. "Why isn't that Mr. Ingham? She better be careful not to dance with him a third time. Even though it's not the same event, she moves off the wall so seldom people will talk."

Aubrey stifled a sigh at having his hopes dashed. It seemed the young man had value enough for one dance, but no more than that.

Isabella seemed not to benefit from his efforts any more than those of his mother, and the last thing she needed was to be scolded for doing what he had encouraged. She needed to choose to engage with more than just Mr. Ingham. Until she did, events would be wasted on her no matter who stood at her side. At least their mother would steer her away from errors Aubrey cared too little about to notice.

It wasn't as though he had any other purpose for being here. Of all of this year's debutantes, only Lady Barbara had sparked more than the mildest of appreciation, and she'd left London all together. Those that remained held little interest, if they didn't actively repel him as did Lady Emily.

Again, his thoughts turned to linger on the one who was absent. He'd been too quick to judge her before with the result that he'd lost the opportunity to discover his error. Yet somehow he'd managed to offend her even so.

Maybe his judgment had been damaged by the sudden urgency to find his match, making him both too eager and too critical all at once.

He'd seen Jasper's love for Daphne grow until it became a motive force. Aubrey wanted just a fraction of that for himself, no longer willing to wait some indefinite amount of time for his own moment to come to be. Perhaps the Lady Pendleton was a true original, a unique property never to grace the London scene again. Still, he refused to lower his standards and pick a companion at random. He'd been instrumental in bringing the two of them together. Surely he could do the same for himself.

His gaze wandered to where Isabella danced with only a little stiffness to show for her lack of experience outside the schoolroom. She had so much to offer if only given the chance. But with all the bright flowers, those able to laugh, tease, and draw attention, she'd been easy to overlook.

She'd compared his status to that of Lady Barbara with a flock of hopefuls surrounding him at all times. Where he'd been quick to call her out to Jasper as the master of her fate, Lady Barbara could as easily have said the same of him, though he did not seek the attention of any lady beyond herself.

Just as he'd wished he'd known a direct approach would work against Lady Emily, how many of those eager girls would have been delighted to discover a telling glance and a quick thrust spur could secure his notice.

Aubrey laughed aloud then had to shake his head at his mother's inquiring look. At least the dance seemed to be coming to an end. He'd be no fit company this night or any other with his inability to learn the cause of Lady Barbara's cut. Likely he'd try a sharp tone on the next mother to drag her daughter forward to meet him, offending them and his parent.

Denied the chance to solve his mystery, he might do best to follow her lead and leave London all together. Perhaps the time had come to take Jasper up on his offer after all.

Chapter Eleven

"We'll make a country girl out of you soon enough," Georgie said as Barbara wiped her brow free of sweat with a dirt-encrusted hand. "Already you've lost the squeamishness of a Londoner."

Barbara dropped back onto the unturned soil around the kitchen garden and laughed up at her youngest cousin. "If ever I had such. I doubt my parents thought on the risks when they sent me here." She lifted one hand, the sun having brought a darker color to her flesh and calluses beginning to form on her fingers after a week of helping her cousins with the chores. "I'll be quite the vision on the ballroom floor."

"Oh, pish. You'll be a vision even with freckles marking your nose and you know it."

Barbara fought down a desperate need for a mirror and knew she'd failed to hide the response when Georgie melted to the dirt next to her, tears rolling down her face from the force of her laughter.

"If you could only see your expression," Georgie gasped out. "As though freckles were a symptom of a disease and next you'd lose your limbs."

Fingers curled into the soil, and Barbara tossed a handful of dirt at her cousin in retaliation for the teasing.

Georgie was quick to respond in kind, both trying hard not to laugh for fear of some landing in an open mouth.

"Girls, really. Must you carry on so?" Charlotte stood over them, a grin on her own face despite her words. "And no, Cousin Barbara, you have no freckles on your nose or elsewhere, though if you lie down so the brim of your bonnet doesn't shade your features, I can't speak for the future. Now get to the weeding with both of you or the vegetables will be choked out and there'll be none for our meals."

"Yes, Mother," Georgie said, sticking her tongue out once her older sister's back had turned. "She's not that much older than either of us, but you wouldn't guess it from how she comports herself."

Barbara swallowed a protest, knowing better than to get between the four sisters. Charlotte had taken on the task of managing the household and raising her sisters when their mother died of a sudden illness. It was an unenviable responsibility, and one she should be lauded for, not condemned.

Her thoughts halted for a moment, and Barbara had to admit didn't know if she'd feel the same with her sibling, had she had one, elevated from sister to parent between one day and the next.

"We'd best be back at work," she offered instead, standing up to shake the dirt from her dress and hair. She settled the bonnet more firmly around her face as well, remembering Charlotte's warning.

The beginning of her visit had passed quickly, full of learning new tasks and following her cousins around. They'd yet to have the chance to ride, as they'd done when much younger, but Charlotte led many an expedition into the surrounding countryside, and even the forest, after berries, flowers, and all manner of herbs.

Her cousin had been studying with the village midwife whenever she could spare a moment, saying only that knowing how to fix a body could prove useful. Barbara suspected the interest came from a lingering guilt for not being present to tend her mother, though from what Barbara understood, not even the most skilled of doctors could have changed what occurred.

In watching the focus Charlotte gave to every task, even managing her unruly sisters, Barbara saw the lack in her own existence. Her parents might not have intended the calluses, but this they'd hoped for her to see, or so she suspected.

Life held much more than an endless round of balls and poetry readings, not all of it good, but every moment precious. What they saw as a lightness of spirit, though, she knew to have been spite. The further Barbara came from that time, the more she regretted letting a harsh word push her to such actions.

Having Aubrey St. Vincent absent from her view surely helped Barbara gain some perspective, though still he lingered in her thoughts and not always for his condemnation. She'd spent too long developing her feelings for them to vanish so quickly, but she had no intention of ever seeking out his company and would avoid his presence as much as possible once she returned to London. She might have come to regret her actions, but she refused to forgive him his.

This time away had opened her eyes to the truth of the situation. More than not suiting, the two of them made a toxic combination as dangerous as some of the herbs Charlotte had them gather.

Her cousin had carefully explained how, in small doses, something strong could be an aid as much as a danger and so worth gathering. Such might be true of herbs, but Barbara found the reverse in people. A little of Aubrey's presence only drove her to worse frivolity. Whether a stronger dose would prove to make her even wilder or would become as nothing, she had no way of knowing, nor any intention of finding out. The man had, after all, been a true louse.

Jasper and Daphne greeted Aubrey's arrival with delight even though he had not taken the time between decision and setting out to send a messenger ahead.

"Nothing worse than the season to send a man running for the hills," Jasper said over dinner.

Daphne gave him a sharp look that held so much love any anger had been wiped from it. "You think it's so much better for the girls? There are as many who would flee if given the chance as look forward to their season."

Aubrey speared a piece of roast chicken with his fork as he nodded. "Isabella is surely one of those. If not for my mother's pressing, she'd have avoided coming out altogether." He stared down at his plate as he added, "Not that it's doing her much good."

Jasper brushed a hand over his wife's fingers. "I'm happy to have saved you from that."

She laughed. "As if you had any intention of doing so. Your mother pushed me as much as mine did, throwing me into a contract without even the chance to spin across the dance floor."

It was almost as though the two of them had forgotten Aubrey's presence all together. He'd teased Jasper about having grown tired of each other's company, but any fool could see their attraction had only deepened. The skeptic had found just what Aubrey sought so fruitlessly.

"It is not your type of dance," Aubrey said. "Much too confined."

"Refined, you mean. With every step known and even training on what to say to your partner should the chance to speak occur. It's a wonder anyone thinks to choose a mate when every attempt is made to make all of the debutantes conform to the same standards."

Aubrey laughed to hear his own thoughts from a woman. "Though one would think a nature of distinction would break through even so. I can't imagine you'd have faded into the background."

"Just ask Jasper how well I hid my nature. He dismissed me without a single moment of consideration."

She laughed, but he detected the smallest hint of irritation beneath her statement.

"And now I know my true purpose in coming here whatever I might have thought. I can relieve that lingering annoyance as I tell you without a single doubt in my mind Jasper did not dismiss you one bit. He may have wanted to, he may have tried, but from the moment he described his first encounter, I knew the man was in trouble."

"Hey, now. You're supposed to keep my secrets," Jasper exclaimed, though with no force behind the words.

"Like you kept mine?" Daphne said, her eyebrows rising.

"Until I'd obtained your permission."

"You would have been gratified to see it, Aubrey. The badgering, the seemingly innocent comments about how much easier it would be if you only knew the truth. Of course I gave in. I wouldn't have had a moment of peace otherwise."

So it went through the rest of the meal, Aubrey becoming ever more aware, no matter how much they tried to include him, he'd entered a place that revolved around the two of them so neatly he'd be forever reminded of his lack.

Daphne pushed to her feet. "Though we don't follow London rules here on most days, tonight I think I'll put in some extra practice and let you gentlemen talk."

"That isn't necessary," Aubrey protested though he appreciated the gesture.

Daphne waved off his objection, already on her way out of the room. He saw in her determination both the stubborn nature that had frustrated Jasper, and the conviction that secured his friend's heart.

"Don't argue when she gets that look in her eye," Jasper counseled. "It's the secret to a happy marriage. Now you better have something fascinating to tell me, because I love to watch my wife dance."

They rose as well, Aubrey grinning at his friend. "How well I know that. I'd thought for a moment last year you'd give up everything for the privilege."

"And so I would have had I not discovered my heart and fate had fallen in the same trap as impossible as it would have been to imagine at the time."

A fire crackled in the study, making the room inviting. Aubrey settled into one of the chairs as he wondered just how to entertain his friend.

"So what's the true reason you've come," Jasper said before Aubrey could find a good enough topic. "I know you too well to think you'd have abandoned your little sister to the dangers of society without cause. No matter how grueling the season may have been, there are entertainments enough to keep you away from the debutantes should you choose without quitting the environs to bury yourself in the country. You never were one for the country life."

Aubrey accepted the glass of fine cognac to gain a little more time, but he stared at the rich brown liquid instead of taking a sip. "I had little choice in the matter. Not all of us were raised on a country estate. It's not enough to miss my best friend's company?"

Jasper burst out with a laugh. "No, not in the slightest. Especially when I was up there to see you not so long ago. Unless I miss my guess, from your sideways glances whenever my wife and I tease, it has to do with a woman. Don't tell me you've found your perfect match and are now dragging your feet? You've been planning this since you grew out of a tutor's care."

Aubrey scowled at his friend, though he shouldn't have been surprised at Jasper's perception. "No, nothing like that. It's more the opposite what with none of the young ladies inspiring more than a passing glance. Daphne is correct in stating their natures are trained out of them, but how's a man supposed to find his match? I even had one mother suggest I could not know the truth of my bride until after the vows are spoken."

He dropped his gaze to the amber liquid, spinning the glass in a slow circle. "It seems chance has more to do with matches working than any deliberation. Why even my parents said their accord came into being as they settled into a life conjoined." Aubrey's mouth twisted up on one side. "I heartily question whether your parents planned on struggling to tolerate each other's presence long enough to bring forth a child, much less three."

"And I doubt you came for courting advice. From your sour expressions, observing wedded bliss to convince yourself that mother had the right of it was not the aim either."

Aubrey offered his friend one of those sour expressions right then but soon gave up in face of Jasper's intent look. "I don't know why I came. Really, I don't. I just couldn't spend one more moment there."

Jasper finally settled into a chair, leaning forward with his elbows on his knees. "So what changed? You were determined to see this through when last we spoke despite your qualms about the available ladies, and I doubt your mother is so fully recovered that Isabella would not appreciate your company … or perhaps she'd appreciate it more with your mother well once again."

A chuckle broke through Aubrey's glum mood as he considered the idea. "True enough, though she felt me a traitor this past week as I eagerly sought the very events that plagued her."

"You?" The chair creaked as Jasper leaned closer. "What brought about this change?"

"Would you believe a cut direct? Though she wasn't as direct as all that."

"Ah ha! Now we get to the heart of it. This is about a woman."

Aubrey leapt to his feet, unable to stay still any longer. "About a woman, perhaps, but not really. It's just the first thing to catch my interest this season. She shied her horse to avoid meeting me. I know nothing much about her, or why she would find me so repellent. I've never even spoken to her." The mocking he'd suffer should Jasper learn her name would only be worsened if his friend sought The Dowager Lady Pendleton's help in procuring an answer. Aubrey chose to keep that piece of information to himself for the time being.

Jasper shook his head. "If only all those hopefuls understood the way to catch your attention was to reject it. I'll bet many an aspiring mother would be thrilled to be listening in at this moment."

"Mock me all you like, Jasper Pendleton, but you stand on unstable ground. How was it again your weathered heart found it could be claimed? Your lady wife had to parade about in a mask."

"Don't let Daphne hear you speak so. She'd be the first to correct your assumptions as she donned the mask to avoid our happiness much more than to lay claim to it."

Aubrey shrugged, conceding the point without a battle. "It's just that mystery won your attention when no other young lady had achieved success. Now I have a mystery of my own to solve, and I'm at a loss as to how."

"That I don't believe. Your sister may struggle to talk with those outside the family, but you've never suffered from that weakness. Simply catch her off guard and get your answer before she remembers whatever reason she has for wishing you gone. Perhaps she was caught up in her own thoughts that day and didn't even notice you coming."

"You make it sound so easy."

"And you make it all too hard. If you've never spoken to this lady, how can the offense be so great? Speak with her and you'll find it's nothing. Mystery solved, but perhaps the start of something more."

"You think I haven't tried to see any other reason for her actions myself? There was little question she meant to avoid me and me alone, but that's not what makes this near impossible." He tossed back the remainder of his cognac too quickly and began to cough.

Jasper snatched up the glass and pounded Aubrey hard between the shoulders with his other hand until Aubrey shrugged his friend off.

"Nothing is impossible, and something's wrong for you to give up so quickly," Jasper said as he returned to his seat to observe Aubrey's struggles.

Wiping the water from his eyes, Aubrey gave Jasper a bleary look. "You're so quick to doubt my persistence that you fail to consider the other possibility. The lady in question has left London behind, sent away by her father for any number of reasons if gossip were to be believed, though none match my own observations, or those of my sister."

"Isabella is involved in this as well? No wonder you ran from London as fast as your feet could carry you. Next your mother will be making inquiries on your behalf." Jasper started to laugh then stopped, an odd look on his face. "You say she was sent from London during her season? Aubrey, seems to me this lady is already taken, a mite prematurely."

"And now you. There could be any number of causes beyond that she's carrying some man's get. I don't believe it of her."

"You don't believe it of a lady you know only by reputation, having never spoken a word in her presence? Seems to me you found your match as handily as I found mine. Now you must take steps to convince her of that fact, a bit difficult with her gone."

"Which lands me here watching the two of you cooing over each other like a pair of doves. I could not face another moment in London with all those eager mothers when the one who had piqued my attention had made herself, or been made, absent. I'd hoped to find distraction here, not more of the same."

Jasper braced his chin on steepled fingers as he studied Aubrey once again. "A week or two in the country may be just what you need to clear your head after all. And if you're right, you may just find your lady love has returned in your absence all the better for whatever sent her away."

He stood, waving one arm in a grand gesture. "I make the library and stables available to you, my friend. There's fields a plenty, forest, and valley to explore should you tire of reading. Unlike you, I have not the luxury of leisure, but will set aside what time I can to spend with you. I seem to recall a certain horse I'd suggested we visit."

Aubrey accepted the gracious offer, grateful for the conversation to turn to other pursuits. Talking with Jasper had solved nothing. He remained plagued by a woman who saw fit to disdain him and he'd no hope of uncovering the cause. His best chance of relief lay in focusing on other things, though he held out little hope based on his experience so far.

Chapter Twelve

As they finished breakfast the next morning, Daphne turned to Jasper. "I think it's time. I've been thinking about it since Aubrey came down, and I've decided it is."

Aubrey looked between the two of them, wondering what this could possibly be about.

"If you're sure."

"Your staff has been endlessly willing to let me practice my teaching, but I need to use that practice. And with Aubrey here, you'll notice my absence less."

"Very well, then. Bettie, please send for Willem."

"What is this?" Aubrey asked as he lifted his cup to drink the last of his tea.

"Daphne plans to teach dance to the local girls as I told you when last I came to London. Perhaps someday she'll open a dance school there as well."

The look of pride Jasper bestowed on his wife was something to be seen, but Aubrey worried of the consequences.

"Won't your secret be threatened if you go teaching others your arrangements?"

Daphne laughed, waving a hand for patience as she got it out of her system. "I'm not teaching performance dance, Aubrey. I'm not the fool you think me. No, I'll teach them the proper steps, and maybe a little grace. Wait a season or two and you may find the ballroom floor transformed."

"Now that would be a sight."

"You called for me, mistress?"

Annoyance swept Daphne's face, though Aubrey suspected the address not the interruption as its cause. From what Jasper had told him, this young man had been raised practically alongside Daphne from an early age, only taking on a servant's place once her father brought the two girls to London. With Willem's involvement in Daphne's schemes, Aubrey suspected the formality something no less recent than her wedding.

"Yes, I did. I need you to go down to the village and speak to the landholders. Ask them if their daughters would be interested in formal dance training. Whether a season in London or country dances, a little grace can go quite far."

"Very well."

He turned to go without further comment, but Jasper caught his arm. "Could you go to the Ferrier household? If I recall correctly, he has some four daughters for my lady's purposes, but I would ask you to carry another request as well. Ask when it would be a good time for me to bring Aubrey down to see that new yearling put through his paces."

"Very well, my lord."

Daphne sighed as he left the room. "He's grown so formal."

Jasper gave her a look that spoke of previous discussions. "You asked if it would pain him. He said no. He is only trying to find his proper station in the household."

She shoved her plate away. "And I'd thought he'd have found it by now."

Aubrey heard the layers of meaning in the words though he lacked the context to comprehend them.

Jasper caught her hand. "It's not so easy to redirect a heart, especially when there's not one to give it to. Give him time, and perhaps your friendship will renew. But perhaps not. If it pains you, I can have him return to your father's household. Lord Scarborough was sad to lose him."

Daphne pulled free with a quick jerk, only to restore the touch a moment later. "I would not send him away just because his discomfort vexes me. If he feels the need, I expect him to come forward. I just miss our friendship."

Aubrey shook his head, thinking on the complexity of life. Clearly Willem had more than friendly feelings toward Daphne, and had for some time from the sound of it. He might bemoan his lonely state, but how much worse must it be to watch the bliss the woman he loved had found with another. Station had little to do with the heart.

Jasper rose from the table, putting an end to the discussion of Willem and his fate. "So, Aubrey, what's it to be on this bright day? Care to come with me on a tour of my holdings? There are some fences in need of consideration, or so my men tell me."

"I'd be happy to." Learning the extent of the land and getting his bearings could only serve him well should Aubrey choose to escape this company for a ride. Besides, he suspected Jasper would give them the chance for something more exhilarating than a simple amble. The confines of London offered little for those in need of a run without bringing censure down on their heads.

"**A**re you sure you don't need a hand with that bucket?" Sarah asked Barbara.

Though the metal bit into her palms, Barbara kept going, head down so she could have warning of potential splashes. "I milked it. I'll bring it in."

From the corner of her eye, she saw Sarah shake her head as she too carried a bucket, though a much lighter one.

"If you'd stopped when told, it wouldn't be so heavy."

"And would you have expected me to," Barbara teased as she slowed her step so the thick milk wouldn't spill over and be wasted.

Sarah stopped all together, putting her bucket down in the yard as she started to laugh. With as much effort as she put into the merriment, even her more reasonable level would have been threatened.

"Excuse me, young misses."

They turned toward the unfamiliar voice to see a good-looking young man dressed much the same as they were, though his clothing showed none of the wear on the cast-offs her cousins had lent Barbara.

Her mother would have been horrified for Barbara to be mistaken for a commoner. She'd worked far too hard raising her daughter as a lady despite her own background. But in that moment, the mistake seemed delightful.

Barbara offered a quick curtsy.

A heartbeat later, Sarah followed the gesture without giving Barbara away.

The young man, though, had eyes for Sarah alone for all he tried to include both of them in his greeting.

Barbara didn't blame him.

With Sarah lost to laughter when he first came upon them, she'd have shone with good humor. Even now, a blush lingered on her cheeks and her eyes glittered in the morning light.

"You have a message?" Barbara prompted when it seemed the two of them would do nothing but stare. She'd have to remind Sarah of proper comportment when they were once again alone, as ironic as that might be considering the roles were all too often reversed.

The young man blinked as though returning to awareness all of a sudden. "Yes, of course. I'm Willem Anderson from the Pendleton Manor. My mistress sent me here to speak to the mistress of this house, and I'm to meet with the master as well."

Barbara tensed at the name, but had no cause to deny him. "The mistress is Charlotte, I suppose. She's off in the milking barn. I don't know where my — the master is, but we can find him for you."

If he'd caught her slip, he made no mention of it. His gaze had turned upon Sarah once again.

Barbara glanced around the yard.

Cook stood within earshot, and one of the stable hands bathed a horse nearby. As chaperones they would have to do.

"Why don't you wait here with Sarah as I go fetch Charlotte?"

Sarah flushed a deep crimson. "I could not."

With a quick nod to the others in the yard, Barbara pointed at the buckets they'd been carrying. "I can't very well carry my milk pail back the way it came, not with any speed. Someone must watch over them.

Surely you don't expect Willem to take on the task. Or perhaps he'd be willing to carry mine the rest of the way so you can get him a glass of water. It must have been a long walk from the manor."

"Not as long as all that," Willem assured her, "But a drink wouldn't go amiss. I'd be happy to lend Miss Sarah a hand."

Barbara sent her friend a wink as she turned toward the barn. "Just make sure you don't spill any," she called over her shoulder only to hear Sarah's warning of the same.

"She overfilled the bucket so take care. You wouldn't want milk to sour on your trousers."

Barbara went after Charlotte with measured steps, wanting to give the two of them a chance to talk. No harm could come of it when they'd be here such a short time, and why shouldn't Sarah have some fun. After all, she had not been the one to get them cast out of London, nor had she suffered to learn the object of her affections had the manners of an oaf.

"**P**erhaps she's planning to hold grand balls and wants us all to make a good showing," Jane said later that night, hands smoothing her skirt after sitting down to the meal.

"She could bring gentlemen from London and it would be just like coming out." Marian got a dreamy look on her face.

"Or perhaps she's just seeking a diversion, and nothing will ever come of it," Barbara said, her mind on the discovery of who lived in the manor. Remembering just whom they had invited down from London, she hoped that when he finally availed himself of their request, she'd be long gone from here.

"Really, Cousin Barbara."

Marian's censure shook Barbara from her dwelling on Aubrey long enough to be embarrassed. "I'm sorry," she said, "but don't you find it the least bit odd for the lady of the manor to be offering to teach any comer the polite dances?"

"Are we so far beneath you, then?" Georgiana lashed out.

"I didn't mean it that way."

"Girls, I haven't even decided if any of you will be allowed to go," Charlotte said, her voice sharp. "Can we at least have a meal in peace?"

That drew the attention off Barbara but without bringing the hoped for peace as Jane jumped on her older sister with, "Why should you be the one to decide. You had a season proper in London before Mother died. Who are you to deny us the shadow of that when it comes calling?"

"Perhaps Lady Whitfeld will send for one of us to return with Barbara and have a season of our own," Marian said, her good humor restored quickly as it always did.

"Perhaps you should spend less time dreaming and more on your chores. A season, in London or elsewhere, is not the glamorous round of balls and events you might think it. It's confusing and complicated, and can haunt you for a lifetime."

Charlotte pressed both hands to her lips as though to catch the words that had already escaped, her normal calm shattered. A deep sorrow showed in her eyes before she closed them and drew a shaky breath as she struggled for control.

"Girls, you will listen to your sister in this," their father broke in from where he examined the paper come down from London on the stage. "Be happy with your lot in life. Looking for something beyond you means only grief in the end."

What followed Charlotte's outburst and his words could only be termed a somber meal.

Barbara did not know what had happened during Charlotte's season to produce such an aversion, but she couldn't very well plead that hers had been all lightness and joy, though she'd brought her banishment upon herself.

Still, what harm could there be in letting the girls dream a bit. Or in learning proper dance. Her studies in art and dance had held more joy than those in comportment for all poetry and politics held her attention the most. If her mother wouldn't have fainted dead away at the thought, she'd have sought out some bluestockings to further her understanding.

Barbara vowed to speak to Charlotte on this topic alone.

Without the complaints and dreams of her sisters battering her ears, surely she'd see no harm in the training. Not that Barbara planned to set foot in the manor herself, but once she'd returned to London, it would provide a lovely diversion in a life that centered around chores.

And should her mother decide to bring one of the cousins out as she had Charlotte when Barbara had been too young to care, at least they'd have a chance at making a good showing. Perhaps that had been at the root of Charlotte's disappointment. If she'd stood out too much as a country girl, the London gentlemen might just have thought her too simple to take on a life in society.

Happy in the decision, Barbara snagged her uncle's paper once he'd finished with it and set it aside to peruse later in her room. She had chores for now, helping the others clear the table and set the kitchen to rights for the early baking.

Chapter Thirteen

The next morning, Barbara and Sarah lined up with the rest of the girls for Charlotte to list out their chores. This life had little in common with Barbara's London existence. While she missed the poetry and discussing politics with her father, there was peace to be found in a world where one's worth was measured not in how others saw her but in her own actions.

Though Uncle Ferrier rebuffed any attempts to engage him in discussion of what she studied in his paper, even regarding farm economics, she'd learned many skills so far that might just someday come to use when she had a manor of her own to tend, her father's or that of the man she deemed worthy to marry.

Charlotte handed out wicker baskets, each of the cousins grinning as she reached for hers. Though the baskets had some meaning, Barbara and Sarah shared confused glances. They had to wait for the explanation to understand.

"The farmhands reported a raspberry bramble gone ripe early. We'll have to be quick to get there before the birds, but if we manage enough, Cook will make us a pie."

"And tarts," Georgiana added to Charlotte's pronouncement with a smack of her lips. "You've not tasted anything until you've had one of Cook's tarts fresh out of the oven.

"If you manage to taste anything with your mouth all burnt to a crisp." Jane caught Barbara's sleeve. "Don't listen to her. Wait until the tarts are cooled a bit."

"If there's any left by then," Marian added with her eyebrows arched and a nod toward the youngest of the four.

Charlotte pushed Georgiana then the rest of them toward the farm gate. "Don't count the number of tarts until we've gathered the berries. And don't any of you snack on more than four, no six. One for each of us." She leaned toward Barbara, her mouth twitching to counter her stern tone. "If I set no limits, we'll come home with berry-stained hands and reddened lips, but empty baskets and no hope of even one tart. The worst of it, though, is explaining to my father how we spent the whole day out in the fields and he gets not even a single berry."

She managed a passable imitation of Uncle Ferrier with the last, and they all laughed their way out into the countryside.

They found the bushes the farmhands had seen soon enough. Though the birds had collected the outer layer, Marian took Barbara in hand, showing her how to bump the branches apart with a fold of her skirt and find the ripe berries hidden deeper inside where thorns protected them.

Barbara pinched the first one as Marian had shown her only to have it squish between her fingers.

"That's one," Jane called out as Barbara licked the juice from her fingers.

All the others stopped long enough to pop a berry into their mouths, a ritual Sarah quickly caught on to.

Barbara swore she wouldn't have only juice for her remaining five and used much more care to tug those that followed.

Soon, she'd mastered the technique enough to add layer upon layer to her basket quickly, pausing only to tease the other girls and enjoy a stretch in the sun.

"Time for luncheon," Charlotte called, making Barbara aware of how far they'd spread in the raspberry bramble.

She made her way to the others to discover the extra basket Charlotte had carried held a large blanket, and bread and cheese for them to share.

"Did you go on picnics in London?" Jane asked, looking to Sarah as much as Barbara for a glimpse into life in the city.

While Sarah explained how outings worked in London, and the

differences between a servant's life and a lady's, Barbara leaned back and let the sun kiss her cheeks. Her cousins might have found London and the season fascinating from a distance, but she couldn't imagine giving up such freedom for uncomfortable clothing, judgmental society members, and the limited conversation allowed at most events.

A hand tugged her bonnet down across her face.

"You'll end up with freckles so dark no weight of powder can hide them if you're not careful."

Barbara sat up at the sound of Charlotte's voice, the others leaning close to listen to Sarah. "One more reason for the other girls to avoid a London season. It's taking care every moment not to make a misstep, not to talk too loud or be too enthusiastic, but at the same time somehow sparkle and distinguish yourself all within the constraints of society. Freckles are the least of the strictures I've broken since coming here." She raised her berry-stained hands as evidence.

Charlotte got a faraway look to her eye as she said, "It's the lure of the unknown. You feel it here where our chores are delightful explorations for you and Sarah. They want to feel the same, only their unknown lies in London with its fancy dresses and grand balls. I remember how dazzling it all seemed when your mother took me up."

Her cousin had avoided all mention of the season that had been cut short so Barbara kept her lips pressed closed, hoping for another hint as to what happened.

Charlotte gave a quick headshake as though in response to Barbara's hope and pushed to her feet. "Come on, girls. Our baskets are barely half full. If we return with so little, Father will declare the tarts for everyone but the six of us for our slacking."

"Can we at least have a berry each to sustain us?" Georgiana asked, her expression denying the filling meal Cook had prepared for their luncheon.

Her playacting brought a smile to Charlotte's lips, wiping away the hint of melancholy whatever thought of her season had caused. "As if a single berry could sustain your energy, Georgie, but you're right to mention it. Everyone has been so careful" — a sideways glance at Barbara marked the exception — "we've yet to have a second."

Each of them snatched up the largest, ripest berry they could find in their basket before heading into the bushes once again. Barbara matched her speed to Charlotte's, the talk of seasons reminding her of the vow to convince Charlotte to let the girls have their dancing.

Chapter Fourteen

The tour Jasper gave him the previous day allowed Aubrey the confidence to venture out on his own upon discovering his friend had paperwork to accomplish. The stables boasted many a fine horse, and Aubrey had been testing the paces mastered by the beast he chose.

Aubrey let the horse amble through the fields on his way back to the manor, both he and the beast pleasantly tired.

The sun burned down warm against his neck but not too hot, the birds chirped, and the horse had a comfortable gait. After the strain of London during the season, attempting to help his sister find her mate, keeping his father's estates running smoothly, and all the rest, he could see the appeal of a country retreat. He'd never sequester himself out here, though.

His place was in London, and he knew the quiet would soon grow unwelcome as he itched to do something more complicated and with greater impact. Nothing could hold the same draw here where the biggest concern — weather — was out of human control and so beyond his reach.

Unlike many of his peers, he'd been raised in London proper, having only visits to tour the estates for his country experience. His father's interest in politics started even before inheriting the seat in the House of Lords, and little could be accomplished without a solid presence in the capital. Unlike some, he preferred to keep his family at his side.

A glint of color drew Aubrey from his thoughts.

He urged the horse forward to investigate, faint memories of childhood jaunts returning the nearer he came to the decorated bushes. He'd discovered a large raspberry patch at the peak of ripeness. Aubrey swung down and tossed the reins over the horse's head to use as a lead rope, unwilling to let this treasure pass untouched.

The first berry dropped into his hand as though it had been waiting for his arrival, and faster than he would have thought possible, three more gave way to his eager fingers and even more eager lips. This the country could offer which had no parallel within the bounds of the city.

Sun-warmed ripe berries.

He mourned the lack of a basket to bring some to the manor, but swore he'd do his best to mark the placement so he could alert Jasper and Daphne to the bounty.

Aubrey collected what he could in a clean handkerchief as he made his way around the bramble.

Laughter and joyful cries reached his ears.

For a heartbeat, he wondered if forest nymphs had burst free from some of the poetry he'd been reading, but no. He rounded a corner with his cloth full of berries and his horse trailing after to see a vision.

A young country girl filled his sight. Her riot of dark brown curls danced around a head tossed back to reveal an open expression and wide smile. Her bonnet hung loose from around her neck. The sheer delight of her laughter caught hold of something deep inside him, washing away the melancholy that threatened him of late. It didn't hurt that she shared some features with Lady Barbara Whitfeld. If he could not ask his question, at least he could admire her country copy.

Here was someone so at peace with her place in life that she found joy in the simple pleasures of berry picking, though from her dress, she'd likely been set to it by a master rather than of her own will. This girl seemed as far from the constrained young ladies of London as possible, and yet she, not her refined equivalents, was the first to spark an instant attraction in his breast.

The laughter fell silent as the girl and her companions noticed him one by one, as though his presence wiped the joy from their simple world.

His thoughts soured. He had no right to pursue his interest, even so far as to make it known to the girl in question. The distance between their lives measured longer than the miles between here and the city proper. The very joy that captivated him would be crushed in the strictures of his world, while a simple country girl would find no peace among the responsibilities of a London lady. She no more belonged in his life than the sun-warmed berries he'd plucked from the branches.

Their curious smiles grew stiff as he stood locked in his own indecision, a further sign of how harmful his presence could be. He couldn't very well turn around and go back the way he'd come, though. He'd been raised a gentleman, and it was about time he lived up to the title.

Tugging on the reins, Aubrey stepped forward to greet them. "Good afternoon, misses. I apologize for the intrusion. I see you're more prepared to enjoy this bounty than I." He raised his stained handkerchief in explanation only to freeze as he met the gaze of the very girl who'd caught his eye.

She stared at him as though she knew him, as though she shared the instinctive connection he'd felt when first he came upon her.

All his careful thoughts of consequences and difficulties vanished, leaving him to gaze at her as though struck dumb. He lowered his hand a moment later, having forgotten it, but he did not break her gaze until she turned away, a delicate blush rising up her neck to color cheeks much too pale for all the time she must have spent in the sun.

Barbara could not believe her luck.

Here she'd been laughing at the enthusiasm with which her younger cousins met the news that she had convinced Charlotte to let them dance, and he had to appear to destroy everything. She needn't have worried that the dance lessons would bring her to Aubrey. He had come here on his own to haunt her.

Her whirling thoughts settled around the last as she recalled his expression when he gazed upon her. Confusion, yes, but she'd seen not a hint of recognition.

He'd seen fit to spread tales about her, to condemn both her comportment and nature, but he'd never bothered to pay enough attention to identify her features even when they'd crossed paths in the park.

The cousins moved closer, introducing themselves and asking if he came from the manor, but Barbara had no curiosity about the man. She'd thought she knew him so well, but everything she'd known had been proved false in one fateful moment when she heard his true nature revealed. She did not understand why his dismissal continued to burn, or why his failure to mark her presence here, even in simple clothing, confounded her. If anything, she should be happy he came by accident and not to plague her.

"And this young woman?"

Barbara spun around, sure he meant none other than herself.

Driven by a wild urge to stave off her cousins' efforts to make her known, she said, "I'm called Barbara," before any others could make the introduction.

He met her gaze with an intent look that warmed her to her very bones. "A pleasure to make your acquaintance, Miss Barbara." He smiled then, and it seemed the sun itself grew brighter.

A blush rose to burn her cheeks despite what she knew about him. In her own life, he'd thought her a waste of time not even worth securing an introduction, yet here, he seemed all interest and intrigued.

The heat drained away as she realized the only possible meaning to his regard. He must have been one of those who found their entertainment among the lower classes, knowing he wouldn't be held accountable for his actions beyond a coin or two, and certainly not forced into marriage as he would be if dallying with a woman of position.

Under the weight of his gaze, though, she wondered what it would be like to be pursued by him.

Barbara turned away a second time, almost faint with the heat rushing through her. She did not want to be compromised by any man, and certainly not by one who held her true nature in disdain. She thought more of herself than to chance her future, her reputation, and her heart on the attentions of a lust-filled young lord no matter how attractive her eyes might find his form.

"You must join us in our berrying, Lord Aubrey. Charlotte has a basket to spare, should you need one."

Barbara opened her mouth to protest Georgiana's enthusiasm, but Aubrey spoke before she could.

"As much as I'd enjoy the company," he said, "I must be on my way with my meager gathering. It does a man poorly to linger among enchanting nymphs."

The others laughed at that, high-pitched giggles much unlike how they greeted the thought of learning proper dance.

Barbara frowned at them. Could they not see his meaning? He might have used pretty words as an excuse, but once the opportunity for a quick tumble in the field was lost with so many gathered round, he saw no need to waste his time among those well beneath him.

The cousins called out farewells and watched him ride off, but Barbara turned back to the bush, venting her anger on the stiff branches that sought to block her way.

"You'll only crush the berries if you continue in this way," Charlotte said, coming up on her side. She glanced over her shoulder in the direction Aubrey had gone before continuing, "Someone from your past come to haunt you?"

Barbara gave a sour laugh as her cousin mirrored her earlier thought. "Anyone of significance to me would recognize my features as surely you saw he did not. He's nothing but an arrogant lord who sees all of us as beneath his notice."

Her cousin nodded as though in agreement, but Barbara shifted, uncomfortable under the accompanying gaze. She waited for Charlotte to question further, for her to pry free the whole sorry story of Barbara's attachment to a man who had proved no more real than the nymphs Aubrey had called them.

Charlotte said nothing further.

She turned back to the gathering and drifted away to let Barbara recover herself alone.

If only thoughts of Aubrey would prove equally as obliging. Instead, they lingered and rose at the least opportune moments. Even worse, rather than the annoyance and anger she should dwell upon, what came to her was the sense of a bond between them in that first glance, the heat that rushed through her at being his entire focus.

Chapter Fifteen

Aubrey had no intention of sullying Jasper's reputation by tying him to stories of lords who came on country visits only to deflower the local girls and vanish to London. All the more reason not to test his restraint by spending more time with the enchanting Barbara. He'd known her for only brief moments, and yet every word from her lips clung to his memory. The unrestrained laugh he'd come upon made him want nothing more than to inspire the same himself.

No, better he'd left the field before this connection could develop further. She had no place in his world, and he had no business disrupting hers.

His decision did not change as he cantered to the manor and sequestered himself in his room after exchanging the raspberries with Willem for the latest newspaper on his way in. Even London politics failed to distract him, though, from lingering on the sparkle in her eyes, the twitch of her lip as she tried to suppress her merriment, or many other tiny details he hadn't known he'd noticed.

By the time the deep bell sounded to announce dinner, Aubrey had started to wonder if this would forever be his state, to yearn always after the women he could not have. Perhaps in his envy of Jasper and Daphne's happiness, he had become obsessive. Perhaps he'd created a cut by Lady Barbara when she'd simply turned away, and the strength of his link with the country girl never truly existed.

He froze, one hand on the staircase rail, as he realized they shared more than a superficial resemblance. They bore the same name, his rigid London mystery and his wild country girl, as though taunting him. The vision of them meeting was enough to give his lips a twist when he joined the others, a merriment as poorly suppressed as Barbara's from the way Jasper raised his eyebrows at the sight of Aubrey.

"Just what are you reading, my friend, that it brings so much life to your expression."

Aubrey took his seat with a nod of greeting to Daphne. "The paper." He passed the same object to Jasper, having appropriated it before any other could peruse the contents.

Jasper ignored the offering to examine Aubrey as though he were a puzzle to be solved. After a moment, he shook his head. "As much as you aspire to politics, there's nothing in that volume to bring forth such enthusiasm, I'd guess. You seem happier somehow. Happier than since your arrival."

The presentation of an aromatic soup offered a distraction, but once his portion had been served, Aubrey noticed Jasper still eying him with an expectant look. He gave his friend a shrug. "I went for a ride today seeing as you were busy with managing your estate. I finally breathed in enough of this elixir you call air to clear London from my lungs."

"No," Daphne said, drawing the word out. "Jasper's right. It's more than that. You've a touch of sun to your cheek, but even our beautiful country isn't enough to bring a haze to your eyes. I'd guess you weren't thinking on our company at all as you came through from the hall. Something happened on your ride."

Under their combined stare, Aubrey shifted in his seat, feeling much the schoolboy facing charges of misbehavior. This had been part of why he'd left the girls rather than enjoying their company. He did not want to receive his friends' censure, and though her presence in his life measured a short year with few encounters, Aubrey had the feeling Daphne was rapidly becoming a member of his inner circle much as Jasper had when they first met at Oxford.

"Enough. It's no grand mystery, I swear. As I've already confessed to Jasper, shepherding my sister through her season and then seeing the two of you together just made me aware of the lack of love in my own life. While your husband saw marriage a trial before finding you, I've always thought having someone at my side would make my day brighter."

Daphne raised one eyebrow. "And a simple country ride made you reach acceptance?"

Her tone could not have been less doubting, nor did she have any need to call him out more specifically.

"If I tell you, can we enjoy our meal before the soup goes cold?"

"Perhaps you should take a bite first. I've seen this look on my wife's face, and she won't be satisfied until she's heard the full of it," Jasper injected with a chuckle as though he hadn't been the one to start their inquisition.

Not willing to waste the advice or the soup, Aubrey took not one but three spoonfuls, pausing to savor the creamy asparagus and letting the others do the same before telling his sorry tale.

"You'll most likely enjoy some of the rewards of my ride, and I've informed your staff of the placement, but I found a large patch of raspberry bushes with berries plump and ready to be consumed."

Daphne's eyes widened. "I knew some should have come into season soon. There's nothing like fresh berries."

Jasper's chair creaked as he leaned forward. "But not enough to explain your joy, for all we appreciate the treat. What happened out there?"

In quick, short sentences that attempted to give away nothing but failed from the expressions on his friends' faces, Jasper explained how he came upon the farm girls out picking the self-same berries he'd been enjoying. He deliberately avoided names in favor of description, only noticing his mistake once Jasper grinned.

"So you met a girl. No wonder your eyes are dreamy and a smile plays around your lips."

"Tell us about her," Daphne broke in, shooting her husband a mock-irritated look.

Aubrey shrugged. "There's not much to tell. Yes, she caught my interest, but that means nothing. I can no more marry a simple country girl than you chose Willem over Jasper here."

She glanced around the room, clearly caring enough for the man to keep him from the pain of Aubrey's unintentionally cruel statement. He'd meant only to deflect the attention from himself, an effort that proved no more worthy than his attempt to call out Daphne's servant.

"Why I didn't marry Willem had more to do with my own feelings, though my parents would have suffered greatly had I chosen to do my sister one better. I'd like to think I would have proven as strong in love as she did, but my heart settled on one of my own station so I never had to test this."

Jasper arched his eyebrows. "And is it such a burden then?"

She reached over and smacked his arm in retaliation for his teasing, but even that could not distract her for long as she turned on Aubrey to continue, "It's not unknown for a man to marry outside his station, though more choose mistresses there." She sent a dark look Jasper's way, but he only laughed it off. "Why, I suspect there's more women with pedigrees lower than you'd have thought. Given enough incentive, the trappings of station can be learned."

"Or so you are relying on with your dance teaching."

Daphne silenced her husband with a look and focused in on Aubrey, her expectant expression showing he had no choice but to offer a reasoned response.

"No, it's not unknown for some of the wealthier trading families to exchange their coin for an elevation in standing, and you're right that many things happen in the name of love that would be frowned upon by the society matrons, your mother among them, Jasper. But there's a world of difference between a London merchant's daughter who has some sense of how the city process works, and a country girl used to open fields and laxer rules. She'd be nothing but miserable in London, and my future is tied to the city. I'd find nothing to do out here and would die of the tedium."

"You'd be surprised how busy one can be in the country, or maybe not so surprised with me abandoning you to your own devices for the day. Still, if your mind is set against this, neither of us has any right to steer your path." Jasper turned back to his soup, signaling the conversation had ended.

Daphne gave Aubrey one last look, but held her tongue as she too turned to the meal.

"Have you had much response to your request for students?" Aubrey asked as the soup bowls were taken away by the staff, the topic chosen as much to draw the attention from his doorstep as because he had any curiosity.

Daphne complied with his unspoken desire and started in to the accounting of Willem's quest as though she had not been quizzing Aubrey only moments before.

"I hear we have you girls to thank for the delicious tarts … though Cook did also mention how quite a few went missing barely out of the hot oven." Uncle Ferrier shot a glance at Georgiana, but his smile softened the reprove.

"We deserved them," his youngest daughter declared. "Our restraint when faced with the fresh-picked berries was nothing short of angelic. Just ask Charlotte."

"Barbara showed the greatest restraint of all," Marian added with an arch look at her cousin.

Before Barbara could do anything to turn the conversation, her uncle shifted his attention to her.

"Oh? I suspect this has little to do with berries."

She smothered a sigh, wondering just what had been in the message announcing her arrival.

"She caught the eye of a nobleman visiting the manor," Jane said. "Who would have thought her season successful even out here?"

Marian reached for the basket of rolls as she finished her earlier thought with, "But she hardly gave him a glance, though he would have liked that and more if my eyes didn't deceive."

Uncle Ferrier had kept his attention focused on Barbara as her cousins supplied the story she'd hoped to forget. She waited for the lecture to follow, but her uncle only shrugged.

"Seems to me Barbara behaved all right and proper, though I suspect the same cannot be said for the rest of you."

Barbara wondered if now, with him singing her praises, would be an opportune time to ask about riding his horses knowing as she did her uncle would allow a proper saddle for safety if not propriety. With his mind on appearances, though, her timing could not have been worse so she said only, "They simply offered to help him gather berries for the manor. He declined."

"As so he should have." He cast his gaze around the table. "You have no business gathering about unattached young men, girls. We might not be noble stock, but your reputations are worth enough not to squander them."

Georgiana tossed her head. "It's not like Charlotte wasn't there with us the whole time. We were chaperoned as well as any at the fancy balls in London."

Their father shook his head, gathered up his paper much to Barbara's disappointment, and rose to leave the table. Before he'd passed through the doorway, though, he called back, "You forget that while your sister plays the role of mother, she's an unmarried young woman as much as any of you. I'll not have rumors spread that my girls lack decorum."

He didn't wait for an answer.

"Though I suppose it's no different from London in more ways than one," Georgiana murmured, her father's censure having little effect. "From what we were told, you have a long list of suitors all begging for an answer which you refuse them."

"Georgie!"

Charlotte's attempt came too late to prevent the blush that rose to heat Barbara's cheeks. The message had held more than she would have hoped if it spoke both to her success and her indecisiveness. Her parents had likely assumed he'd keep the contents to himself, but having been here long enough now, Barbara suspected her uncle had read the letter aloud over the breakfast table to share news of London before realizing discretion might have served better.

"Aubrey St. Vincent is nothing like those suitors," she said, her tone sharp. "They came to my father proper. He didn't even know me from a simple country girl, and his intentions were unlikely to include a proposal."

A hurt look crossed Georgiana's face before Barbara realized the way her words could have been taken.

"I didn't mean anything by it," she whispered.

"Maybe that's the problem," Georgiana snapped. "Maybe you consider yourself better than all of your suitors like you do the lot of us. I'm just grateful not all share your thinking."

Jane put a hand on her sister's arm, though whether to soothe or restrain, Barbara couldn't tell. Either would be welcome. Her cousin's words burned, but she'd drawn them out herself with her own ill-thought speech.

Marian gave a forced laugh. "If he doesn't know who you really are, maybe you should do some kissing behind the hay bales. Your reputation would be sound, and you'd lose some of your arrogance."

Accepting the attempt to deflect with grace, Barbara chuckled. "I'd prefer to adopt a country girl's saddle than her kisses."

"Oh, but that's only because you haven't tried them," Georgiana said, the transgression apparently forgiven.

"Georgie!" Charlotte cried again, this time shock coloring her tone. "Don't tell me you have."

The youngest of them gave a wink. "I won't. Tell you that is."

Charlotte put a hand to her forehead and pretended to faint. "Guiding the lot of you will put me in an early grave."

"Ah, but you heard Father," Marian chimed in. "You're no different than the rest of us. An eligible young woman ripe for the picking. Like the raspberries. Perhaps the next young lord will fall for your favors."

Their sister turned a deep crimson and thrust to her feet hard enough to make the dishes rattle. "I think it's time to clear the table," she said in a tone that allowed no argument.

Barbara joined the others in completing the chore, enduring teasing glances though nothing else was said. Nothing needed to be.

The image of Aubrey bending toward her in the shelter of some haystack and of her rising up to meet him seemed firmly embedded behind her eyelids. An odd heat flooded her body at the idea.

Sarah gave her a look that seemed all too knowing each time they passed in the hall between the dining room and kitchen, having eaten at the formal table.

As much as her friend could not possibly know what lay in Barbara's thoughts, the knowledge did little to stop another blush from heating her cheeks. If only he had stayed in London as he should have. Now he infected her visions of the country as much as he ever had those of London proper.

Chapter Sixteen

"I have some letters still to write," Jasper announced as they rose from the table after a lovely meal followed by cheesecake topped with the few raspberries Aubrey had managed to bring back. "I'll see you come morning, Aubrey. Have pleasant dreams if you won't allow yourself more than that."

Aubrey gave a sour laugh and went to follow Jasper from the room, but Daphne caught his arm.

"You forget. When Jasper fell for me, he thought me only a public dancer. My proper self he'd decided to throw over despite the repercussions because it wouldn't have been fair to either of us if he spent his married life pining after another. Only chance made the dancer and my noble form one and the same."

Aubrey shrugged, the story still a bit miraculous and much harder to accept when he'd set a simpler task of finding a mate through proper circumstances and failed. "Maybe I should have haunted the dance halls instead, though seeing as I was the one to bring the masked dancer to Jasper's attention, it seems even that path is barred to me."

She poked his arm much as she would have done to Jasper, her brows lowering in annoyance. "You miss the point, though whether on purpose or because you're blind, I do not know. I will spell it out for you. Love comes where it may. You have no need to haunt the dance halls. You found it here out in the fields. You'd be a fool to throw it over just because she's not of your station. The path to finding your match is rarely an easy one. You have to be willing to make the effort, and your country girl is less of one than my husband tread.

You envy what we've found, but you're ignoring the chance for your own."

He took a quick step to stay free of her sharp digit. "It's not her rank that worries me, it's her experience. Jasper may have been willing to tie himself to a dancer, but he could retire here to let the scandal die down. I have no such plan. She would be dragged from the country into the heart of society. She'd be crushed beneath the scorn of those more experienced, and isolated from all she's ever known."

Daphne planted both hands on her hips. "Would you risk losing your chance at love to this? How are you to know she won't take to society as a natural and become their darling?"

For just a heartbeat, he considered her point. Had he been too hasty? Then a laugh burst from him long enough to provoke a glare. "I've only seen her the once. I've barely exchanged a handful of sentences with the girl. More likely desperation than love."

She paused as though to ponder his words, but he should have known better than to think her concession won so easily.

"Then there's no reason to worry about how well she'll blend with society, is there? Not every courting ends before the altar, and you respect Jasper too well to damage this girl's reputation or compromise her being. Why not find out just what drew you to her? Maybe your response is more because you've been looking than because of this girl. You'll never know for sure if you don't take the risk. If not to prevent regrets for something that never was then for the chance to discover how shallow your feelings for the girl truly are. You could walk away from her now, but thoughts of her would linger as they have this day and you'd never have a better opportunity for putting them to rest. Wouldn't you prefer to know it is lust rather than something more lasting?"

Aubrey stared at the woman who had captured his friend's stone heart and didn't know whether to laugh or frown. She'd spent her moment of thought well and had presented an argument where he could not say no without being either a cad or an idiot. He shook his head at her skill even as he gave the only answer left to him. "You are wiser than I. I'm wrong to put so much weight on a passing moment without question. Had I stayed longer, I might just have found my true feelings, but now I cannot seek her out without raising expectations I have no intention of meeting. However …" He held up a hand to still her protest. "Should our paths cross again, I won't shy away. I'll let fate take me where it will and only then decide what needs doing."

Daphne once again showed both her wisdom and strength of character as she responded with a sharp nod rather than pressing her point or crowing over her success. "Until the morning, then."

He watched her leave, thinking not for the first time how lucky his friend had been to find someone with the confidence to defy society and the intelligence not to be caught doing so. She showed the same qualities now as she assessed his situation, and for that, he held her in awe.

His thoughts turned inward as he made his way to the guest room assigned to him. What if Daphne had been right about more than just his haste and this girl could best not just him but society as a whole? He knew her beauty would claim them, and she had shown reserve as well.

His book worked hard to capture his attention while his mind preferred to wander through the possibilities should his feelings prove deep and his country girl even deeper.

"So why didn't you tell him?" Sarah asked as they prepared for bed, the farmhouse boasting a single room for guests and Sarah so much more than a simple maid to bed down in one of the servant rooms.

Barbara pulled back the covers, worn out by the day in the sun and helping with the household chores. "It didn't seem the right moment." She'd have to ask her uncle about riding when he was in a better mood.

"You finally have a chance to speak with the man you spent weeks pining after, and it didn't seem the right moment? Sure you became enamored of others soon enough, but I wouldn't have thought you so fickle."

Barbara stared at her friend for a moment before connecting the question with earlier events rather than asking about riding of which Sarah knew nothing. Not for the first time, she wished she'd confessed her humiliation that very night. Instead, she'd held it close where it festered and made her vulnerable to both her cousins' teasing and now even Sarah.

"You don't know the whole of it," she blurted, unable to hold it in any longer. "Aubrey St. Vincent is a fraud of the worst sort. He pretends to be wonderful only to mock those who fall for his illusion."

Sarah rounded the bed and pulled Barbara into her arms, her friend kind enough not to criticize Barbara for holding the secret.

"Just what did he do to you? Is this why you behaved so poorly in the park before we were sent out of London? All this time you let me think it was from a foul mood after your morning visit and let me condemn you for it."

In as few, succinct sentences as she could manage, Barbara explained overhearing exactly what he thought of her. She spared herself not at all, each cutting phrase as clear to her now as it had been the moment she'd overheard.

Sarah pulled away to look Barbara in the face. "What they say of eavesdroppers is true, though from the sound of it you'd had little intention of listening in on what must have been a private conversation."

Barbara jerked to her feet. "And does that make it more worthy? That he would mock me so in private when I spoke nothing but his praises? He never even took the time to introduce himself before he formed a judgment so rigid he felt it worth sharing."

Sarah reached out, but let her hand drop when Barbara moved away. "So this is why you withheld your name."

"I did not. I gave him a name that is my own, just not the whole of it. I saw no reason to let him add a cut direct to the pain of hearing exactly how he saw me."

"So you thought to punish him?"

Sarah's gaze became intent enough to cause Barbara a measure of discomfort. She shook her head and tossed herself down on the coverlet. "I didn't plan on staying unknown. I didn't think it through at all. I just wanted him gone. His presence only makes his words burn the sharper. I'd thought myself free of that pain here. He has no business following me."

A chuckle escaped Sarah's lips, and even Barbara had to fight a smile at how petulant her words had sounded.

She had no control over Aubrey's movements, and with him unable even to recognize the one he'd scorned, he'd clearly not come here to plague her further.

"It doesn't matter," she said at last. "We're unlikely to cross paths again while I'm here. It's not like Uncle Ferrier travels in the same circles as the manor."

"Except you encouraged your cousins to take lessons there."

A frown pinched Barbara's forehead at the reminder. "I couldn't have known. And it matters even less. I have no need of lessons. Perhaps I can convince Uncle Ferrier to lend us some horses to entertain ourselves while the others are training for something they're unlikely to experience. I'll be sure to stay on the far side of the manor fields either way rather than hear one more word out of his mouth."

Sarah considered Barbara for a long moment before saying, "The words might be different if he knew you."

She laughed. "He wouldn't be likely to try any more now than then. He thinks I'm some country girl up for a dalliance in the fields. That's how little he tried to discover anything real."

The look in her friend's eye held a mix of consideration and mischief. "Why not give it to him then?"

Whatever she'd expected, that had never crossed Barbara's mind as something Sarah might have spoken. "Spend my virtue on someone who has so little respect for me that he didn't seek to discover my full name? What has come over you? If my parents ever heard of such a thing, I'd be bound for life to the horrid man."

Sarah had raised her hands between them before Barbara came anywhere near to the end of her statements, and they waved furiously until Barbara ran out of words.

"I didn't mean to compromise yourself. Never that. I meant only to give him the chance to know you without … well … knowing you." She grinned. "It seems an appropriate **retribution** for him to have lost your regard out of arrogance and to learn the truth of what he cast away without even trying because of ignorance."

Her friend's words made all too much sense as Barbara pondered them. "And here I thought you frowned on punishing him for his wrongdoing."

"This isn't punishment exactly." The words came out in a drawl as Sarah considered her answer. "It's more to offer an education. You said yourself how you wished to reveal his true nature to the ton. How he deserves for the innocent girls he deceives to know the truth. Well, you cannot manage that without revealing his statements about your own person, which would only raise gossip with you at the center as a spurned woman. This way, he's taught the lesson and suffers for his arrogance while you're left the innocent party who stood fast against his advances."

Barbara shook her head, though not in disagreement, as she rolled off the bed so they could both tuck under the covers. "My mother would be shocked to find such a devious plot came from your making. She's sure I have been at the root of every bit of trouble we've ever been in."

Sarah turned to her side so she could look at Barbara. "She'd be right. My parents would shudder to learn how you've rubbed off on me. I'm sure they dreamed our friendship would elevate my station, never knowing what a troublemaker you were. Your mother would have me cast out on the streets."

"Never. I wouldn't let her. You'll be at my side when we're both grey-headed and beyond all this."

"You may be happy to settle into a spinster life to the disappointment of all your suitors, but I hope someday to find my own match."

Barbara laughed as her friend's gaze turned inward. "I have a suspicion you just might have already. But you'll always have a place at my side, and in my household. Your imagined husband as well. I cannot afford to lose you. Who else would be daring enough not only to call me out for my errors but to concoct plans such as this one to revenge me on my detractors?"

Sinking to her back, Sarah drew the coverlet up to her chin. "No one else, I'm sure. Not that you listen except when my suggestions match so perfectly to your own thoughts they might as well have come from you. But we have a full day ahead of us tomorrow, I'm sure, and we'll regret having spent all night in chatter soon enough."

Though she went to return with a teasing phrase, Barbara's face split into a yawn that she changed to a laugh. "Whatever my mind may say, my body is matched to your words."

"Dream of Aubrey St. Vincent," Sarah murmured. "And of teaching him a lesson he'll never forget."

Chapter Seventeen

"So they're coming here now?"

Aubrey walked in on his friends in conversation at breakfast the next morning.

"Did you doubt it? I'm offering a grand opportunity few would have the chance of otherwise. Why wouldn't they?"

Jasper held up both hands. "Of course I didn't doubt you capable of doing whatever you set your mind to. You've proved it often enough. I just didn't think it would happen so quickly. These are not ladies of leisure after all."

"What ladies?" Aubrey asked, hardly paying attention as he collected his breakfast from the board.

Daphne gave him a smile that could only be characterized as smug. "The young women of the neighborhood. The first lesson will be today."

Anticipation shot through Aubrey with enough force to jerk his arm so he almost lost his breakfast roll. "All the young women?"

She read more in his expression than he'd have liked, despite having been the one to encourage his attraction, but her pitying look gave little hope. "While not ladies of leisure, those who come are the daughters of landholders."

"And not simple servants who have more than enough to keep themselves busy." He finished her sentence, trying to sound disinterested and not let the disappointment show.

"Exactly," Jasper cut in, unaware of the conversation between his wife and Aubrey the previous evening. "A bunch of barely educated girls who have yet to find a husband. You came here to escape the season only to have it thrust upon you. If even half the tales you've told us about young ladies and their mothers trying to secure your interest are true, Daphne's pupils must fill you with dread. It's not much of a consolation, but I'm off to inspect the mill repairs after some damage from a lightning strike. You'll join me of course. Maybe afterward we can go down to the local tavern and hear a tale or two of the old days when the fields were richer, the women more lovely, and the ale stronger than any man would want to sip."

Aubrey laughed at the description, conceding when he had no good reason to linger about the manor. From the state of her dress compared to the others, and the way she hung back in his presence, she was unlikely to be a wealthy man's daughter. As such, she was sure to work every waking hour just to keep bread on the table. Though conditions out here where even the poor could scratch out a piece of land were better than in London, still survival meant working hard with neither inheritance nor significant farmland to keep a body.

"The man I brought out from London has some innovative ideas on gearing. The lightning struck at just the right angle to shift the stone and damage the mechanism so it needed major repairs. I thought why not try something new if we have to do the work in any case."

Aubrey forced himself to concentrate on what his friend was saying, pushing all thought of the lovely Barbara from his mind. "I remember now. You mentioned him as why you'd come up to London."

Jasper nodded then shook his head. "To employ him was part. Things tend to accumulate when you're isolated in the country. There's always a dozen or more things to attend to on such a trip."

They finished the meal with Jasper waxing eloquent about the man and his grand ideas, almost as though Jasper could claim some form of ownership over them. His friend's enthusiasm proved catching, and by the time they headed out for this inspection, he'd come to terms with the trip and even looked forward to seeing how the new mill worked.

"We'll just have to hope someone brings over grain so we can see a test right then and there. Our stores were running too low to wait so

I sent the grain to the next closest mill already."

Aubrey suppressed a smile at how quickly his mind leapt to the possibility that a servant would do such a task where she wouldn't attend a dancing lesson. It had little weight though, what with the mill only now becoming usable. No master would send a servant to verify the fix, especially not with word sure to spread about the new workings. Like Jasper, anyone with the wherewithal to get his grain mill ground would most likely come himself.

"I have no need of dancing lessons, Uncle. You know that. And for all Charlotte has been teaching me, you wouldn't want me trying to do the farm work on my own."

Uncle Ferrier brought his hand up to pinch the bridge of his nose as though suffering from a headache. He'd been resistant ever since she caught him in his study this morning.

Barbara could only hope this showed a sign of him weakening. "Besides, if I followed my cousins to the manor, I'd prove nothing but a distraction as surely the lady would want word of London from one more recently there. Little teaching would occur with us chatting about things my cousins have no experience with."

He lowered his hand to look at her in a silence long enough to become uncomfortable.

Just when she thought he'd never speak, he said, "Your parents put you in my charge, Barbara. They sent you here to cage your wild tendencies, not so you could indulge in them."

She twisted her fingers together as she sent him a pleading look. "It's only a ride. I did the same in London often enough."

His bark of laughter startled her into taking a backward step.

"Well I remember your idea of a simple ride, and I doubt you did anything like it within the city parks. Had you done so, word of your exploits would have arrived much faster than your parents' letter begging me to get you in order when they had given up hope for the task."

Barbara's shoulders slumped. "I wasn't as bad as all that, Uncle," she said, her voice barely above a whisper.

He raised a hand to tick off on his fingers. "You toyed with men's affections. You held them wanting even after they'd attempted an offer, denying them happiness with any other. You kept them from choosing other girls, and even set them against each other from what your parents implied."

"I did none of those things," she burst out. "I neither encouraged them to propose nor gave them any hope when they did. Is it my fault that they could not engage my interest?"

Again he observed her as though considering the truth in her words. A tiny spark of hope came to life that he would look beyond her parents' missive to see her true self.

Uncle Ferrier shook his head. "Whether you did so on purpose or because you didn't know how to discourage them once their interest was set matters little. You were well on your way to gaining a reputation, and not of the good sort. You need ruling by a firmer hand than my sister possesses. She put all her hopes into the one child she brought living into this world. I won't betray their trust in me on a girl's whim."

"You'll force me to go to the manor?"

He quirked an eyebrow. "Is it such a punishment?"

She could offer no answer to that, or at least none she wanted to share.

Then he shook his head. "But no, your arguments have the ring of truth. I wouldn't spare you from tedium, but there is little point in sending my daughters for some refining when the opportunity arises and then make sure to distract their teacher. I've sometimes wondered if that lack weakened Charlotte's standing when your mother brought her onto the scene."

He shrugged, dismissing his thoughts in favor of narrowing his gaze on her. "However, you're right as well that you have not the skill to work on the farm alone. I'd have you work alongside Cook with as much baking as there is to be done, but I'm off to the mill to see the repairs and get some more flour ground since our supplies are running low. Besides, with the other girls freed of their chores, it seems more punishment than not to have you and Sarah still labor."

"So giving us horses would be the perfect solution. It's been many summers since you've seen me ride, but I promise you both of us can keep our seats on a sidesaddle."

His hands slapped flat on the desk. "If you think I should recall your skills, then you know full well I put no truck with sidesaddles. They are a danger to horse, rider, and anyone in reach."

Barbara smothered her smile to give a contrite nod. "It's only that we can because we must. Our skills would be so much greater astride, and the dangers lessened."

He heaved a sigh. "You should have been born a boy, Barbara. You think I haven't noticed you picking up my paper when I'm done. Politics are no place for a woman. Had you been your father's son, you'd have persuaded the most resistant in your path."

A warm glow overtook her at his praise, though he thought her gender should confine her as did most. "Does this mean you'll allow it? The ride, I mean?"

Uncle Ferrier shoved to his feet. "Yes." He paused at her delighted squeal. "And no. Your parents would never forgive me if I let you go riding wild with only Sarah, another young woman, as escort. As I mentioned, I'm off to see the mill repairs. The lord brought in some innovator from London itself to design the gearing. You and Sarah can join me on horseback."

The prospect of a canter vanished, but at least she'd get some time riding, and her uncle boasted a refined stable for a man of his station thanks to careful breeding rather than expensive purchases. Whereas the likely sedate pace failed to bring forth a protest, a sudden memory of her cousin speaking on the mill almost did. Charlotte had been concerned about the state of the flour stores and mentioned the mill stood firmly on the Pendleton Manor lands, just where Barbara had not wanted to go. But how could she cry off now after having pleaded for the chance of a ride?

"It's settled then. Gather Sarah and your bonnet. We leave short-ly."

Barbara wandered from the room, caught up in her tangled

thoughts. As much as she'd wanted to stay far from the manor, surely Aubrey St. Vincent had little interest in farming matters, of which a mill would count as one. She doubted he knew where the flour he consumed came from, not that she would have either without her cousin's lessons. He'd shown no interest in country matters from what she'd seen, focused much more on the events in the political realm.

Satisfied in her thinking, she ran off to find Sarah and apprise her friend of their plans. Not that Sarah had expected to go to the manor anyway though she might have wanted to for the chance of a glimpse at that servant who had caught her eye the other day.

Chapter Eighteen

After an awkward moment of Barbara and Sarah figuring out how to spread their skirts to maintain decorum, something she hadn't thought much of when a child, they set out, each horse carrying a sack of grain to be ground slung over its withers.

They rode alongside the wagon carrying the cousins to their dance lesson at first, but to Barbara's relief, the paths split, taking the wagon off to the manor while the riders sought the mill.

The warm late morning sun made for a pleasant ramble if not the canter she'd been hoping for.

Uncle Ferrier pointed out different landmarks, and though she knew some of the earlier ones from her work in the fields with her cousins, soon they passed beyond where she had been.

"That hill yonder is said to have been claimed by the fey in olden times," he said. "Some think forest nymphs, called dryads, still linger there."

Barbara gave the space a close look, reminded of how Aubrey had claimed them nymphs when he came across them. Perhaps he knew more of the country than she'd thought.

A spike of nerves thrust through her as she considered whether that meant an interest in the mill, but she laughed aloud at her foolishness. Had she not heard the many mentions of the fey in poetry and play alike? More likely he had picked up the phrase from the theater than the country folks, especially considering his quick dismissal of the cousins' offer of a basket. Gathering berries and grinding flour would be as far from his interests as they'd been from her London life.

She thrust her worries aside, determined to enjoy what the day had to offer without the specter of Aubrey hanging over it. "So tell me about this mill then," she told her uncle, maneuvering up to his side on a path meant for farm wagons.

Though all attempts to draw her uncle into conversation regarding politics or economics had failed, it seemed mechanisms had become as much of a focus as his horses. He entertained them for the rest of the ride with descriptions of the gearing at every stage, having been a frequent visitor since he'd heard the lord thought to bring up the mill in a different fashion than it had been.

His enthusiasm proved so compelling, Barbara was startled to see the tall stone structure appear before them as though by magic, her attention firmly fixed on him rather than the land about her.

"It looks like we're not the only ones who wish to see its first working." Uncle Ferrier kneed his horse faster in his eagerness.

Barbara followed the path of his gaze to see two men standing beside a third who wore a thick canvas apron. It took only a moment to recognize the nearer of the two, but the delay was long enough for Aubrey to glance their way.

His gaze unerringly sought out hers as though he'd somehow known she would appear.

Her heart pounded faster as he stared much too boldly to be proper, and her hands grew slick against the reins.

The horse, a steady if unimpressive ride up to this point, gave a small buck and half-reared in response to the sudden tightening of her knees against its sides, sending the grain sack hard against her chest.

Barbara fought for control, not wanting to chance being thrown and injured, but just when she lay on the brink of achieving it, she realized success meant continuing down the path toward Aubrey. She was not ready to meet with him, not with Sarah's plan lingering in her mind with all its temptations, nor with her own responses suspect as they had been since Marian suggested she take advantage of his ignorance for an unladylike exploration.

She let the horse rear a second time as though a snake lay in her path, nudging the beast with one knee so it twisted to land with its head toward the fields rather than the mill.

Her palfrey needed no further encouragement, especially with the sack slamming down on its shoulders. It broke into a run, soon taking her out of sight.

Even knowing the scolding she'd receive, Barbara let the horse settle into a canter from its panicked flight, giving the horse its head. She'd paid good enough attention to the landmarks her uncle described in the beginning of their journey. She would not get lost, though she doubted her knowledge compared to that of her horse who would be eager to return to the stable and a measure of feed.

The wind rushing through her hair and the muscles moving beneath her gave Barbara such joy she threw back her head to laugh only to find she couldn't stop, an edge of hysteria having captured her. She imagined the look on Aubrey's face as she turned from him and ran for the second time though he remained unaware of that fact. She'd always seen herself as a grounded, serious sort. Adding Aubrey to the mix seemed to strip away those qualities in favor of yet another flighty girl.

The thought finally calmed her enough to hear the pounding hooves coming up on her. She twisted in her saddle, a feat only possible because she sat astride, to see Sarah charging up.

"Glad you can find reason to laugh," her friend said when she reached speaking distance. "Your uncle is not pleased."

That drove the last of the humor from Barbara, hysterical or not. She lowered her gaze to avoid Sarah's reproving look and slowed her horse even more than when she'd heard Sarah coming, chastened.

They completed the journey in a solemn walk, the absence of a grain sack on Sarah's palfrey a further strike against Barbara.

Her friend had clearly taken the time to deliver the grain before coming after her, the reason for the delay and further sign neither Sarah nor Uncle Ferrier had been taken in by the illusion of a snake. They had not feared for her well-being, only her behavior.

Aubrey St. Vincent brought out the worst in her no matter what she intended.

At that very moment, Barbara decided to put Sarah's plan into effect. Today had shown her folly in thinking she could avoid the man and proved how little control she had when trying to do so. Instead, she would act on her feelings to draw him in. She would not be the one to suffer from his presence any longer.

That honor would fall on his silky head as he unwittingly revealed his true nature to one who had both the position and the connections to expose him to the ton and to all those eager girls he sought to beguile for his own mockery. When she finished with him, he, not those still in white dresses, would be the one subjected to scorn, and she would be the instrument of his downfall.

"Pity your engineer couldn't come down again now the work is complete," the miller said before shooting Ferrier a grin. "You have another sack of grain?"

Ferrier and Jasper mirrored the miller's expression, but Aubrey couldn't share their enthusiasm, distracted as he was by the near accident he'd witnessed.

"Sarah's a good girl. She left hers before taking after Barbara."

"Are you sure Barbara has the skill to get a wild horse under control?" Aubrey could no longer hold back the question, unsatisfied by the farmer's even demeanor.

Ferrier gave Aubrey a tight look and clapped him on the shoulder. "Why don't you come with me to fetch it? Those two will just have to make do discussing the previous grinds." Though his words implied disinterest, he'd been the first to exclaim at the finely ground flour the new machinery achieved.

Aubrey followed the man out, unsurprised when he paused next to the grain sack and showed no interest in picking it up. Instead, Ferrier stared along the path Barbara had taken, a direction that claimed Aubrey's attention as easily.

"You needn't worry about the girl," Ferrier said after a moment. "She's got as good a seat as the best of them. Been riding since she was able to walk, and on a proper saddle too."

Aubrey didn't glance at the other man, but nodded. "I could see as much myself when the horse reared, but it still took her off too fast to get my horse to follow."

Ferrier shook his head, his frown making Aubrey nervous. "Your care for the well-being of those around you is fine, Lord Aubrey, but she is not your concern. You wouldn't have reached her had you been on horse, if I know my Barbara. She and I will exchange a word or two when I return."

The underlying message came through clearly.

The man suspected her of pretending trouble to get out of her duties. Aubrey hadn't seen any sign of the snake that could have startled her horse, and if she were as good a seat as Ferrier believed, she should have been able to stop any bolt before they'd gone out of sight, no matter how perturbed her palfrey.

He said nothing further, not wanting the farmer to grow even more irate at the poor girl than he was already. She hadn't seemed the type to run from simple labor, whether she found interest in the mill improvements or not, but without a half-crushed snake for proof, he had no way to show her innocence, and with the careful use of his title, Ferrier made it clear what he thought of Aubrey's interference. Barbara would be the one to suffer for it as well should he persist.

Saying nothing more, Aubrey swept up half of the sack and let Ferrier lift the other end.

The awkward burden bridged the silence, and by the time they laid it on the shelf so the miller could load more grain onto the edged grinding surface, the farmer seemed caught up in the innovation once again.

Aubrey could not contest the efficiency or elegance of the gears as they maneuvered a heavy stone over the grains and crushed them to powder. On any other day, he'd have been the first to need a warning not to lean too close. Today, though, the vision of dark curls streaming free as his country girl beat a swift retreat kept pushing to the forefront until he barely noticed the events before him.

"So you have the time to put your horse through its paces on the morrow?"

Jasper's voice brought Aubrey from yet another daydream, the contents of his speech too important to miss.

"In the morning will do fine. He'll be rested and eager for the exercise."

As they'd worked the mill, Aubrey learned Ferrier was none other than the breeder with the remarkable stock, a better explanation for the quality of the horses both he and the two girls had ridden than that he had the funds to purchase same. No wonder his servant knew her way around a horse. She'd likely grown up beside a stable many a nobleman could not boast and had a hand at exercising the beasts when necessary. Aubrey smiled to hear Ferrier's agreement, though not at the prospect of admiring even prime horseflesh.

He'd wondered just how he would put Daphne's plan into effect, having no idea where Barbara came from or how to cross paths another time. Now he had the hope of seeing her the very next day, though she'd be busy about her chores and he'd been committed to the viewing.

Chapter Nineteen

Barbara noticed her uncle's return first, her senses tuned toward the stable though she shelled peas with Sarah and her cousins in the kitchen. The cousins had come back from their dance lessons excited and chatty, so her distraction didn't stand out until she tensed, the blood draining from her face.

"What's wrong?" Sarah asked.

Before she could answer, Uncle Ferrier burst in the kitchen door, his arm filled with not one but two flour sacks.

He dumped them on the table sending pea pods flying and casting up a cloud of grey dust. "Your parents sent you here to learn to consider others, not pretend a snake and go off on a half-wild horse," he ground out, not even acknowledging Cook or his daughters. "And in your time here the best you've learned is how to choose your moment to disobey, knowing I could not abandon the mill to track you down."

She shrank away from him, hard peas springing out of the pod in her hands.

He planted a hand on either side of her from across the table, looming over Barbara. "Did you think my anger would cool? Did you think coming back to find you hard at work would free you of what you've done? I know full well how good a seat you have. Even had there been a snake and I'd put you on the most flighty of my stable, you could have gotten the horse under control within sight of the mill. You didn't think my stricture of a simple ride to the mill worth your obedience."

Barbara said nothing, her breath caught in her throat by the force of his anger. Had she been able to put two words together, she still would not have spoken. He had no idea what caused the panic — hers, not that of her horse — and she had no intention of enlightening him. She had done everything he charged her with, and this distress was no more than her due.

If anything, though, her quiet only seemed to enrage him further.

A vein in his forehead began to pulse at an alarming rate. "You didn't think my command worth following either. You play at being equal to your cousins, but you hold yourself to different standards, or perhaps to no standards at all."

"No, Uncle. I swear. I deserve your anger." She'd meant to stay silent, but his charge brought the words forth, words which only worsened the situation from his glare.

"You mock me now? You think I'll tolerate such behavior? You were a good girl once. If this is what London does to a soul, perhaps I should be grateful Charlotte's season was cut short despite the cause."

A gasp from one of the cousins reached Barbara but she didn't turn to look, her gaze locked with her uncle's in a kind of terrified fascination.

His face an unhealthy shade of purple, her uncle leaned even closer. "You will learn respect if nothing else while you are here. And you will learn to obey, whether you want to or not. Since my horses brought us to this space, they shall be your punishment. You are banned from my stables. You will not ride again no matter how long your parents think you should stay to learn your lesson."

This time, the dismayed cry came from her own lips, the punishment worse than any she imagined. To lose this chance for freedom before returning to the confines of London society burned, especially when she could not reveal what lay behind her actions.

"Oh, Father, no." Georgiana put a hand on his arm, and for a moment, it looked as though he would shake it off. "Please don't be so harsh with her. She doesn't mean to harm, I'm sure of it. Only look at how she tried to bear your anger as her due. She just doesn't think through how her London ways are hurtful."

Barbara turned a stricken gaze on Georgiana, aware of exactly what the younger girl referred to.

"Surely she didn't mean it as it seemed," Jane chimed in a heartbeat later, as did Charlotte and Marian, rising to her defense in an endearing manner when they chanced him turning his rage in their directions.

"She did not think to disobey you," Sarah said, her quiet voice ringing with authority.

Uncle Ferrier looked from one young woman to another, his gaze resting speculatively on Sarah for a long moment.

At last he turned to Barbara, his natural color restored and his gaze calm. "Did you not mean to flaunt your disobedience?"

Heat swept her face as she heard the pain behind his words. Barbara half-rose from her seat to say, "No. Uncle, no. I acted without thinking, and once done, it was too late to return."

His eyes narrowed as he stared at her, then he nodded once, recognizing the confession in her statement. There had been no snake. "Your punishment stands."

A shared sigh came from the girls.

He raised a hand to silence them. "But I'll soften it thus. You can ride only in the company of your cousins, and you're to stay with them at all times. One more incident, and I'll do more than just withhold the stables. I'll tan your hide myself if you prove so reckless again. No matter how good the seat, accidents happen to the best of riders, and I'll not be returning a coffin where your parents entrusted me with their daughter."

Stunned at the reprieve, Barbara leapt from the table and rounded it to give her uncle a hug. "Thank you, Uncle Ferrier. I swear I'll not betray your trust again. I will stay with my cousins always."

He looked down at her and laughed, giving his head a rueful shake. "How you survive in London, I have no idea. You have little sense of decorum and share my love of horseflesh. But under all those little arrogances, you're a good girl. Be careful that doesn't get lost in the run of suitors trying for your hand."

Uncle Ferrier froze. He glanced first at Sarah then looked to his niece, his gaze turned thoughtful. "That was the noble from the field,

I suppose. He spent the afternoon trying not to ask after you. Just what happened on that day?"

Barbara choked, fearful of what her uncle had begun to suspect. "Nothing. Nothing happened in the fields or any other time."

The cousins came up on either side to provide a wall of support as they agreed.

"There wasn't time for anything."

"His interested was marked, but Barbara would have none of it."

"She behaved only as you wished."

Charlotte waited for the others to quiet before adding her own statement to the mix. "She found his attention inappropriate then, and would have been driven to discomfort upon seeing him again."

Uncle Ferrier waved them away. "So your parents sent you here to think on the nobles who press you in London, but one found you here and is just as pressing." The last of the pinched lines in his face eased. "While I can't condone your choices, I understand better why you reacted as you did ... and why you could not just recover the horse and return. Still, he's the lord's guest and will be about on the land. You must learn to control yourself. I spent the afternoon with him, and he's not the type to force himself on a young lady unwilling." His gaze narrowed once again. "You're to do nothing to encourage him, neither flight nor flattery. He will soon give up the chase."

Somehow Barbara doubted it would be that easy, but she smiled her agreement and returned to the task of shelling peas as though it were resolved. She had no plans to defy her uncle's ruling. She would neither encourage Aubrey to give chase nor flatter.

This showed more than anything she needed to gain the upper hand in the situation between them. Her uncle said nothing about letting Aubrey succeed in his pursuit, at least enough to teach him a lesson. And if that wouldn't drive away the hold he seemed to have on her emotions, at least she wouldn't have to worry about him pressing her after she'd revealed him the cad.

Chapter Twenty

Barbara lingered as she carried her milk bucket past the stables, hoping to catch more of the stable boys' conversation. It seemed Uncle Ferrier would be putting his prize stallion on display. She'd heard him speak of the beast, but had yet to see which one it was.

"Hurry up, Barbara, or the milk will sour before we reach the kitchen." Marian laughed at Barbara's expression, a sign she'd only been teasing about the last, but from the lack of others crossing the yard, she'd been serious about the hurrying.

The chance that she'd be allowed to watch offered enough to speed her steps. She need only find Uncle Ferrier before Charlotte declared their next task.

As she stepped through the door, though, Barbara discovered she would not have to search for her uncle after all.

"There you are. We've been waiting for you," Uncle Ferrier said.

"Oh? I had hoped to speak with you as well."

His eyebrow rose, and whatever he'd meant to share, he nodded for her to speak first.

Under his close attention, especially with the disaster of the previous day, she found herself reluctant to ask. The enthusiasm she'd felt outside had drained away.

But she'd already spoken, and if she didn't ask a question, he'd be sure to suspect her of something far worse than wanting to watch his horse.

"The stable boys were talking about how you'd planned to run your favorite through his paces. Would you mind if I were to watch?"

Uncle Ferrier started shaking his head even before she got to the question, and only determination kept her going.

"I am sorry about yesterday," she added, her voice soft. Clearly he'd held on to more of his anger than she'd thought.

Again he shook his head, but this time his eyes softened. "It's not yesterday on my mind, but today. I'd come to tell Charlotte to take you all to the forest. Grannie mentioned she's low on some of her herbs."

Charlotte's brow furrowed. "She said none of this to me yesterday. I'll go check with her to see what she needs."

Uncle Ferrier put out a hand to bar her way. "Grannie's off helping a birth. Just do a general gather. There's never enough, and she can dry the extra for the winter. Besides, it would do your cousin good to know her way around the simple remedies. I have little doubt such was neglected in all her preparations for London society."

"But Father, wouldn't it be better to know what Grannie needed so much that you want us gone on the task right now?"

Father and daughter exchanged a look full of meaning if only Barbara knew more about this Grannie and her herb lore. From the nod Charlotte gave and the end to her protests, though, her cousin understood his intent.

A light blush heated Barbara's cheeks as she wondered if the reason had little to do with not knowing and more to do with the types of herbs they had been sent after. She'd heard some stories from the other girls in London regarding the impact of certain herbs, but surely her uncle wouldn't send Charlotte and the rest of them on such an errand.

As she considered the possible meanings, Uncle Ferrier announced they would leave this very moment. The cousins clearly knew his tone because they left the milk for Cook to deal with and gathered their things.

Barbara accepted both the basket and shawl thrust into her hands when she saw Sarah do the same.

"It can get cold under the trees," Marian said as she released the cloth. "Come on now. We wouldn't want Father to learn we'd dawdled."

When they stepped into the yard, Charlotte and the others turned away from the stables, but Barbara could see a magnificent young male being led out. "Can we not just pass by the stable yard," she asked.

Charlotte followed her gaze to see the horse then met the pleading look Barbara gave her cousin with a shrug. "I suppose there's little harm in it, though the stables are out of our way."

"Must we truly?" Georgiana said. "It's far enough to the forest."

Marian gave her sister a shove. "No purpose in whining. Our cousin sickens to the same bug that our father suffers. Let her get an eyeful and then we'll be on our way without her dragging her feet." She turned to Barbara to add, "Only we'd best make it a quick glimpse what with Father specifically making this task the more important one."

Barbara didn't wait to be told twice, Sarah not much further behind her. The cousins put no speed in their steps, most likely because they'd grown up alongside these horses, and Georgiana at least had little interest.

Aubrey was suitably impressed with the horse as Ferrier ran through its gaits. Perfectly executed high stepping and controlled turns that would be ideal in a carriage horse. Had he been a twin birth or raised alongside another with equal skill, the horse would have made half of a wonderful pair. Even now, he could be trained to work with another, though the bond would be less.

For all that the horse proved to be everything Jasper had described and more, Aubrey struggled to stay focused what with the possibility he'd catch sight of Barbara.

A chorus of laughter rewarded his vigilance just then.

He turned to see a group approaching with their arms full of baskets, his country girl in the lead.

Ferrier followed his gaze, and out of the corner of his eye, Aubrey thought he saw a scowl. When he twisted to see more fully though, the farmer laughed. "It's hard to think on horses when pretty young women are about."

They neared the fence when Barbara caught sight of a well-set figure and stumbled, almost taking Sarah to the ground when her friend collided with her back.

Barbara steadied Sarah but turned her in the other direction. "Perhaps Georgie is right after all. Surely Uncle Ferrier will let me watch next time, and I wouldn't want to anger him again."

The cousins sent her confused looks until Marian glanced past and clearly had the same realization.

"You cannot avoid him forever," her cousin said with a glance to Charlotte, "but somehow Father's efforts to rush us about now make more sense. I suspect he'd be angered for a different reason should we continue."

Barbara linked arms with Marian and tugged her the way they'd come. "All the more reason to get on with the chore he set for us. You can teach me all about nature's bounty."

Marian shook off the hold with a laugh, her sisters joining in. "For that you need Charlotte. She's the one with the herb lore. We gather what she points us to and don't nibble on anything we don't know as well as our own names."

Charlotte fell into step with Barbara and Sarah both as they crossed the fields. "It's an important warning, what Marian said. There are herbs and fungus we collect that can aid in a healing if prepared the right way, but nibbled in the wild can kill you as dead as any toss from a fevered stallion."

Turning his attention back to the girls, Aubrey found the group had changed direction and were now crossing the first field on the farthest side.

Ferrier clapped him on the shoulder. "I remember what it's like to be young, and my daughters make for a good distraction, but my horse deserves your attention."

About to agree to be polite, the middle of the man's statement caught Aubrey. "They're all your daughters?" he asked, stunned at the sheer number.

"No, only the prettiest four."

Ferrier shifted to look at the horse again, and Aubrey followed suit, but his mind was not on the feats before him. He didn't share the farmer's fatherly eye judging from the various stages of wear on the girls' clothing each time he'd seen them together. The most arresting of the group was the least well dressed, but that did little to diminish her appeal.

. He wanted nothing more than to stride after them right then, before they could get out of sight. Without realizing it, he'd twisted once again to mark their path.

"Now that is a thing of beauty," Jasper said in a reverent whisper. "When you're ready, assuming you plan to sell the beast, let me give you a hand in finding the right buyer. I'd take him on myself, but I have no space in my stables at the moment. He should bring you enough to manage the larger stables and training area you've been mentioning over the past year," he continued, facing Ferrier.

Aubrey realized the two must have spoken on many an occasion, further complicating his situation with the servant girl. He no more wanted to ruin Jasper's friendships than his reputation. At least she wasn't the man's daughter, though a landholder's daughter would likely be somewhat educated and more capable of taking on a life in London than a servant girl.

He smothered a groan at how his desire chose so poor a focus, though if it turned out to be simple lust or frustration, better the object prove unsuitable than that he raise expectations only to dismiss them out of hand.

With more effort than the situation warranted, he forced his thoughts to the horse as Ferrier launched into an explanation of the bloodline and his breeding choices. Aubrey would have enjoyed this opportunity on any other day. With thoughts of Barbara crowding their way into his mind no matter what he tried, he could not find more than a faint sense of wishing he were somewhere else. At least Jasper was capable of holding up their end of the discussion.

"I'm enjoying our conversation," Ferrier said at last, "And I could keep going all day given the chance, just ask my daughters. But as much as I am, I have other tasks to see to, as I'm sure you do as well."

Jasper laughed. "True enough. My lady wife will be wondering just what became of me."

Aubrey stirred himself enough to add, "I doubt that. She most likely anticipated what would occur and won't send runners out until dark falls."

The statement drew a chuckle from the farmer even as he shook his head. "You're lucky to still have your wife with you and should treasure this time, not squander it on horseflesh. I'll consider your offer of assisting in the sale. I've yet to decide if I'm willing to part with him. I have a bit of a bond with the beast, and if he breeds true …"

"Or if he would have and you had him gelded. I see your quandary. He's a magnificent beast."

"You're welcome to come view him again some other day," Ferrier said with a smile. "I appreciate time spent with a man who knows his horseflesh."

Jasper accepted the compliment with a nod. "But we've taken up enough of your day. Until later."

They strode to where their horses were tethered and headed to the manor in silence, Jasper most likely thinking on the horse while Aubrey's thoughts unerringly returned to his country girl.

"Jasper, I'm weary of standing around for so long, and the thought of sitting holds little appeal. Would you object to my going off for a canter?"

His friend gave him a long look, one eyebrow raised. "And this sudden desire has nothing to do with the gathering of young women, I suppose? You plan to ride out to the mill?" He waved in the opposite direction.

Aubrey shrugged. "Perhaps I have some thought to encountering them as I ride, true."

Jasper laughed. "I'd join you if only to see just what this servant girl has to distract you so much, but as I said, Daphne will be waiting to hear about the horse and our visit. She must be something for sure to make even such a prime example of horseflesh lose your interest. Be careful or you'll find yourself well and truly caught."

"Little chance of that. A servant girl does not fit into my vision of the future, and I'd no sooner torment myself with the struggle than I would any young woman who caught my eye."

"So you've said. It would seem you feel the need of repetition, a habit more revealing than any other." Waving Aubrey off rather than continue their exchange, Jasper called after him, "If we were in White's, I'd lay odds against you in this."

Aubrey kneed his horse around and set off across a pasture in the general direction he'd seen the girls headed. Jasper's comment lingered, bringing a smile to his lips that had more to do with daydreams of a miracle proving the man right than collecting his winnings.

Chapter Twenty-One

As the day wore on, it became clear the cousins had spoken truly about their oldest sister's knowledge. Charlotte pointed out each plant, showing Barbara its unique characteristics and telling her of how it could be used when she saw only green leaves, or sometimes grey.

"You know so much about this. Have you always planned to be a healer?"

Barbara saw a shadow cross her cousin's face and wished she could withdraw the question.

"When my mother fell sick, I was off in London. Grannie let me help her when I returned though the doctor wanted both of us kept from her side. I couldn't do anything then. I was too late and too ignorant. But Grannie has been teaching me in the spare moments since. I don't plan on becoming what she is, but I'll never be caught unable to help someone I love again." Charlotte's words came out quiet but filled with strength.

Barbara could think of no good response.

She'd been paying only half attention to the lessons, knowing she'd have little use for it once she returned to London. Her easy dismissal made her chest ache now when she imagined Charlotte desperate to help but unable. Though Grannie had also failed to save her mother despite having the knowledge, that fact would not change the emotions driving Charlotte.

"Cousin, come see."

Grateful for the excuse, she hastened her steps to find Jane and Georgiana had not found some new wonder but had paused in their labors to enact the steps of a formal dance.

"So? Are we doing it correctly? Why do we stumble?" Georgiana demanded. "Lady Pendleton said we were to practice. She'll be disappointed if we come back worse."

Barbara shook her head and pulled the two to the same line. "You're trying to pair when you should be paired to a man. The steps are different."

Jane's brow furrowed. "Then how are we supposed to practice? It's not as if Father can practice with us. Even if he had the time, I don't think he has any idea how beyond country dances."

"You won't have much need for the skill anyway," Charlotte said, her voice unnecessarily harsh. "No need to perfect it."

Georgiana planted both hands on her hips. "And what if I don't want to disappoint my teacher? Lady Pendleton is sweet to be teaching us."

Charlotte looked like she had more to say on the subject, but the sound of horse hooves distracted every one of them.

The rider came fast, but not so fast as to hint at a panic, though from the expressions on her cousins' faces, Barbara knew that had been their first thought. Her own panic, rather than easing, grew stronger as the rider came into view.

"Aubrey St. Vincent." She hadn't meant to speak his name aloud, but it came out in a hushed whisper as she knew her time of avoiding the man had come to a sudden end.

"Look, Barbara," Georgiana squealed in an overly loud voice. "It's your nobleman. Just what we need."

Barbara turned to hush her younger cousin, but at least the girl offered a way to gain a momentary breathing space.

Demonstrating his skill on horseback without being showy, Aubrey rode up close at speed then brought his horse to a slow halt so he could swing down to stand at Barbara's side.

What she'd expected Barbara couldn't say, but to fall under his gaze and meet a confusion matched to her own had not been among the possibilities. He seemed at a loss for words once he joined them, neither claiming an accidental meeting nor stating intent.

Barbara stared back, her mind a haze despite what she knew about the man. Her body warmed to his presence even with a chill breeze from the nearby forest. If he could find no words to break the silence, neither could she bring forth a single coherent sentence.

Georgiana broke the impasse when she jostled Barbara's elbow and whispered loud enough for the distant birds to hear her, "Well, are you going to ask him?"

Barbara shook herself to dispel his effect, for a heartbeat lost to her cousin's meaning.

Georgiana executed a turn as though aware Barbara needed the reminder.

With a laugh, Barbara glanced up at Aubrey.

The warmth of his smile struck her dumb once again, but she marshaled her strength, knowing she must stay strong against his presence if the lesson she planned to teach would fall on his head rather than once again on hers.

"Can you stand in for their practice?" she asked, her voice sharp and abrupt.

Again confusion swirled in his deep brown eyes as he followed her gesture to take in the cousins, all but Georgiana waiting patiently for his answer.

"The dance lessons," Barbara added when he showed no signs of understanding. "Lady Pendleton asked them to practice, but they have no man to take his part."

Had she not been closely attuned to his expression, Barbara might have missed the wince before his smile widened.

"As you wish. I only hope I can do such lovely company justice."

Though he held his arms out to pair with her, Barbara took a rapid step away and moved Georgiana into position. Even had he known her true station, she had little need of practice, and no need for his touch, or so she tried to convince herself.

Still, the warmth he'd brought soon drained from her, and she pulled the shawl off her basket handle to draw about her shoulders as she watched him move from one cousin to another. Had she still been ignorant of his true nature, she would have found his willingness endearing. As it was, she could only wonder at what he hoped to achieve.

Charlotte called a stop to their play soon enough. "We have more herbs to gather, and other chores await us at the farmhouse. We cannot spend all day dancing with a handsome gentleman." Even she gave Aubrey a sweet smile, taken in by his accommodating manner.

Barbara could only be grateful their time had come to an end for surely he'd get back on his horse and ride off to the manor for some activity planned with the others of his station.

He caught up his reins, but only to loop them around one arm as he moved to her side, the horse keeping up with them. "What kind of gentleman would I be if I left you young women to wander on your own?"

"We do so all the time," Marian said, but Jane quickly hushed her, sending a pointed glance between him and Barbara obvious enough to bring heat to Barbara's cheeks.

"Surely you have responsibilities at the manor," she said, her face turned half away to hide the response.

Out of the corner of her eye, she saw him shake his head. "I am a man of leisure for the time being at least, and the same cannot be said for my friends. I'd be grateful if you would accept my company rather than abandoning me to lonesome pursuits."

He sounded so sincere that Barbara had to struggle to remind herself of his sharp condemnation of her and all others of her nature. But how could she reject his request without seeming a shrew, and even had she not decided to put Sarah's plan into effect, her cousins would plague her endlessly should she give him harsh treatment after he'd been so helpful.

If she were being honest, Barbara enjoyed both his enthusiasm and apparent interest as the day wore on. He left her side only to admire whatever plant the girls pointed out, and she had the chance to demonstrate — to Charlotte, not Aubrey — that she had been listening earlier as she answered some questions with only small corrections from her cousin.

He made for a good companion, though she knew it to be but a mask, and when the time came to part ways, she felt his absence no less than the others. Her weakness where Aubrey was concerned made the decision of how to treat him harder.

It seemed the choice to stay distant had been taken from her hands, though, and so Sarah's plan offered the only hope of reclaiming her confidence. Still, she feared it would not be as easy as all that.

Aubrey left the girls much later than he'd expected. Who would have thought a day spent walking at Barbara's side would have brought such contentment.

His feet ached in his riding boots, but his heart ached the stronger.

She'd been nothing but proper as she let him keep company, hardly speaking to him at all except when he caught her with a question.

Her knowledge of the plants surrounding Ferrier's farmland should not have surprised him, but her polished tones surely did. He'd suspected as much before, but now he felt sure she'd been raised among the farmer's daughters despite her station, giving her a smoother, cultured nature than the general servant girl could claim.

Still, they'd spoken hardly at all, and he had to wonder if shyness held her tongue or if she had no thought beyond those necessary to complete her chores.

How she drew him would seem to make that worry false, but what proof had he?

The day had shown little more than that his preference lasted beyond the stray moments of their first meeting. It offered nothing either to boost his confidence in her suitability, or to cull her from his consideration once and for all.

He laughed aloud at the last, the action startling his horse into a sidestep. If nothing else, he could be sure his interest held more weight than a passing fancy, though if it had true endurance, whether she turned out to be capable or not, remained to be seen.

Daphne would be delighted in this event no matter how unsatisfying it had proved for him. She saw the possibilities without the barriers, but what could he expect from a lady who had defied both society and family to make her dreams a reality.

He had a more pragmatic approach and so did not plan to tell his friends of the encounter for all Jasper knew he'd sought it out. He had little need to pore over every aspect, and would better serve his thoughts and sanity if he contemplated the meaning on his own — at least until he had more to consider than as of yet.

Chapter Twenty-Two

Baskets full of the various plants they'd gathered, the girls headed to the farm. The cousins were laughing and teasing as they were wont to do, leaving Barbara and Sarah to grin and enjoy the spectacle. Or so Barbara thought until Jane turned her attention on Barbara with a speculative look in her eyes.

"He's not seeking a simple tumble in the hay, dear cousin."

Barbara gave Jane an innocent look, pretending not to understand.

"No wonder you had too many suitors to choose from and couldn't make up your mind." Marian came up on her other side, slipping between her and Sarah. "You managed to secure the interest of the one unattached nobleman for miles, and in Charlotte's worn castoffs. He might think you an ignorant country girl, but he's willing to waste a whole afternoon just to be at your side."

Georgiana skipped past them. "I'd be burning with envy, but he's so sweet and smitten. Besides, you turning shades whenever he catches you off guard is precious."

Barbara ignored the others to glare at her youngest cousin. "I am not some newborn kitten to stare at him with wide eyes and beg his favor," She turned a pointed stare at Jane.

The others burst out in laughter at a description too close for the meaning to be missed.

Jane pouted for a heartbeat, but the souring of her mood didn't last long before her lips cracked into a twisted smile. "Perhaps that's the answer. A direct approach makes them scatter to the winds while turning your gaze and hiding the truth of your history brings them right to your doorstep."

"While I've no doubt Barbara has made a conquest," Charlotte said, catching hold of Jane's arm, "What begins in falsehood rarely ends well, so don't you go concocting stories to trap the local men."

A deep red swept up Jane's neck to color her face.

"I didn't say a word," Barbara protested, as much to defend herself as to rescue her cousin.

"No, you didn't. You didn't have to." Charlotte frowned. "You might not have told him you were a country girl, but you're dressed in castoffs and doing chores with the rest of us. What is he to think but that you're our servant? Be careful it does not come crashing about your head."

As much as she wished she could reject her cousin's words, what Charlotte said held only the truth. She hadn't intended this to happen, but neither had she done the least thing to stop it. Though if she had, Sarah's plan would have been worthless. Whether he recognized her or not, he knew her name well enough to slander it.

"Besides," she said after a short pause. "If he were a conquest as you say, he would have followed us home to speak with your father about me. Instead, he called it quits and went back to the manor. That is a sure sign of how devoted to me he is not."

Marian put a finger against her chin and tapped twice. "Perhaps our father gave him the same speech he gave you. He went out of his way to ensure you did not meet when showing his prize horse. I'd have thought nothing short of disaster could keep him from watching your expression as you realized what he'd managed to breed."

Georgiana giggled. "A forbidden romance, like that play you told us of. He must steal moments with you far from Father and is willing to risk wrath showered upon his shoulders just to share a few sweet words."

Barbara gave her cousin a shove. "Now don't you be making up stories and telling them to your father. It's no more than a bored nobleman preferring any female company to the prospect of entertaining himself. You heard him. His friends are busy so he sought other pleasures."

"Pleasures indeed," Jane repeated.

"Really, sisters. If this is how you think to behave it's no wonder the man sought out the servant among us. He'd fear for the consequences with such wild girls as the likes of you." Charlotte followed her words up with a stern gaze that swept from one of her sisters to the next, shaming them for their behavior.

As much as Barbara appreciated the rescue, she couldn't suppress a faint thrill at the thought that Aubrey had denied her uncle just to spend time with her. She should find the suggestion laughable, and would soon enough, but first she had to get herself under control, something that proved harder than it should have.

Sarah moved up next to Barbara once again, leaning close to say, "Are you going with the plan to teach the man a lesson then?"

Barbara hardened her spine and stared straight ahead for a moment, but the answer seemed the only clear aspect of this whole muddle. Why else would her pulse race when he appeared if not because she anticipated bringing him to his knees?

"I am."

"You are what?" Jane asked from the other side of Barbara.

Her mind spun through possible explanations until she found one her cousin might accept. "I am tired of all this talk of pairing and noblemen. Charlotte is right. We'd do better to focus on our work."

Barbara ignored the fact that her oldest cousin had said nothing of the sort, but when Jane accepted the dismissal, Barbara's thoughts returned to what Charlotte had said in truth.

A connection built on falsehood and lies could bring only trouble.

Barbara comforted herself with the knowledge trouble was her true purpose. If she could get Aubrey to commit himself, she could then use the truth to prove him no better, or perhaps even worse, than those he saw fit to scorn.

If her thoughts lingered on him, the need to plan out her next steps had to be the cause. He held no other interest, and certainly no fascination, for her.

Aubrey had failed to account for the bond between husband and wife, and the enjoyment they seemed to share at his expense, with his hope to keep the encounter to himself.

No sooner had he left the stable and set foot in the manor proper than Daphne descended on him from wherever she had been keeping herself.

"So? What did you learn? Is she the true bond for your heart?"

The difference between avoiding a mention and an outright lie gave Aubrey little choice but to admit to how he'd spent the afternoon. Still, he could keep his own musing to himself. "I learned nothing."

Daphne's expression fell. "You didn't find her after all? Jasper had been so sure, and when you were gone most of the day ..."

Aubrey waved off her concern, tempted once more to claim a simple ramble through the forest but allowing a misunderstanding to stand had as little honor as provoking one with his own words. "I found the girls all right. I spent a pleasant afternoon in their company learning the local herb lore, though I can't say whether I'd be able to repeat any of it." He laughed, remembering Charlotte's cautions. "Well, no more than not to pluck a random growth for something to chew on. I had no idea there were such dangers to be found among the greenery."

Daphne added a chuckle of her own as she laced an arm through his and drew him toward the drawing room. "If such a thing interests you, perhaps I should arrange an encounter with the local midwife. They all call her Grannie, though as far as I've been able to tell, she's related to none of them. She has stories in plenty. Practically any plant can be used for a medicinal purpose to hear her speak of them, and as many for harm. It's a wonder any husband strays as easy as it would be to slip him something to quiet the urge, if you catch my meaning."

The image that created brought a flush to his cheek as much for coming from her lips as for the words themselves. She showed no such weakness, her eyes twinkling with delighted mischief.

"I have only to spend a moment in your company to envy your

husband, Lady Pendleton. How he could have mistaken you when first you met is beyond me."

Daphne shook her head, both at his formal address and the words. "I had little enough reason to trust in his nature, and no reason to reveal my own. But our tale is old news by now, surely. I'm more interested in yours. How goes things with your country maid?"

They reached the drawing room just as an awkward step reminded Aubrey of both his sore feet and the stench of horse sweat he carried with him.

He pulled free of her hold. "I'm no fit company at the moment and would not want to sully your drawing room. Any telling must wait until I've washed the horse from me and changed to more appropriate clothing. I wouldn't look askance at a soak for my sore feet either."

Daphne appeared about to protest until he added the last. Instead, she burst out a laugh. "I suppose you couldn't have spent much time with them up on your horse, and those boots aren't designed for rough fields. Better your story waits for Jasper anyway, or you'd just have to tell it all a second time. I'll send a bath to your chambers, but don't think you can withhold the afternoon's events forever. Why, your tale is as convoluted as any drama in the London theaters, and we don't have such entertainment out here."

Aubrey nodded thanks, his lips twisted to one side at her assessment of his pursuit of Barbara, seeking as he did either her hand or freedom from her siren's call. Only the future would reveal it to be a comedy, farce, or drama strong enough to bring tears to his eyes.

The last thought gave him pause as he mounted the steps to his room. His heart wrenched with all too much pain at the idea of her proving to be none other than she appeared, a simple girl with a beautiful smile and an eye for the wonders of their world. If her very simplicity drew him, it also condemned him to leaving her behind no matter how it burned him. He would not kill what made her special by uprooting her. No London hot house could sustain her wild nature.

By the time he reached his room, any amusement had drained from him as his mind turned to more serious paths. Better he flush all thought of her from his system.

She had her life here, and his path had been carved since he was but a boy.

He feared the delightful tale Daphne waited on no longer existed. From this moment forward, his pursuit of the truth about his feelings had come to an end, for the good of both of them.

Chapter Twenty-Three

When Charlotte came in from telling Grannie of the bounty they'd collected for her, she marched right up to Barbara and announced, "Since you're the cause of this extra, you'll just have to help me prepare the herbs for storage." Charlotte looked as though she didn't know whether to laugh or scowl as she made the pronouncement. "Clearly Grannie's wishes had no stake in sending us off."

Barbara soon gained a better understanding of why the scowl.

Even with all six of them working, it took the rest of the first day and far into the second before they'd set out those that could be dried and identified what needed to be boiled into solutions.

Their work had only begun.

After dividing the herbs, they began with more preparation steps than many an apothecary, each instruction given by Charlotte in a stern voice that allowed for no complaints and warned of dire consequences should they make a mistake.

Only when they finished did Charlotte relent as she took in the results of their labors. "There'll be no more chores today. Take yourself off for some relaxation."

The cousins scattered faster than Barbara had expected, perhaps fearing Charlotte would find some other essential task should they linger.

"What would you do?" Charlotte's gaze swept both Sarah and Barbara.

Though her back ached and her hands were red and sensitive, only one thought came to mind. "I would ride."

Sarah laughed at that, though Barbara read the agreement in her friend's face. In London, they'd spent what time they could on horseback, the only way to be free of any social restrictions, though riding there had little in common to the wild tear she'd accomplished the last time a horse stood between her knees.

Barbara's smile sank as the consequences of that freedom came back to her. "But with the cousins gone, I cannot. Your father was very specific that every one of you must accompany me or I may not go at all."

"Surely he didn't mean to be so strict," Charlotte said, her tone soft. "If any deserves her choice of rewards it is you and Sarah. Never would I have expected one so recently from London to put herself wholeheartedly into every task I set. The both of you are to be commended."

That brought life into Barbara as she stated, "Commended, maybe, but not on horseback."

Charlotte gave a rueful headshake. "No, I suppose not, or commended would unlikely be the response my father offered. I'll promise you this though. If you help me with the remaining chores today, I'll make sure Father agrees to a morning ride."

Barbara exchanged a glance with Sarah, and the two of them burst out in laughter, much to Charlotte's confusion. Though she could hardly have predicted their humor, her statement only proved the desperate flight of the others a true act of self-preservation.

"I won't speak for Sarah," Barbara said as soon as she got herself under control, "But that seems a worthy exchange to me." She didn't even mind that the other girls would get a second chance at freedom from chores when she did not. A true ride without incurring her uncle's wrath would be worth the work.

"Well, then, I think we should catch up on the sewing. We've spent enough time out in the sun, and from the look of your hands, they need to rest and repair as much as the whole of you."

Though sewing had never been Barbara's favorite, she could manage a decent stitch, and it meant sitting down most likely with a cup of tea. There must have been other things that needed doing, so she chose to be grateful for her cousin's kindness.

Sarah followed them in rather than finding her own pleasures, and the three of them spent a quiet afternoon repairing clothing Barbara felt sure she'd wear before her return to London. At least her handwork would not embarrass, not herself nor any of the cousins who donned the clothes.

The others returned at nightfall without speaking of how they'd chosen to spend their time, though from the blush on Georgiana's cheeks, Barbara suspected Charlotte would soon have to give the girl a stern talking to.

Without hesitation, they each poured a cup of tea and pulled something from the sewing basket, talking on the state of the fields and how high the river was running. Barbara let the conversation flow over her, focused on the possibility of a ride in the morning.

She refused to admit to herself how much the desire stemmed from the hope of crossing paths with Aubrey. After spending the day with him when they were gathering, she knew she wouldn't shy from his company, but she'd had no opportunity to put it to the test. With the herb work, they'd kept close to the house, and Aubrey had made no attempt to seek her out there.

Barbara pushed away her disappointment, reminded of how the cousins suspected her uncle had warned him to stay back. His absence could not be taken as an already waning interest any more than her feelings showed anticipation for his company. She only wanted to put Sarah's plan into effect and teach Aubrey not to judge without evidence.

If her thoughts rang hollow, only she could hear them. The cousins and Sarah had no reason to suspect and tease her for what consumed her attention much more than the measured stitches as she repaired a sprung seam. At least her hands obeyed her command, making even, tight loops that could provoke no complaint.

Just then, her uncle came in from the yard and the girls leapt up to greet their father with an abandon Barbara had cause to envy. She loved her parents, but such boisterous affection had long since been discouraged as she became a young lady and left childhood behind.

Just one more way the country differed from London society much like her canters would be soundly condemned there.

Charlotte pulled her father out of the bevy of sisters and spoke so softly Barbara could not hear her words. Still, what else could she be talking about but the ride? Barbara had seen enough even in her short time among them to know catching him in the first moments come in from the stables meant the greatest chance of whatever request they made.

Uncle Ferrier glanced her way then back to Charlotte, but when he spoke it was in a voice loud enough to fill the room and cut through the chatter from the girls. "You can all go riding tomorrow. I'll leave word with the stable boys as to which horse for each of you." He turned to face Barbara fully. "You are all to stay together. No wandering off and getting into trouble."

Though she'd been sure the last had been a reference to her attempt to escape Aubrey, he pivoted to glare down at Georgiana who turned a deep scarlet. Perhaps the behavior that brought a flush to her cousin's cheeks had not passed unnoticed after all, nor had all of Charlotte's whispers to her father concerned Barbara.

At least things couldn't have gone so far as to compromise the girl, or her uncle would have done more than glare, but Barbara hoped her cousin took this warning to heart. Even out in the country, a young woman's future, and whom she chose to spend it with, had much to do with how good a reputation she maintained.

Barbara could not imagine Uncle Ferrier giving her off to someone at random if no one of standing would have her, but neither could she think of a woman less suited to spinsterhood than her youngest cousin.

Aubrey's decision to stay clear of his delightful country girl passed without challenge in the two days since he'd met the girls at the forest's edge. That he'd noticed the absence did not bode well for his conviction, however, nor did how he chose a path near the Ferrier farmland to complete his morning ride.

A clear voice cut through the background murmur of nature, rewarding his vigilance with, "You heard your father. We must stay together. So keep up."

He tugged on his reins just in time to enjoy the spectacle of Barbara astride a well-muscled horse, her head tossed back and hair streaming behind her as the horse sped from a quick walk into a full-out canter.

The wisdom of a proper saddle, especially at those speeds, did not escape him though she'd be shunned if ever she rode so in London.

The other girls from the gathering trip charged after her, equally skilled, perhaps, but less capable of drawing his gaze, which had stayed with their wild leader as though bound to her with stout leather.

He kneed his horse to follow at a more sedate pace, not because the challenge of a canter failed to appeal but so he wouldn't startle the girls, as Barbara had been that day at the mill. They seemed oblivious to his observation as first Barbara and then the others pulled up their horses into a trot then walk to cool down.

"Morning," he called out as he neared. "Nothing like a fast ride to start the day off well."

As he'd thought, from the way they twisted to face him as a group, his arrival had passed unnoticed. Their expressions ranged from surprise and embarrassment to delight, but he cared only for the one painting Barbara's features.

Her eyes had widened, but the blush that colored her cheeks did not make her turn away. Instead, she stared right at him, their gazes locked for what seemed like an age. If she were as a siren to him, it seemed he did not suffer alone.

"How is it you happened to be crossing this field?"

The question, from one of the other girls, broke his concentration. Aubrey struggled with an answer for a moment before realizing she'd meant to tease. "There are only so many directions to a compass, and I've roamed a bit these past two days."

"Searching for our Barbara, I'd guess."

"Jane!" The oldest of the farmer's daughters gave her sister a sharp look and saved him the trouble of a reply when he did not want to admit she'd said nothing but the truth, especially when he'd hidden that knowledge from himself. Seeing Barbara now, though, made the circuitous nature of his rides all the clearer.

The girls swung down from their horses, Barbara the last to follow suit as though reluctant to give up her perch.

Aubrey refused to take advantage and so joined them on the ground, his feet having recovered from the abuse of last time in the long days between.

"Would any of you girls like some water after your hard ride?" he asked instead, pulling his flask free from its bindings.

Barbara sat nearest, and he watched as she tipped her head back and swallowed twice. The movement accentuated the slender length of her throat, so pale despite her labors under the sun.

Instead of returning the flask, she passed it over to another servant, a further sign the rules of class and station did not hold much sway in this company.

"I should not be surprised from the quality of Mr. Ferrier's stables, but you all ride with skill," he said, collecting his wandering thoughts in an attempt to appear unaffected.

Barbara's lips curled in a grin that sent heat to his very core. "Shouldn't you be shocked and upset to find yourself in the company of girls astride?"

He blinked twice, perhaps giving the impression of shock as he admired her pluck. "I see nothing wrong in setting the right tools to the task," Aubrey said after a moment. "The sight of you, any of you, thrown down as your saddle gave way at such speed would be pleasing to none."

"You sound as though you know a thing or two about sidesaddles," the oldest broke in.

"I have three sisters. You'll have to trust I've heard their curses often enough to know the failings of a woman's saddle. Besides …" He turned to Barbara. "This is not the first time I've seen you astride."

He'd meant to compliment her on regaining control without being thrown, but before he could continue, Barbara flushed a deep red, and this time she did turn away.

From her response, it seemed the farmer had been closer to the truth than Aubrey had thought in claiming the snake a ruse. "You were running from me." The words came as he relived the moment their gazes crossed, the same moment her horse reared up as though attacked from beneath.

He'd spoken under his breath, but the way she jerked back to stare revealed he'd been heard. The sharp need for her answer prevented him from any pretense of not having spoken. That need more than anything put paid to his vow to abandon the pursuit. He was caught in her clutches as sure as Odysseus had longed to hear the sirens, only Aubrey's friends had not seen fit to tie him to the mast.

Barbara gave him every opportunity to deny what she'd heard, or even turn the conversation to other topics. He only stared at her as though expecting a response, ignoring any chance of withdrawing with the steady nature of a horse wearing blinkers. She couldn't believe he'd meant to confront her on this, but neither did he seem willing to let the moment pass.

"If I did, it is because I find your attentions disturbing," she said finally, losing patience along with control of her tongue.

Her mother would have charged her with shrewishness, but she spoke only the truth. His seeking her now, when she'd have given anything to catch his interest before learning what he really thought of her, drove Barbara to erratic behavior that spiraled between rage and confusion.

Though her words came out sharp, a wide smile split his face. "I do as well, but that doesn't seem to have the least impact."

Confusion won as she shook her head, unable to comprehend his statement.

"I came here to get away from the marriage mart, the constant press of girls and their mothers. Certainly not to find myself drawn to someone new."

In one simple statement, he reminded her of exactly why she'd decided to follow through on Sarah's plan as her emotions swung once again to rage.

If ever a man needed a lesson, this one did. His pretty words held as much meaning as the dust his horse kicked up to dig free a fresh growth.

And he wasn't offering the simple country girl he saw anything more than a loss of reputation and a broken heart. He'd come to escape the marriage mart and certainly wouldn't make an offer here, especially not to someone so unsuitable after he brushed aside all those other girls.

She glanced away, not wanting him to see the flames that must have been shooting from her eyes, but he caught her chin and tugged her back. The touch, as light as it was, stole the breath from her lungs and sent tingles down her neck.

"I did not mean to spurn you. Only to admit to being driven by something greater than myself. I cannot promise to leave you be." His shoulders raised in a shrug. "I tried and failed. But I'll do my best to help you become more comfortable with my attentions."

Barbara cast about for her cousins to beg a rescue, unsure just what he'd meant by that but suspecting her uncle would be none too pleased.

They had moved aside to give Aubrey and Barbara the illusion of privacy. Whispers interrupted by the occasional giggle, though, revealed what could only be enjoyment at her expense.

She sent a scowl at Marian, the closest, who surely knew better. Some help they were. If this were the way of sisters, Barbara could only be grateful she had none.

Marian flushed a bright pink and called in an overly loud voice, "Just look at the berries on that bush there. We should all collect some for Father. Coming, Barbara?"

Barbara regretted her bitter thought as she spun away from Aubrey's intent gaze to cross over to where the girls had gathered. It seemed the bush did hold plump, deep purple berries, a fortunate circumstance with Aubrey following close on her heels.

Georgiana cast him a bright smile. "It can be just as how you first met Barbara, only now none of us have more than a handkerchief to hold our bounty." She cast a sideways glance at her older sister. "And I doubt Charlotte will be quite so strict on the number we consume, especially when we can carry so little."

Aubrey collected the reins of all the horses, looking like nothing more than a servant walking the master's dogs on the streets of London, only his charges stood many hands higher. "I'll tether the beasts to that sturdy tree. Without baskets, we'll all need our hands, I suspect."

Finally, he chose to act the gentlemen and put aside the uncomfortable intensity he had been pressing on her.

Barbara allowed herself to relax. She ignored the little voice at the back of her head that expressed regret at the moment passing. He made her so turned about. She'd have to be much more careful if she was to escape from her plan unscathed.

That, if nothing else, made her even more determined to bring him to his knees. She found the sensation of being out of control disturbing at the very least.

"... And everyone at the manor enjoyed a delicious piece of cheesecake with one bruised raspberry clinging to the top. Even such a small treat proved so good Lady Pendleton sent out servants to pluck a full measure. Though how they followed my directions, I do not know. I've been so far unable to return."

Marian laughed and brushed his sleeve with already sticky fingers. "It's because the servants took all the berries so the bush seems nothing more than a bramble now, I'm sure."

"Or maybe," Barbara cut in as she touched a decidedly ripe and plump fruit, "the manor servants know the area much better than some gentleman fresh from London."

Charlotte shot her a reproving glance, but Aubrey took no offense, throwing back his head to laugh with infectious abandon.

Barbara watched him from the corner of her eye, most likely fooling no one but herself as she enjoyed a humor that in no way connected with the person she'd discovered in London. If he wore a mask here, it fit like a fresh-boiled glove. Perhaps he saw this as a space out of time, much like she had become another person in Charlotte's cast-offs and with chores making her hands red.

"Perhaps," Aubrey said, as though in answer to her musing until he continued, "but they'll be happy for some of these despite the bounty." He proved himself pleased enough by plucking two from the bush and dropping the first onto his tongue.

Though she'd turned to watch him openly, Barbara ducked away when she realized his intention for the second berry. She could just as well pluck her own, and the thought of accepting a treat from his fingers, of his fingertips brushing her lips as he had her chin, made her insides shaky.

Unwilling to chance another such opportunity, Barbara moved close to Charlotte, the only one of the girls she could trust to shield her rather than offering her up to him much like the berry he'd savored so openly. She allowed herself sideways glances but nothing more as they took what they could carry and went their separate ways.

Chapter Twenty-Four

Barbara woke the next morning with a sense of well-being at odds with the hard work Charlotte had put them to upon their return from the ride.

They'd gone through a long list of chores that kept them close to the farmhouse so surely their tasks today would take them into the fields and beyond her uncle's narrowed gaze. He'd welcomed the gift of berries the previous day, and by some twist of fate or luck, had not inquired as to why they'd stopped during their ride long enough to discover the fruit.

His distraction had been so noticeable Georgiana asked after him, but when he'd started to speak of some decision regarding his breeding program, his youngest daughter quickly turned the conversation to speculating on what Cook would do with the berries this time.

Barbara would have liked to hear about the horses, but she was happy enough to avoid another lecture on engaging in activities with Aubrey.

"You're looking quite lively this morning," Sarah said, pulling herself to a seated position with obvious effort. "One might wonder just what — or who — put that smile on your lips."

With a glance to the window, Barbara shrugged. "It looks to be a beautiful morning."

"And you can tell this through the gingham, I suppose?"

Barbara focused on the space she'd used as an excuse only to find the curtains pulled closed. Of course. Sarah was the one to open them each morning, forcing Barbara to rise, and her friend was still abed.

Instead of answering, she slipped out from under the covers and crossed to the basin of water to begin her morning wash.

"It isn't for thoughts of seeing your nobleman, is it?"

"If I have any thoughts of seeing him, it's for the chance to give him a taste of his own nature using your grand plan," Barbara said.

She glanced over to Sarah, but instead of the mischievous expression she'd expected, her friend wore a frown.

Sarah rose as well. "Perhaps I spoke too hastily before. Perhaps it would be better to tell him the truth and let him discover his mistake now in a gentler way."

Barbara had not expected her friend to have given in so quickly to Aubrey's pretense, not knowing what she did once Barbara had told her. And yet, hadn't she experienced the same trouble? Though she'd not admit it to Sarah, the hope of seeing Aubrey once again had brought her awake with anticipation, and her response had more to do with the chance for his company than any punishment, deserved or not.

Her voice sharp more against her own fickle heart than Sarah's, Barbara snapped, "Aubrey St. Vincent caused me no end of heartache. Who knows how many other girls have suffered from his cutting wit? And he is the root of any worries my parents suffer as well. God sent him here so I could give him a taste of his own medicine, not so I can soften the blow and cater to his already overblown sense of superiority."

Sarah had flinched when she started speaking and showed no more signs of comfort now that Barbara fell silent.

A twinge of regret passed through her.

Sarah deserved her rancor no more than her parents had for sending her here instead of letting her finish out the season. Aubrey lay at the root of everything, and she'd do well to remember it.

With a familiarity from their shared childhood as much as the forgetfulness of station this place provoked, Sarah caught Barbara's arm when she would have turned away. "I know you believe that to be true. I do not doubt what you heard him say, or that he meant every word at the time. And yet, you said yourself he spoke in confidence

to his friend, unaware anyone stood close enough to listen. I've seen
no sign of such a disregard in the time he's spent in our company, and
I have seen how you are drawn to him no matter what you'd like to
pretend."

Barbara pulled away, wishing for a mirror so she could watch Sarah without looking in that direction, but the simple chest of drawers
had none. She stared resolutely at the wall instead. "I'm not the one
pretending. You hear my words, but you don't listen to them. How is
his gentle nature now any different than his mask worn in London?
Tell me how you can see through to his heart when he has all of society fooled?"

This time when Sarah touched Barbara it was to offer a soft hug
to her shoulders. "I didn't mean to state I could see what you could
not. It's only that being out of London can bring out true natures in a
way society prevents. You, yourself, strained at its strictures. Why
couldn't it be the same for him? Why couldn't this be whom he would
be if he didn't have to conform?"

Though Barbara tried to shrug off the touch, it wasn't much of an
attempt and had little effect. Sarah said nothing she hadn't thought
herself. It took more effort than she could have imagined to keep herself from succumbing to his playacting. When he'd touched her those
few times, her whole body joined the chorus begging to accept his
deceit as truth.

"I can only think on your cousin's warning," Sarah said as though
reading the answer in Barbara's tense form. "No good comes from
scheming and lies, no matter how good the intention."

Barbara forced a smile to her lips ignoring how strained it must
have appeared as she turned to meet Sarah's worried gaze. "Then it's a
good thing I have not deceived in the slightest manner. It is no fault
of mine if he looks on my clothes and assumes without asking. I
promise you, should he seek my background, I'll be truthful. That
should calm your fears. Though if he thinks to ask and looks beyond
the judgment he made without my consent, no one will be more surprised than myself."

She pushed her friend aside gently so she could collect a dress from those Charlotte had lent her, ignoring the quiet words that followed her.

"But when you told him your name, you chose not to tell it all. Is that not enough of a lie?"

The berries were as well received at the manor the second time as they had been the first, and Aubrey suffered the sideways glances and knowing looks from his friends in silence. He might not have gone out of his way to seek her, but some part of him had been aware of the greater possibility when he'd chosen the direction he had.

Aubrey found little value in self-deceit. He could call her a siren, claim she had mystical nymph-like qualities, or however else he chose to explain why the next morning he turned his steed toward the farm once again, but that she — and no other — drew him could not be denied.

He mused on where this attraction would take him as he rode, determine to break through her reticence and get a glimpse of the thoughts in her head. Whether she could survive in London became more imperative as he questioned if he would survive leaving her behind. Part of him dreaded the discovery that, like any wildflower, once plucked from the country she would shine her bright colors into his life for only a few short days before beginning to fade.

Aubrey laughed at himself, always planning so far into the future when too many twists and turns lay in his path for him to see the truth of such a plan. After all, he'd always thought to find his mate the traditional way, at the marriage mart, and yet he'd fled from the scene after less than a full season, unable to stomach it.

As though an echo of his humor, he heard faint laughter.

He pressed heels to the horse's sides. No doubt of the source ever rose, not with the way his heartbeat quickened at the teasing sound.

"I found some!"

His faith rewarded, Aubrey rode up to the forest edge to find his country girl calling the others over. She knelt in the dirt, her hands pressed to the soil as she stared at something beneath her.

"Fine morning," he called, swinging down from his horse. He paused only long enough to tether the beast to a tree before joining the gathering. "What have you found?"

Barbara had looked up at his greeting, and from the moment their gazes locked, had not shifted.

He could see the confusion at his question and when she blinked to clear her mind of the effect they seemed to have on one another. The sight offered hope where nothing else could. It confirmed she was as affected by his presence as he was by hers.

"Mushrooms," she said after a short pause.

He suspected she read a match to her earlier expression on his face with her reply.

He'd been so caught up in whether she shared his interest he'd forgotten asking the question at first, but he followed her pointed finger to see the small brown caps against the ground.

Charlotte approached with her sisters, and Barbara moved back to give her room. The farmer's eldest poked the fungus, inspecting its features as the others stood by, waiting for her assessment.

Aubrey had nothing to offer in this. The only mushrooms he'd ever seen had been carefully prepared by a cook and presented in their most savory forms.

"Yes, these are good for eating. Collect half of them, Barbara, no more. We want to keep the patch growing, and it's only right to share some bounty with the wild creatures," Charlotte said as she dusted her hands and stood. "The rest of you get back to looking. She needs no help in this. It's been a wet winter, but the finds are still rare this early in the season."

Charlotte had a commanding tone that would have served a naval officer well.

Within heartbeats, all the girls had returned to their searching.

Aubrey dropped to his knees, hoping the servant Jasper had lent him for this visit wouldn't scold for the stains. "Can I help you? You'll have to tell me what to do."

Barbara glanced at him, her eyes sparkling with some aspect of humor she chose not to share. "Don't pull them from the ground. Break them off just above it. And you heard my … Charlotte. Only half of the patch."

He understood her hesitation all too well. If she felt even a fraction of what he did, the reminder of their differences in station only served to point out how unlikely their connection had to be. And yet, he'd observed often enough the close bonds between nobles raised alongside their common staff. Such didn't happen in London, or if it did, much more rarely, but his contemporaries who had been raised in the country seemed to consider this happening commonplace. He had only to look to Daphne and Willem for an example, her London life beginning when she'd been almost grown.

When Barbara tucked the caps into her basket, he took the woven handle from her. "I know how to carry, at least. You'd best do the searching."

Though one of the other girls had called out a success while they carefully plucked the mushrooms free, from the time passing, Aubrey suspected finding the fungus had as much to do with luck as skill.

"It's only a matter of walking slowly. You must push the grass and bushes aside with your toes."

The comment sent his gaze to her feet to find them bare and enticing. Slender and graceful despite the soil smudged along them.

"I think I'll leave that task to your skilled digits. I've heard in France they train pigs to find truffles the same way a hunter would use dogs to search out a fox den."

She glanced at him with a wide smile. "Are you claiming I'm a pig, then, sir? Or the same as one?"

In another, her words would have been full of anger, but she offered a challenge of different sort, straining his skills as a conversationalist, an event he'd rarely experienced. Then the call from another of the girls brought the answer to him as his own lips curved.

He caught hold of one of her dirty hands and raised it to his mouth to brush a kiss on her skin. "No, my fine girl, there is little chance of mistaking you for a pig."

Aubrey waited for the blush he knew would sweep her features before he lifted one eyebrow to give her a sardonic look. "A pig would be much more successful."

Barbara stared at him, her eyes widened in shock at his words. Then she jerked her hand free and planted both on her hips. "Well, I never."

He shook his head. "Not never. After all, this basket does not stand empty."

As much as she struggled for anger, he could see the humor tugging at her like quicksand until it won the battle as she threw her head back in a laugh.

Aubrey stood transfixed.

The sunlight burnished her dark curls with hints of copper.

Her skin cried out for his touch, a craving began when he claimed her hand and now grown to a wanting so much stronger.

"Let's see if you are any better," she said once she regained control. "I'll hold the basket, and you can probe the undergrowth."

She stared at him boldly for a moment before he understood her meaning.

"It's no less than I deserve," Aubrey answered with a shrug.

He surrendered the basket to tug off both boots and stockings. "At least this way I won't have blisters from walking in footwear intended to ride."

Where his boots kept him separate, now his feet sank into the rich soil, a twig pressing hard against one heel in a warning he risked more than blisters. He didn't care, though. Somehow, this deeper connection with the earth married well with the bond he felt to his sweet Barbara. If she could not come to his world, at least in this he could join with hers.

Barbara hadn't expected Aubrey to be so quick to follow suit. After all, it had taken her some moments to come to terms with what Charlotte told her was the best way to go hunting mushrooms. She refused to admit how much her reluctance had stemmed from the thought of Aubrey joining them and seeing her as something less.

Instead, there he stood, shifting gingerly from foot to foot as he tested the soil, and the various sharp and uncomfortable objects she knew lay hidden within it.

With her own toes peeking out from between the blades of grass, his state of undress, even in so small a fashion, sent a shiver of heat through her. Barbara forced her gaze to her cousins and Sarah, checking on their progress as a distraction from a man who consumed too much of her waking thought already.

His teasing spoke of familiarity, a comfort in her presence she wished she could deny. Every moment at his side only made her wish an ignorance she could never have again. This, more than the infatuation she'd had in London, threatened her wellbeing.

She understood Sarah's worries better than her friend supposed. The plot had become in itself a pretense, an excuse for spending time with the one man she should stay as far from as possible on their island home. To do otherwise was to put her heart at risk.

Yet here she stood, in an intimacy grown of bare feet, and the distance between them and the other searchers.

Aubrey cleared his throat as though he'd recognized the same circumstances that now plagued her. "Probe the undergrowth, you say?"

Barbara nodded, not trusting her voice to be even.

"Well, then, we best be at it. I need to prove I am as skilled as the average pig. Not the trained ones, mind you, but dogs only go after foxes because it's in their nature."

"And hunting fungus is in yours?" she teased, her voice returning as mischief took the place of discomfort.

He shrugged. "Hunting dinner certainly is, though this is the first time I've gone after this part. Do you think your mistress will allow me to bring some home with me?"

Barbara supposed Charlotte was her mistress in most senses for the moment. Her parents had given her over into her uncle's care, and he assigned the task to his oldest daughter from how Charlotte had been keeping her busy. She pushed aside the twinge of guilt in letting the statement stand. "That would depend on how pig-like you are. Or is it how French?"

Aubrey gave one of his deep laughs at that, and Barbara stopped her forward steps to stare.

"You, my dear girl, offer as much entertainment as many on the stage."

Desperate for something to distract her from the connection she felt growing between them, Barbara latched onto the statement with the focus of a drowning man.

"Have you seen much of the theater?" she asked, knowing full well Aubrey St. Vincent was considered a patron of the arts and spent much of his time in the theater district.

"The tales I could tell you," he said with a dramatic pause as though quoting from one of the performances he'd seen.

"Then do." She widened her eyes and tried to put forth the words in a tone appropriate to a young girl locked in the country.

They wandered the forest edge, eyes cast down to catch any hint of the savory mushrooms, as Aubrey told her of the plays he'd seen. She'd been to some of the same, but in his voice, the stories took on a deeper meaning, as though tales of star-crossed love spoke of her and how endangered she'd become while the adventures played on her thrill of a challenge.

"You certainly chose the more entertaining partner," Charlotte said one of the times they'd called her over to confirm what they'd found would rest well in their bellies. "Take care you don't wander too far though."

Avoiding her cousin's stern look, Barbara discovered Charlotte had more than enough cause to question when her averted gaze found Jane at some distance. "I hadn't realized how separated we'd become. Aubrey and I will follow you back."

Charlotte's eyebrows rose at how easily his first name tripped from her tongue, but Barbara almost forgot her cousin's presence when Aubrey greeted the familiarity with a grin.

Her world narrowed to his face. Her heart beat faster, and she longed for him to reach for her, to pull her into his embrace.

"Pick half this cluster first. They're safe for the table, and we'll need as many as we can find if we're to reward his lordship with some in return for his labors."

Her cousin's words, matched with Charlotte rising off the ground and brushing her skirts free of the mossy soil, broke the trance Aubrey had trapped Barbara in.

She stepped away as though to escape him, but stopped herself and instead bent down to the mushrooms, ever conscious of Charlotte still within earshot. The use of such a formal reference had been a warning more subtle perhaps than Charlotte's gaze, but a warning she'd meant not just for Barbara's ears.

They both focused on the task in silence for a moment.

Though she could no more read his thoughts now than ever, Barbara suspected he pondered the warning as well, or maybe he'd felt the same bond between them before Charlotte broke it, an intervention Barbara had to be grateful for no matter how much she'd have preferred to remain suspended there. They spent this time together against her uncle's wishes and against her best judgment. She would not fail herself or her uncle so far as to cost her reputation.

"I guess that answers my question," Aubrey said, his voice light in a clear attempt to ease the silence between them.

Barbara stared, wondering just what question had been floating in his mind. Did he now think Charlotte wary of him?

"That your mistress would let me take some of these finds to the manor as well. The kitchen staff must think I've become quite the scavenger for all the wild fruits and foods I bring them."

She barely heard his last sentence over the reminder again of just what he thought her to be. He was no more than a nobleman whiling away the lonely hours in the company of an uncultured country girl. Perhaps her delight in his tellings amused him, or perhaps he had let himself fall into a bit of a fantasy like the plays they'd spoken of with him as a country role, wandering barefoot and gathering fruits of the dark earth.

Whatever his reasoning, she had to recall her own.

This was not some playwright's fancy where the titled man falls for the lowly servant girl, and moves heaven and earth to rescue her from her rough upbringing. If anything, it played more the farce with him the fool. If she thought any chance of it turning out differently remained, whether she told him now or strung it out as long as she could manage before she lost him, she had taken the fool's cap onto her own curls.

Barbara feared she felt the press of its band already.

Chapter Twenty-Five

Even without a mirror to watch Sarah's face, the way she tugged and jerked the brush through Barbara's curls was evidence enough her friend had something on her mind as they prepared for bed. The ritual had extended beyond the responsibilities of station years ago, but rarely had Barbara longed for it to come to an end. Usually, the brushing soothed her and eased the day's tensions.

Unable to stand it a moment longer, Barbara raised a hand to catch the offending brush and spun to face her friend. "Out with it, then. Whatever you're keeping bottled up, my scalp cannot take more of this."

A flush colored Sarah's neck, but she didn't turn away as she marshaled her thoughts. "I know you don't want to hear my opinion. You made that clear enough this morning."

Barbara should have known the problem. Through unspoken agreement, the girls no longer mentioned Aubrey once they returned to the farmhouse, a conspiracy grown out of a romantic notion that her uncle was the only barrier between them. While the cousins knew Aubrey had been deceived as to her station, only Sarah understood the full of it, as well she should being its mastermind.

"You might as well speak," Barbara said, rising to drop her brush on the chest of drawers "I'm hearing it anyway though not in words." To emphasize her point, she rubbed a sore spot where Sarah had pulled too hard. The country air and wind had much to answer for in the state of her hair, but Sarah's usually gentle ministrations could untangle the most distressing of knots if she but tried.

"You've grown too close, too comfortable with him. This has to end or you'll wind up compromised no matter what your intentions. You need to tell him the truth and have him seek your uncle's permission in lieu of your father."

Barbara stared at her friend. "I will not. Can you imagine Uncle Ferrier's response should he discover what I, what all of us, his daughters included, have been about?" She pressed a hand to her breast and acted a swoon.

Sarah scowled back, no sign of amusement on her features. "Better that than you returning to London more broken than when you were sent off, and under his watch. Don't try to make this into a fun little game. It's long gone beyond that. I've seen the two of you together, and I know you too well. You need to tell him before it's too late."

Unable to meet her friend's gaze, Barbara twisted to stare out the window, this time lifting the curtain though she saw no more than before. "I won't tell him." Sarah might know her well, but not so well as to realize Barbara had passed beyond the bounds of safety long ago though it took Barbara until today to admit it.

When she told Aubrey, he'd hate her for playing him the fool — more even than she'd hated him upon hearing his cutting remarks. She couldn't suffer that. Not now. Not yet.

She needed to hold on to every connected moment she could for she feared those memories would be all to comfort her through a loveless marriage to any one of the suitors she left dangling in London. Her parents would see to it, and they'd be confident she needed only time for love to grow. They'd never perceive her heart had already been claimed, claimed by one who rejected her once and would do so much more harshly the second time. He'd thought her frivolous for dancing. What would he call her upon learning her schemes?

Sarah caught Barbara by the arm and turned her round. "If you won't tell him, I will. There is nothing to be gained in continuing on this revengeful path, and much to lose."

Barbara barely heard the rest of Sarah's statement as she saw her life crumbling before her. It was far too late to save her from harm. Whether Sarah told or she did mattered not. The game had gone on too long to recover his regard.

She drew herself to her full height and pulled on every moment her mother had taken charge for inspiration. "You will not," she ground out in a low, commanding tone. "You will not speak of this to Aubrey. I forbid it. Do you understand? I forbid it."

In the stunned silence that followed, Barbara did not know which of them was more surprised. Never in all their years together had Barbara so mistreated her maid, never before had she dismissed Sarah as though she were nothing more than a servant rather than a lifelong friend.

She raised a hand to break the silence and rub out her words, but Sarah only gave her a tight nod, not a sign of interest in reconciliation but rather an acknowledgment of the offense.

"Please," Barbara whispered, wanting nothing more in that moment than to have her friend again.

Without a word, Sarah pivoted and walked to the door. She closed it a little too firmly as she left.

Barbara sank to the floor and stared at her hands.

Perhaps it had been Aubrey who'd seen her character clearly when he spoke what she'd overheard.

First she deceived the man she'd given her heart, and now she stabbed the girl who had been her companion since as far back as she could remember.

She'd trapped herself in a situation where any attempt to change things would mean she'd lose. Her blissful plan to teach him a lesson had resulted in a lesson for sure, but Aubrey remained unaware of his part in it, just as he'd had no way of knowing how he'd destroyed her world with his sharp words.

This time, though, she had none but herself to blame. Sarah might have made the suggestion in jest or through some other motivation, but Barbara had been the one to decide to put it into play. She'd kept the pretense, lying to herself as much as to him.

Now she stood in a disaster of her own making where every path only led to a greater tangle and none offered hope of a better outcome.

The sounds of a busy household woke Barbara to a difficult day. Her curtains were still drawn.

She'd fallen into a sleep of exhaustion still in her clothes though no longer on the hard floor because she'd moved to the bed to wait for Sarah's return.

The other pillow remained untouched, nor had Barbara any memory of her friend sneaking in.

"There you are," Marian exclaimed when Barbara made her way to the kitchen, but she said nothing further, pulled up short by a sharp glance from Charlotte.

"You'll have to grab some bread and cheese for breakfast, though there might be some warm tea left in the pot if you hurry."

Barbara stared at her oldest cousin, surprised her tardy arrival would provoke such a cool response, especially since no one had been sent to roust her.

"We'll be heading out shortly. Sarah has volunteered to help Cook sort the pantry and so will not be joining us."

Suddenly, Barbara understood Charlotte's behavior after all.

Sarah had not returned to their room no matter how long Barbara had managed to wait for her. The girl must have gone somewhere, and now Barbara had the answer. She'd gone to Charlotte.

Barbara's shoulders slumped as she turned to follow her cousin's directions, pouring a cup of over-steeped and lukewarm tea on her way to collecting some bread and cheese from the pantry.

Though she'd hoped to find Sarah there, to apologize and beg for forgiveness, her friend proved absent from here as much as she'd been from their room.

This would be her punishment for her sharp tone the night before.

Charlotte's ice seemed nothing in comparison to the absence of her friend, or worse, the burden of injuries given then left untended.

Sarah had done nothing to warrant her ire, wanting only to keep Barbara safe both in reputation and heart. How broken had she become already that she would cast off a lifetime of care for a moment longer with a man who would be sure to despise her for the rest of his life.

Barbara made up the tail end of their wild strawberry gathering expedition, her thoughts on more than the hoped for glimpse of bright red.

She searched half-heartedly as she considered what she could do to repair the breach between her and Sarah. They'd had squabbles before, but never of this magnitude, and never such that Sarah felt it necessary to involve someone else before they could mend things.

A twinge of anger flashed through Barbara at how Sarah had turned Charlotte against her, but just as quickly it vanished under the weight of her responsibility. She'd had no other choice, unless she meant to bed down in the straw of the cow barn, and that would mean more than just Charlotte would discover their falling out.

No, if any were to blame for Sarah needing to seek Charlotte's assistance, it fell on Barbara's shoulders alone. Maybe if she'd chased after Sarah rather than waiting passively for her friend to return, Charlotte would never have known. Had she acted, perhaps Sarah would be at her side now, laughing as they proved incapable of hunting down the rare, but delectable fruits.

Barbara gave a harsh chuckle as she realized Sarah had succeeded in her aim after all.

The break between them consumed Barbara's every thought, leaving none for wondering whether Aubrey would chance upon them this day as he had the other times. When she longed for company, it was Sarah who came first to mind.

But thought of Aubrey, once risen, would not slip quietly away.

There'd been a time when she would have laid the blame for this mess on his shoulders along with the rest. Her parents may not have intended this type of growth, but Barbara had indeed learned something of her own agency.

Whereas she'd thought herself in command before, having secured her parents' promise to choose her future husband, she'd been no more in control of her own self than a newborn calf in Marian's stories as it struggled to stand. She'd let an overheard comment turn her into the worst of offenders, both in London and now here, practicing a deceit Charlotte had warned would only bring harm to herself and others. And it had certainly done that.

She'd lost Sarah as well as any chance with Aubrey.

With none but herself to shoulder responsibility, her future seemed bleak.

That thought, more than any other, opened her eyes to the sole path before her.

If she were to recover her own nature and cast aside her childish revenge, she'd have to stand up to her failings. To win Sarah's regard once more, she'd have to do the one thing she'd rejected, the very thing she'd ordered her childhood friend not to accomplish.

She had to tell Aubrey herself.

The thought brought with it a wash of peace followed by anguish.

The tale told, Aubrey would be quit of her presence, of her life. She'd never have the chance to laugh with him, to discuss poetry, plays, or even pigs. To regain her friend and her true self, she would have to lose the man who had taken hold of her very heart.

"One last day. Surely Sarah would not deny me that much. Just for today, and then I will."

"Will what?" Jane said, coming up on her side. "Will finally concentrate enough to find some berries? You seem a bit distracted." She glanced at the basket on Barbara's arm. "And your weave is empty of a single one. Don't think we'll be quick to share when you did none of the labor."

"Perhaps you'll walk with me and show me how to find them?" Barbara asked her cousin, grateful for the distraction. Aubrey had so far been absent, but if she were to keep up the pretense for even one short day, she needed to know what a country girl would. Seeking a flash of color seemed much too simple a direction for her to have any success.

Chapter Twenty-Six

Despite Charlotte's warning gaze the previous day, Aubrey had a feeling the four sisters were not opposed to his interest in their servant, a suspicion confirmed when he once again came across them in the fields far from their father's stables.

"There you are," the youngest of the daughters called out. "We were wondering if you'd see fit to grace us with your presence at all today."

"Georgie, don't cause the man grief," her sister Jane said, offering him a smile.

Aubrey scanned the group, finding only the four sisters.

"Don't look so glum," Marian told him as she rose from the ground with her basket swinging from one arm. "We'll think our company not good enough for you."

He struggled for an appropriate response, but before he could appease, she thwacked him lightly on the arm. "It doesn't count if it takes that much effort," she teased. "I last saw Barbara hunting over yonder."

Aubrey gave a nod to each of the sisters, Charlotte reception the only chilly one, and set out after his country girl without even asking what they hunted today. Whether delicacy for the dinner table or medicines to make a man hearty once again, it mattered only the company he'd find when joining them.

His eager step was well rewarded as he came upon Barbara seated in the dirt with her legs tucked under her in all propriety. A flash of regret went through him at the sight, her toes invisible once again.

As he neared, she glanced up with a welcoming expression. Then something changed to make him suspect her mood not conducive to courting.

"Good morning," he said softly. "What are you collecting today?"

Barbara looked to the ground then raised a hand without energy to reveal a small, red berry. "Strawberries. I'd offer you one to taste, but they're so hard to find I fear Charlotte would have my head."

Whereas yesterday her tone would have been full of teasing delight and her eyes sparkling with mischief, today, her voice seemed as flat as the rest of her demeanor.

Aubrey crouched next to Barbara. "What is so wrong that it takes the light from your character?"

Her gaze jerked to his as though she'd been unaware of her affect until he brought it to her attention. Eyes wide, she revealed nothing to ease his concerns.

"Tell me. Whatever it is, a burden shared is a burden halved."

She laughed then, not her usual, entrancing laugh, but a sour, bitter sound. "What troubles me will not be assisted by sharing, least of all with you."

Aubrey caught one of her hands and raised it to his chest. "Try me. You have too little faith in a man raised among women."

That brought color into her cheeks, but not the best kind.

"You think this a simple women's problem you can cure with a brush of your manly hand?" She tugged free of him. "I have fought with Sarah over something large enough to break a friendship counted in years, but you will cure me of the sorrow by offering a few short hours in your company instead?"

Aubrey rocked onto his heels at her vehemence. While relieved a spat between friends caused the melancholy rather than learning someone she loved had a fatal disease, he knew enough from his sisters to understand the impact such could have. "I didn't mean to belittle your upset. Only that it hurts me to see you saddened, and I would do all in my power to ease your pain."

She stared at him then, tears welling in her eyes though she refused to let them fall.

"Come." He took her hand to pull her upright. "While you figure out what is necessary to mend this breach, we can gather a wildflower bouquet to deliver with your apology. What young woman doesn't like flowers?"

She resisted his pull for only a moment before she joined him in standing, a little of her spirit returned to her expression. "You're so quick to assume the apology is mine to give."

He shook his head. "Not at all. But the hurt is yours to suffer, and an apology sincerely meant, no matter who was at fault in the rift, can go a long way to healing it."

He won a smile then. "You are wise for a nobleman with no duties to keep you from me."

"Nothing," he declared with all his heart, "could keep me from you." Despite his concerns, the statement rang with truth not just for her but for himself as well.

A shadow of sorrow returned to her face, but vanished again so quickly, he wondered if he'd imagined it.

She'd confessed the cause for her misery else he'd think her father had found her a suitor, though perhaps some element of that question rose between her and her friend.

"Is she to marry?" he asked, his thoughts translating to words. "Your friend that is."

She gave him a startled look. "No, of course not."

Her sharp rejection raised more questions than it answered, but she showed little sign of wanting to elaborate, and he chose not to push her.

Instead, they sought out wildflowers and strawberries across the fields, the tiny white blossoms hard to find. When they reached the rocks at the edges, they trailed along them in hopes of a cluster more visible than in the grass.

She asked him after London, a curiosity most in the country must share, and one he happily indulged. Though comfortable in the silence when it fell, he found himself telling her of his studies in law and politics, half expecting her interest to fade into ennui.

Barbara probed his statements with the skill of a solicitor, articulating her concerns, asking exploratory questions, and even pointing out possibilities or conclusions he'd yet to consider, her earlier sorrow set aside for the moment.

The more time he spent in her presence, the more intrigued he felt.

Despite the limited circumstances of her birth and station, whether considered part of the farmer's family or not, she had a curious mind and the sharp intellect to act on it.

Perhaps he'd been too quick to assume London would tear the heart out of his Barbara. From what he'd seen today, she'd make short work of anyone trying to cast aspersions and would likely find the amount of information available to her amazing. He wondered if she could, in fact, thrive as his wife.

"I think I see some over there," Barbara said, appearing oblivious to the turn in his thoughts.

He watched her scramble around a large pile of stones pulled from the rocky soil to make the field. Though she'd kept her feet clothed this time, her efforts gave him the opportunity to enjoy her rounded hips and long legs as the cloth of her skirt pulled taut. The sight distracted him enough that he had to increase his stride to catch up with her once she vanished from sight.

"I knew it."

The delight she found in overcoming every challenge, whether daring her mistresses to match her riding skills or finding an elusive flower, astounded him. How could he have been so quick to dismiss her character, to think London stronger than the woman he found before him?

"Are you going to help?" she demanded, forgetting their differences in station and life as she leaned up to pluck the ripe strawberries nestled in the very cluster of rocks she'd clamored over.

As Aubrey moved to join her, he realized she must have glimpsed the flowers through a crack in the pile. The rocks blocked everything on the far side from view, including the other women.

The hot sun beat down, mixing their momentary privacy with his thoughts of tying his life to hers to concoct a wild notion in his head, one he could not deny.

She twisted to look at him, most likely to take him to task for not helping, but the movement brought her face so close to his he could feel her breath against his neck.

Her gaze softened as she tipped her head up to see him more fully, presenting such an appealing picture even a monk would be hard pressed to resist. Aubrey, though particular, was no monk.

When she'd turned to find him so close, Barbara had been startled, but not enough to back away.

He bent slowly, giving her ample time to turn aside, but when his lips met the curve of her own, she sighed, opening her mouth to his exploration.

Her nerves seemed to fire all at the same time. She couldn't have ducked his advance had she wanted to. Her limbs turned to water, but even that could not stop the burning that demanded more.

Sarah's warning repeated somewhere in the back of her mind. She should have stayed with the other girls. She should never have put herself in this compromising position in the first place.

Barbara shifted nearer. The feel of his lips over hers, warm, firm but yet not rough, sent delicious tingling throughout her body and she never wanted it to end.

The thought managed what Sarah's warning could not. It would end, and badly.

She drew in a quick breath, struggling to regain control, but the air came imbued with a rich scent that was uniquely Aubrey.

He pulled her tighter against him so she could feel the firm muscles of his chest.

His arms provided support for her trembling limbs, and she sank into his warmth, unable to remember why she needed to protest. This was where she belonged. This place over anywhere else in the world no matter what Sarah, her uncle, or the whole of society might think of her.

The blood rushed through her body, warming with a deeper heat somehow than the sun's rays. Unfamiliar desires swept over her, and she wanted something more than the caress of his lips against hers though she did not know what.

She needed his hand to stroke her cheek as he had once before, to feel his rough skin beneath her own touch. To melt together and become one, flesh to flesh without the barriers still between them.

The image her unspoken desire brought to mind cut through Barbara's muddled state with the force of a cleaver, wiping out the fog his nearness had brought upon her.

Barbara jerked free, staggering against the pile of rocks that sheltered them when he did not fight to hold her.

She stared at him, eyes wide with fear, but something more burned in her chest and begged her to return to his embrace.

Her hand came up to touch damp, full lips, her own not his though he stood so temptingly close.

With a strangled cry, she gripped her skirts in both hands and twisted away from him to break into a run as soon as she stepped free of the rocks.

She didn't choose the direction, but when she noticed the forest edge so near, her speed increased to as fast as she could manage while holding her skirts free from her legs. There in the forest, she'd be able to lose him among the tall trees and thick undergrowth. There she'd find a quiet place to measure her sins.

She'd wanted one last day in his company before telling him the truth of her station, her name, and what drove her to hide it from him though she knew she little deserved the gift. Once told, he'd scorn her. He'd never speak to her again.

So why had she come so close to giving him everything, her reputation, her future, and her body along with the foolish heart he'd claimed already? Had he pressed, had he fought her moment of conscience, she'd have lain down with him there in the field without hesitation.

One hand rose to her swollen lips again, losing her skirt enough so she almost tripped and tumbled down one of the many sharp descents this forest owned. Barbara righted herself, but the sensation of her full lips and the way her skin tingled all over drove Barbara to greater speed. Her clothing had served as an all too frail barrier to his touch.

She ran now, driven by how she ached more than anything to be back there with him in the field. She wanted to touch the passion he drew from her, to see how she inspired the same in him.

Barbara stopped to catch her breath, one hand clutched around a nearby branch.

How could she inspire true emotions in Aubrey?

He knew nothing of her. He'd seen only the country girl, a servant in a farmhouse, and thought that to be the sum of her. Why else would he have kissed her there in the field despite his impassioned declaration?

Tears gathered in her eyes, blurring the route before her even as she started off again, unwilling to chance him finding her so vulnerable and raw.

If he were to catch up, with all that lay between them, she'd have to confess, to tell him why she ran from him, and then she'd long for the days he thought her a simple servant girl. Once he knew the truth, he'd never see her as anything but a scheming witch.

No matter how much she now knew her revenge a ploy not against him but against herself, no matter how much her infatuation had deepened until he claimed the full of her, she had lied to him, made a fool of him this whole time. No man could forgive such a thing, not even Aubrey.

She sank behind a bramble, too worn out to run any further and sure she'd lost him in the time it took for him to get over the shock of her escape. He would come after her, to demand an explanation if for no other reason, but she'd wandered the forest with her cousins often enough, both as a child and now on Charlotte's various tasks. He'd have no experience with this one even if he had spent any time in the woods beyond roaming the edge with her that one day.

Memories of Aubrey crashed down on her, each one stabbing with the knowledge that they belonged to her past. She could not stay here another moment, not after this. Let Sarah tell him, or Uncle Ferrier. It mattered not at all.

Tonight, or tomorrow morning at the latest, she'd beg her uncle for transport to London where she belonged, among the frivolous debutantes who had no thought in their heads beyond scheming to capture a husband. She'd take the stagecoach if she had to, or give up a precious piece of jewelry for a horse. She'd ride all the way back to London with her skirts tucked up between her legs if that's what it took to put what she'd done, what she'd lost, behind her for good.

Chapter Twenty-Seven

It took Aubrey longer than it should have to comprehend Barbara's flight.

He'd been in a haze, captivated by her and by the possibility of having found true happiness. He'd pushed her too far, too fast, and all without revealing what had been on his mind. She would have had no way of knowing he meant to offer for her, to make her his wife.

He cursed under his breath, reliving the sheer panic in her expression as she jerked free of his arms. She must have thought him no more than a lusty nobleman after all, as well she should with his lack of consideration for her virtue.

Staring in the direction she'd gone, he thrust a hand through his hair, angry at himself. He'd taken advantage of her vulnerability, especially with her emotions heightened by the conflict with her friend.

His gaze sought her out for all that he should give her time before forcing himself on her even long enough to explain. She'd been moving so quickly, though, that he could not find any sign of her along the forest edge.

He scanned further only to have the same result.

Tension coiled in his gut.

She'd gone at a flat run, but even so she should have been in sight still and would have been if she hadn't crossed from the fields to the forest in her agitation. She could get lost, hurt, or worse in there.

Before he could pause to consider, Aubrey found himself charging across the intervening space with neither plan nor an effort to alert the others. All he could think of was Barbara. He had done this to her. He had sent her into the wild undergrowth, too upset to care where she headed.

The forest proved as unyielding as he'd feared from how a scrap of torn cloth marked her entry point. He had little of the huntsman in him, but a blind man could follow the path she'd cut, undergrowth trampled and branches thrust out of the way, some having ripped free more fabric.

Each marker only proved her state of distress, especially when a deer path cut around one dense bush that she'd clearly charged right through, leaving who knew how many scratches on her skin.

He burned for her pain, feared for her safety, and cared for nothing other than the next hint he could find. Mindless of his own safety, he raced forward as fast as he could in the hopes of catching up to her, or at least of catching a glimpse of her before him so he could know she had not already come to harm.

A sound in the distance drove him faster, though whether from Barbara or some animal he could not tell. He shoved aside bushes, jerked free when he grew tangled as she must have, and charged ahead with little thought to his own safety, only hers.

His momentum cut suddenly, one foot trapped under a raised root.

Aubrey threw his arms out wide to catch himself, already planning how to spring onto his feet and continue forward.

His hands met open air where he'd expected land, and the soil, when he found it at last, held roots, rocks, and no purchase. With a startled yell, Aubrey continued his tumble head over heels down a steep slope.

Trees and rocks appeared out of nowhere, crashing into his sides and his limbs, battering his head as he fell.

Aubrey could not control his descent nor catch hold of anything strong enough to stop him. The roots tore free, and the rocks became yet another object to slam into him.

Just when he seemed finally to be slowing, a sharp pain stabbed his head for a heartbeat before the world went dark.

She'd been right about his woodcraft from the sound of him coming through the forest long after any reasonable sort would have given up, especially with him thinking her a country girl familiar with the area. Her only hope lay in keeping quiet and letting him pass her by, his persistence more damning for the fact that he chased a lie.

Then Barbara heard a great shout followed by curses her delicate ears should not have been party too, but that wasn't what drove her to her feet.

Between the blistering words came thuds and crashes much greater than even Aubrey could have produced on his way through the forest.

Before she could wrestle her way through brush that seemed to grow fingers to catch on her hair and clothes with every step, though, the noise ended as quickly as it had begun, leaving a hushed silence.

Barbara ripped her skirt free of the latest snag, aware she'd have much to answer for in her treatment of the clothing, but she didn't care. She didn't care for her reputation, her secrets, or anything.

She had to find Aubrey.

The place where he went over, as falling seemed the only possible explanation for what she'd heard, was marked with a swath cut through the brush and evidence of a rock fall that made her wince as she thought of the hard stones tumbling around him.

"Aubrey. Aubrey! Where are you?" she called down, waiting for his response or at least a groan.

Still she heard nothing.

"Aubrey St. Vincent, you answer me this very moment," she scolded, anger masking the fear that threatened to steal her breath.

She didn't wait for him this time, instead making her careful way down the very same slope, mindful of its steep nature and the warning in the signs of rocks that sprang free in his passage. As much as she wanted to blame her tight chest on the difficult climb down, she heard nothing from Aubrey any of the times she paused to listen.

At last the slope started to level out, and she caught sight of him, lying unnaturally still with a dark, shiny puddle next to his head.

Barbara leapt the last few feet, staggering as her shoes met uneven ground, but not stopping until she fell to her knees at his side.

"Aubrey, please. Open your eyes. Talk to me." The tears streaming down her face fell to dampen his mouth and offered the only sign of life as the liquid bubbled between his lips. "You have to be all right. This is my fault. You cannot be the one to suffer for it. Please, Aubrey."

Grief tore at her, but she swallowed hard and stood once more, unwilling to wallow in it and chance his only hope for survival.

The branches had done her a good turn in starting tears so she could shred her skirt even more and use it to cushion his head and bind the wound.

No sooner had she covered the gash with her makeshift bandage, though, but the blood seeped through to stain the cloth a dark red. She had neither the tools nor skill to tend to him. She needed to get help.

Barbara called as loud as she could for Charlotte and the others, but she'd come too far within the forest to be heard.

She knelt at his side once more, dropping a chaste kiss on his cheek. "I'd not leave you if I had any choice, my love, but you need more than my tears if you're to mend. I'll be back as soon as I can manage."

With that she had to be satisfied because she could delay no longer though she received no response.

Barbara attacked the slope with more success going up than on the way down, her fear driving her while she'd moved far enough over to have no risk of sending something down to injure him further.

Their path lay heavy in the crowded growth, and all those branches torn aside now eased her way and allowed her to speed toward the meadow, calling as she went.

"There you are," came Charlotte's voice long before Barbara broke free of the greenery. "My father is not going to be pleased with your behavior, and if this is how you take advantage of the loose reins, I won't be party to it."

Though she stood hands on hips, clearly ready for a further scolding, one glance at Barbara's state brought shock to her face. Then

Charlotte wiped her expression clear. "What happened? Are you injured?"

Barbara hadn't realized until that moment how she wore poor Aubrey's blood on hands and skirt. "No, no," she said, waving Charlotte's fears away impatiently. "I'm fine. It's Aubrey who needs your help. I'll take his horse to the farmhouse and get my uncle. Go tend him, Charlotte." She gave what directions she could, ending with, "You can probably follow the trail better than I can describe it. Look for the rock fall." Then she paused, exhaustion and fear breaking through her control for just a moment. "Help him, please." Tears gathered in her eyes once again.

Her cousin waved Barbara past. "I will. I promise," she called after.

Even before Barbara reached the tethered horse and clambered aboard with the use of a nearby rock, she heard her cousin gathering the others. The girls would tend him for her, Charlotte most of all, but from the look of his injury, and his unconscious state, he needed a doctor's care.

The horse shied a bit, most likely from the scent of blood, but no unruly beast would stop her from saving Aubrey, and she soon brought the horse under control, transforming its nervous energy into a fast canter that ate up the distance between her and the help she so desperately needed.

<h1 style="text-align:center">Chapter Twenty-Eight</h1>

Barbara rode up to the farmhouse to find the sound of her frantic arrival had already provoked a gathering. Her uncle stormed over in the next moment, his face a mixture of fury and fear.

"What have you done? Whose horse is that? How did you come by it?" he demanded, making her all too aware of every time she'd thoughtlessly began something that led to disaster, often taking others with her.

He paled as she swung down, clearly having caught sight of the blood still marking her. "My daughters. Where are they?"

She put a hand against his chest to stop him long enough to catch her breath.

He stepped aside, avoiding her touch.

"My cousins are fine, but we need your help. Charlotte and the others are tending him as best they can. We need to bring a wagon and make a sling to bring him up the slope."

Her words eased the fear, but his anger remained visible in the pounding vein on his forehead. "Who is he?"

His gaze passed from her to the horse and back again, his jaw firming as he made the connection. "I told you to leave that be else trouble come to you, and to my family."

Barbara's eyes itched with tears, but she blinked them away. "I know you did. You were wiser than I am, but there's no time. The blood is his. He needs a doctor's care and fast."

Uncle Ferrier grew still for a heartbeat only before he turned away to set things in motion.

"Peter, get the wagon. Kevin, grab a pallet from the servant quarters and several lengths of rope. Come on, boys. Hurry now. A man's life is at stake."

Barbara released her breath on a shaky sigh. She reached for the reins, knowing the horse already worn out, but what choice did she have?

Her uncle closed his hand around hers and plucked the treated leather from her fingers. "He's worked hard enough for this already. John will have the tending of him."

She nodded, stepping aside as one of the stable boys came to take the exhausted horse. On a fresh horse, she'd be able to ride ahead and tell the girls their father came with help.

A hand came down hard on her shoulder when she turned to the stables.

"You have no need to be in there," her uncle said, his voice deep and rough. "You are going nowhere except to your room. I will take the nobleman to the manor where he belongs. You will stay here and consider your actions while in my care."

"You'll need me to find him." She saw no value in reminding him she too held noble blood from her father.

"Unlike a foolish nobleman and girl, I know these forests, as do my men. I know where my daughter goes hunting the wild strawberries, and doubt not I'll find one of my daughters waiting to take me the rest of the way."

His answer made it clear where the fault lay. His daughters were too clever to have done something this foolish.

Barbara wanted to protest her exclusion, wanted to see Aubrey to safety herself, but her hands started shaking now that the crisis had been taken from them. She could not claim innocence in this. Even had he not followed her, she'd risked herself and done no good service to her borrowed clothes either. Anything she said would only make her uncle's opinion sink lower.

He stared down at her with a harsh gaze until she gave a nod and turned toward the farmhouse. He had no need to tell her how she'd caused this injury. She could think of nothing else. If his opinion of her hung low, her own stood no higher.

She lingered at the doorway until they headed out, two on horseback to ride ahead. A heartfelt prayer for Aubrey's health when they found him seemed little enough penance for her hand in all of this.

When her parents sent her to the farm, she'd thought their opinion of her nature untrue, but here she'd proven them right more than wrong. They'd warned her against playing with a man's feelings, leading him on, and having little regard for the pain she caused.

That was exactly what she'd done with Aubrey, all the while keeping her true identity a secret to use as a bludgeon against him. And now, when her conscience finally awoke to the wrong she did to him and herself as well, her need to cling to her game, to hold on for just one more day, may have cost him not just the day, but every one to follow.

The realization proved too hard to bear.

She twisted away from the sight of his rescue party and raced through the farmhouse to throw herself down on the bed she had shared with her friend until her unruly tongue drove Sarah away. Whatever control she held over her tears broke, and Barbara cried until she thought she'd pour every drop of liquid from her body and become a dry husk.

At some point, Sarah appeared to rub Barbara's back as though the break between them never occurred. She didn't ask what had caused this outburst, nor could Barbara marshal the strength to tell her as she twisted to throw herself into Sarah's open arms and cry some more as though her heart had broken.

She'd believed life lived separate from Aubrey could not grow more painful. How foolish that seemed now with the chance of a life lived without Aubrey even on the earth.

In the long hours before her uncle returned, Barbara told Sarah the whole story, about how her friend had been right from the start, how she'd stolen just one more day before confessing the truth, and then how the kiss had broken through her control and sent her running off into the forest where Aubrey got hurt.

"You truly love him, don't you?" Sarah said, her face filled with none of the elation the words should have offered.

Barbara gave a sad smile. "Had I any thought to how my feelings would deepen, I would never have hesitated in London. I wanted everything to be perfect when I met him only to learn he wasn't perfect himself."

"No one is perfect."

"I know that now. Certainly not myself. It shouldn't have taken a risk to his life to figure it out though."

Sarah laughed softly. "Consider that part of your own imperfections. And without them, you'd be intolerable."

Barbara threw her arms around her friend and gave Sarah a tight hug. "I've been almost so anyway. You could see what I could not. You tried to warn me, but I was too arrogant to listen."

Sarah pulled away, not in rejection but so she could meet Barbara's gaze with a steady look. "Love, not arrogance, drove you to deny the truth. And before you take all the blame, remember the revenge came first from my lips, not yours. It's what you do now that counts."

Barbara gave a stiff nod.

She already knew exactly what she had to do. She'd been offered a gift, and in her thoughtlessness, she'd broken it beyond repair. She had no choice except to carry out her plan to leave, but not until she knew him to be all right.

The sounds of the returning wagon broke through the silence that had fallen between them. They turned to the window, but their room faced the fields rather than the yard.

"Go to the wagon," Sarah urged. "You'll have no peace until you learn what has befallen your love."

Uncle Ferrier gave Barbara a dark look when she emerged from the house, but he said nothing about his directive, perhaps reading in her expression she'd done as he'd asked and pondered her fault in everything that had occurred.

"We found him where you said. Charlotte did what she could for him, but he still had not woken when we delivered him to the manor." He didn't even wait for her to ask the question. "Lord Pendleton has called for a doctor. Your nobleman will be in as best care as can be acquired."

She didn't know whether to be relieved or more upset at this news, having never been around anyone with a serious injury before in her life.

Uncle Ferrier caught her arm. "I'm sorely disappointed in your behavior. You had no business running about in the woods with an unattached man, ignoring that I'd specifically forbade you to seek him out. Charlotte and the girls say I should go gently, that you could hardly have cast him out of the field when he came, but your parents will be told exactly what a wild child they have, mark my words." He shook her hard. "Your foolishness may have cost the man his life."

Her skin all of a sudden felt too tight against her face and the world seemed to spin violently. Only her uncle's grip kept her upright.

"Hold now, Barbara. More likely than not he'll recover fully."

Whatever caused him to soften, she didn't need to be coddled. She needed the truth.

"There was so much blood," Barbara murmured, mindful of how she had failed to change out of her bloodstained and torn clothing.

"Head injuries bleed profusely. It's that he's still unconscious which provides the worry."

He used his hold to pull her through the farmhouse to his study. There, he pressed her to sit while he leaned against his desk to loom over her.

"Barbara, you did what you could in getting help. He's in a doctor's hands. What happens from now on is none of your concern."

"But —"

He shook his head. "No. No exceptions. You must put this nobleman from your mind. You must never see him again. Neither of you is innocent in these events, and what came before them. If you're to preserve your reputation and not bring shame down on your mother's head, you must listen to me. You must obey no matter what."

Barbara could not bear to meet his gaze for another moment. She stared down at her twisted fingers, wanting to protest, to argue more than anything, but she knew he was right. She'd already decided the same for herself.

Even if he knew her true standing and forgave her the deceit, she'd proved nothing but trouble and a danger to him. He'd been right in his earliest judgment. Had Aubrey only recognized her that first day in the fields, he would have kept his distance. He would not now be lying unconscious and fighting for his very life.

Her uncle caught her chin and raised it until he could see her eyes once again. He said nothing, but she understood what he waited for.

"Yes, Uncle. I promise. I will not seek him out, nor will I let him do the same when he's able."

He gave her a gentle smile. "I know this seems harsh, child, but some day you'll understand. It's the way of the land. Your reputation is all that stands between you and ruin. I'll not have my sister lay the blame at my feet when I should have kept a closer eye on you. Sometimes the best way to work the wild out of a horse is to let him run." Her uncle gave a sharp laugh at her expression. "From your look, I think maybe you were much the same and had to learn your lesson the hard way. Sheltering you only made the costs higher when you were set out on your own."

As much as she knew she should take this moment to beg him to send her back, Barbara couldn't find the strength. She felt as though she had run from the field with her own two feet. Every bit of her ached and felt drained from the experience. There would be time enough to ask. For now, she would prove to her uncle that she could listen. She would hold to his strictures as rigidly as any found in London society and do whatever he told her to do.

Chapter Twenty-Nine

The first sensation that broke into Aubrey's consciousness made him think he'd drowned his marriage sorrows in far too much cheap ale.

He brought a hand to his pounding head with a groan.

"He's up."

The shout brought forth another groan.

Aubrey lifted first one eyelid then the other to scowl at his friend Jasper. Of course it would be Jasper. Who else would have encouraged him to imbibe past his tolerance?

"How do you feel?" Jasper asked, thankfully in a softer tone.

"Like I should have left whatever ale house you dragged me to some drinks before."

Instead of the laugh Aubrey had half tensed against, Jasper's brows drew together as he frowned.

"You seem no worse for the wear, curse you."

Again no laughter. Not even a hint of humor graced Jasper's expression as he asked, "You have no memory of the events?"

"Is that so unexpected? Stop hovering over me," Aubrey snapped, despite the pain it triggered.

"I've sat vigil for half a day and all of a night, except when Daphne took a turn so I could be rested if you needed me. Until you woke, the doctor could not assure me you'd survive."

"Well, I'm awake, aren't I?" Even as he gave his testy response, Jasper's words filtered through the pain to raise questions that triggered their own answers.

"Barbara!" Though the cry caused a spike through his head, Aubrey struggled to rise, memory returning in a crash of images and fears.

Jasper pressed him to the mattress. "You need to rest. The doctor said —"

"I don't care what the doctor said." Aubrey tried to fight the hold and found the effort more than he'd expected. "I won't lie here and rest with Barbara still lost. I need to find her. I need to know she returned safely. Get off me, you oaf."

His words had no effect, but he dragged the strength to fight Jasper's hold from the very depths of his being. "I must know what happened to her."

The energy vanished, leaving his body aching and his head swelled to five times its size from the weight of it. He sank back to the mattress with a groan, but marshaled his strength for another try. His pain-muddled brain decided if he could only throw Jasper off, he'd be free to go find the answers he sought since his friend seemed determined to ignore his demands.

"What's this?" an older man said as he shoved through the doorway.

Aubrey spared the newcomer only a quick glance as he surged upward, using Jasper's distraction to win free. He rolled to the edge only to find himself incapable of stopping the movement.

The floor came up to slam into his bruised body without even the brace of his arms to cushion it.

"Restrain him."

Hands seized him, more than just the two Jasper possessed, and Aubrey started to struggle in earnest. Having won this much, he would not surrender it without a fight.

"Barbara. I have to find Barbara," he gasped out, as much to remind himself as to tell the others.

They showed no more sign of listening than Jasper had. He was lifted back to the mattress and held there by Willem and two others of the servants, his efforts undone.

Aubrey glared at the one who'd orchestrated his failure, the unfamiliar face too serene for what he'd cost Aubrey. "I could have bested

Jasper. Let me up. You can't hold me here." He thrashed from side to side, but these men showed no signs of slacking, and each movement sent jolts of pain through his battered body until he had to stop if only to catch his breath.

"Something might have been knocked loose in the fall," the man was saying when Aubrey finally quieted enough to hear.

Aubrey went to send an icy glare only to find the man had pulled Jasper to the side.

"Sometimes in cases like these, even if the patient recovers consciousness, he'll never be the man he was."

Patient.

Suddenly Aubrey connected the man's black frock coat with his statements and realized the stranger had to be a doctor. A doctor who told Jasper to expect a madman where he'd once had a friend.

Aubrey realized he'd harmed his own cause when reacting to how Jasper wouldn't listen. He drew in a few deep breaths and stilled his body, though the servants showed no sign of relaxing their hold, another indication he'd appeared the madman.

Only when he could be assured of an even, normal tone did Aubrey attempt to speak once again. "I went into the woods to find a girl. I'd upset her and worried for her state. Before I could find her, I fell down the slope. She could still be lost in there. I have to know she's all right." His voice rose on the last despite his efforts, but the words came out sound.

"What is the meaning of this? Jasper? How could you treat him so?" Daphne appeared in the doorway with a tray and glared at each of the men in turn before meeting Aubrey's relieved gaze.

Jasper stepped between his wife and friend, a move that sent pain of a different sort through Aubrey. "He's agitated. The doctor thinks he might be a danger to himself or others."

Daphne pushed her husband to the side with the tray and marched to Aubrey's bedside. "He doesn't look agitated to me, or at least not unreasonably so. You're not, are you?"

Aubrey gave her a slight headshake that ended in a groan.

"I heard what he said before coming in to find all of you manhandling him."

Willem flinched from her sharp look, and he and the other two released Aubrey to back away.

Daphne gave a satisfied nod. "It seems a simple enough request, and if this girl is still lost in the woods after a full night, reason enough for agitation if you ask me."

Finally, someone had listened.

A tension Aubrey hadn't recognized before relaxed with the knowledge he'd gained an advocate at last. Had he been feeling more himself, he would have laughed at the contrite expressions that took over all but the doctor.

"My lady, with an injury of this type —"

She waved a hand to cut him off. "You'd set his injury over another's life?"

The question threatened to send Aubrey surging to his feet for all he knew he wouldn't make it upright if his last attempt had been any measure. He fought the urge only to ask again, "What happened to Barbara?"

Daphne turned to face him, placing one hand on his cheek as she met his gaze with enough understanding for him to know she recognized the significance of his interest. "I don't know, Aubrey, but I swear to you I'll find out."

She pulled away to look at the others. "Did the man who brought Aubrey make mention of a girl?"

One after another, the men shook their heads, Aubrey's hopes sinking lower.

"Well, what are you waiting for, Willem? Run down to the village and seek an answer. It was Ferrier who brought him, was it not? Ask at the farmhouse first. Take the cart. It's faster. If he came across her, he'll know."

Aubrey added, "She's a servant there. He will know."

"You heard the man." Daphne's tone offered no room for protest. "Get down to the Ferrier lands and find out her state."

"Ask for her to come if she's able," he called after Willem's retreating back. "I want to see her myself."

He accepted the tea Daphne offered him if only for a distraction as he settled in for the wait. With the effort to get him his answers begun, Aubrey had to admit he was in no condition to discover her state on his own. He had no choice but to be patient, though fear continued to gnaw at him as he suffered the doctor's examination.

"He's as well as to be hoped," the man said at last. "But he'll only recover if he rests. No more of this, whether the girl comes or not." The final sentence was directed not at Daphne and Jasper but at Aubrey himself along with a stern glare.

Aubrey gave a stiff nod, suppressing a wince. He was not ready to forgive the man for pronouncing him insane when no one would listen to his very real concerns. He held on to the realization that had escaped him when he'd charged after her.

The girl grew up next to this forest and worked both at its side and within her whole life. While he'd been risking his own, she most likely had come out a different way and rejoined the others. Only by a miracle had he been found at all.

Barbara saw the young man first as he swung down from his cart and tied the reins to the fence before entering the yard. She stopped too suddenly and felt the splash of warm milk as it soaked through another borrowed dress.

He hurried toward her, and her heart stumbled then started again. Why hurry if the news told of Aubrey's loss, and why come to tell her at all?

"I need to see Mister Ferrier. It's urgent."

She gave him a grim nod even as she bit her tongue to keep any questions from coming out. She'd promised her uncle, and what right had she to badger this man anyway?

"He's by the stable," Barbara said at last, turning to show the way. Even if it meant carrying the milk back and forth a dozen times, she would not chance missing any news the man might impart.

"Where do you think you're going?" Marian asked as they passed the barn, but when she saw the manor servant, she picked up her skirts and rushed after them, catching the attention of the others who did likewise.

By the time they reached the stables, they'd become a crowd.

"What is this?" Uncle Ferrier asked, scanning the faces before him. "Have my daughters decided to rebel?"

Any humor in his expression vanished when his gaze tripped over the servant. "Willem, right? What brings you down from the manor?"

Despite her best intentions, Barbara stepped closer, not wanting to miss a word.

Luckily, her cousins did as well, Sarah joining them, so her choice did not stand out.

"It's Lord Aubrey St. Vincent."

A gasp she could not smother hung in the air, but her uncle gave an impatient wave.

"What about the man? I'm no undertaker, so I presume you have not come to announce his demise."

"Father!"

Which of the girls made the cry, Barbara couldn't tell. She had no objection, finding relief in his confidence if not in his blunt nature.

"No, nothing like that, though he's like to do himself further injury if you cannot aid me in this request."

Uncle Ferrier gave a knowing laugh. "What then can I do to protect the lord from himself? Out with it, man. My girls have more important things to do than listen to your gossip." He swept them all again with a stern look that landed the heaviest on Barbara.

"He needs to know the fate of the girl he went after into the forest."

This time no one distracted from her gasp.

Barbara found herself, not Willem, the center of their attention, the man catching on a moment later.

"He need not trouble himself," Uncle Ferrier said after an awkward pause. "She came through the ordeal with little more than a scratch on her. Go tell him to rest easy."

Willem stared at her for a moment longer as though expecting her to confess her involvement, but she took the cue from her uncle and kept silent, not even releasing a sigh of relief when the servant finally turned his back.

"If only it were that easy. He has grown quite agitated over his concern and will not rest until he has seen himself that all is well. I was one of those called to restrain him, and the doctor fears for the state of his mind after the knocking it took. Keeping him calm is crucial for his recovery. The only way to calm him was to go seek this girl. I cannot speak to his health should I return with little more than assurances from you."

Though he spoke the last to her uncle, he twisted to lay his gaze once more upon Barbara, making it clear he'd understood their attention well enough.

"I cannot," she said, unable to stay silent any longer. "I only bring trouble to his doorstep. It's best I keep my distance."

Willem caught her arm when she made to leave the gathering, more of the forgotten milk splashing out. "The time for distance has passed, girl. You only bring him more harm by denying this request."

Uncle Ferrier closed a tight hand on Willem's shoulder with a strong enough grip to make the younger man wince. "Let go of my —"

"He meant no trouble by it," Barbara cut in before he could finish the sentence. She did not want word to get back to Aubrey. Better he think her lost to him than that he knew the truth of her betrayal. "And now he has your word to trust in this. As you can see, I am without injury and glad to hear of his restoring health. But it is not to be. I cannot see him again. No good will come of it. He can take the account from your own eyes."

"But —"

"But nothing," her uncle said, stepping between them. "You've heard from me and the girl. You've seen her yourself. Return to the manor and leave my girls to their chores."

"Father, you can't mean it." Jane's incredulous tone brought all eyes to her, but her sisters moved to surround Jane and offer support.

"You heard Willem," Charlotte added. "This could be the request of a dying man. I know you're angry with Barbara, and disappointed too, but you are not stone-hearted."

"I don't want to go," Barbara said, unwilling to be the cause of a disagreement between her uncle and his daughters. "He is not stopping me."

Marian put both hands on her hips and glared at Barbara. "He should be forcing you to go. All this time we thought to give you the chance to see him, and now when he needs you, you turn your back? Did you not notice his injury before you ran off to hide? Do you not remember he hadn't even woken by the time we delivered him to the manor? Do you not care for him one bit? Was it all a lark?"

Barbara flinched under the force of her cousin's accusations, each one hitting like a blacksmith's hammer. She couldn't even protest because the truth, that she sought revenge for a slight, would only show her off worse while the deeper truth of her love for the man meant nothing.

Sarah moved to her side and caught her hand. "She fears for him. Isn't that evident enough. Can't you see she holds herself responsible for his accident?"

Marian looked from Sarah to Barbara and back before she relaxed her stance.

"All the more reason to go to him." Georgiana had kept silent until then, the soft, sensible words not what any of them would have expected from her.

"He asks after you," Willem injected as though sensing how Barbara wavered. "You worry of trouble, but how much more harm can come to him trapped in his sickbed."

Uncle Ferrier caught her free hand and stared down at her for a moment. "Is this true? Do your feelings run as deep as all that?"

Tears gathered in her eyes, but she blinked them away only to nod her confession.

A slight smile played upon his lips. "Then what are you waiting for, girl. Go to him. Georgie can take the milk."

The last startled a laugh from her as her cousin came to pry Barbara's fingers loose. They didn't understand. They didn't know the whole truth, though the girls knew enough to be aware of Aubrey's ignorance.

Still, though she feared her confession would make him more agitated rather than less, Barbara could not stand against the pressure of all of them weighed against her no more than she could hold fast against the need burning in her chest.

"I'll go."

The cousins let out a shout loud enough to startle a horse in the nearby pasture so it reared up, but Sarah only turned to Barbara. "Would you like me to come with you? I'm sure Willem has room for two in the cart he brought."

Barbara put both hands into Sarah's and gave her friend a smile. "Thank you, but no. This is something I must do on my own."

"Do you think it the time?" Sarah asked, clearly catching her full meaning.

Her shrug had nothing of casual feeling to it. "There will never be another."

Once they spoke, he would cast aside the illusion of a country girl and scorn the deceitful lady that came in her place.

"At least take a moment to change your soiled skirt."

Barbara stared at Sarah before remembering how the milk had splashed the cloth. Her words would be sour enough without the stench of old milk rising from her.

Chapter Thirty

Aubrey had been wandering in and out of consciousness all morning. When he glanced up to see Barbara hovering in the doorway, he couldn't be sure it wasn't another dream.

Then a sense of everything settling into place came over him with a relief so great he knew nothing and no one would ever be allowed to stand between them again.

"Out. Everyone leave the room."

Though his voice lacked its usual strength, he found a commanding tone needed volume less than conviction from how the others came to attention, and he had no lack of conviction.

Daphne stood watch over him this time, along with two male servants whose sole purpose, he supposed, would be to restrain him should he get violent and threatened her. In other circumstances, he might have laughed, but now he just wanted them gone.

She glanced at the door, the first to figure out what provoked his sudden response. "Why hello. Welcome to my home."

Barbara ducked her head, clearly embarrassed with the attention. From where he lay, he could see the blush staining her neck.

"Leave off, Daphne. You can meet her later. For now, just go and take your protection with you." His petulant tone drew the gaze of both women, not how he wanted to appear before Barbara, though reclining on a bed offered little better in terms of his presence.

Daphne glanced from one to the other of them. "I can't just leave you two here alone."

A laugh came from the dregs of his humor. "This is not London where everything must be proper, and even if it were, she's no lady to expect such things."

Daphne's lowered brows bothered him less than the gasp from Barbara. He'd meant no insult, though he could see both of them had taken it that way.

He had no intention of apologizing. Barbara would understand his meaning once they were alone, and Daphne needed to go.

Aubrey waved at the bed. "I'm in no condition to compromise anyone. You know all too well I can barely lift my head without feeling like it split open once again."

This time Barbara's gasp held a very different meaning as she crossed the space between them to kneel at his side, her face pale.

He fumbled for her nearest hand. "I'm not so poorly I won't recover. Don't be afraid for me."

Daphne coughed loud enough to serve the purpose of reminding them they still had an audience despite his request.

"I was thinking less of the proprieties so much as that you need to be monitored. The doctor is unhappy with both your progress and your episode earlier," she said, with a nod to the last of the two servants exiting the room.

Barbara's hand tensed in his grip at the reminder of his injury.

Aubrey sent Daphne a scowl both for emphasizing his weakness and the implication that he might harm Barbara. "I am neither so injured as to need a nursemaid nor so dangerous as to require a guard. I'm sure Barbara is capable enough to notice should I lapse into unconsciousness again. Anything less and there will be time enough to see to it. So everyone else can very well quit the room."

"Mistress?"

He was fully aware of the concerned glances Daphne shared with her staff at his irritated tone. Aubrey dragged in a breath, struggling for calm before they started to question his judgment again.

At that very moment, the doctor appeared at the door as though determined to cause Aubrey misery.

He let out a groan that had little to do with pain, or at least not the physical type.

When the man looked to enter, Aubrey held up his free hand to stop him. "You can stay right outside with the rest. Shut the door after you, Daphne. If Barbara has any concern, she can give a cry and you'll be able to rush in long before anything could happen." He lowered his voice with effort as he added, "Now will you please just let us be?"

He sent Barbara a beseeching look, knowing Daphne would appeal to her next.

"I'll watch over him," she said, her voice low.

The quiet words should not have had the ability to command him, but they sent happiness rushing through Aubrey. He might not need a nursemaid, but he'd found his soul mate, and she seemed as tied as he was. Why else would she have agreed to come see him despite his overeager advance before?

He needed to make his intentions clear so no doubt could remain between them. Whether she wanted him to stay in the country or would be willing to chance life in London, Aubrey planned to spend the rest of his life at her side.

aphne paused at the doorway, and Barbara wanted to call back her words, to beg the woman to stay. She'd come to free Aubrey, to free both of them, but his response terrified her. Not the kind of terror that meant she wanted him restrained, but more a fear for his health.

As though his friend could read her mind, Daphne met her gaze with a firm look. "Don't do anything to agitate him. He doesn't want you to see him as weak, what man would, but his injury was nothing to take lightly."

"I won't." Barbara's promise came out in a whisper as weak as Daphne said Aubrey was, all plans dissolving around Barbara and leaving her trapped in falsehood just as Charlotte had warned.

The door closed behind Daphne with a thud.

Barbara wished she could be anywhere but where she was now, wished she'd stood stronger against the persuasion and refused to come see him. Anything she said now could only harm.

He was sure to demand the reason she ran. She'd have to lie once again. Daphne said he mustn't be upset, no idle warning when his condition required a doctor and just leaving him without care for a moment made them all so worried.

"Finally, we can speak."

Barbara had been so caught up in her own thoughts, his statement startled her. She turned to face him then ducked her head. "We have nothing to say that cannot wait." As much as she wished she could add that it could be said just as well in front of others, she couldn't make that claim. Her humiliation would be complete enough with only him to hear her confession.

Aubrey put a hand to his head and winced as though she'd hurt him with the force of her words.

In a softer tone, she added, "Your friend said as how you should not be agitated. Clearly my presence has that effect." She pushed to her feet and moved toward the door only to freeze when he grabbed her arm.

His hold fell away, whether because of her response or his own weakness, she couldn't tell.

"Nothing you do or say would upset me greater than not having you here."

More than his touch, the words spoken with conviction if not strength stabbed at her core. She froze, unable to take another step, but unwilling to turn back either.

"Please."

The groan that followed it rather than his plea had her spinning around to find him in a half-seated position, his brow furrowed in obvious pain.

She dropped to her knees beside him and gently urged him down to the pillow with a hand on his shoulder.

His condition must be even worse than her fears if he could not raise his head without suffering. Daphne had been right in her concern, but anything Barbara did only seemed to agitate him more.

As though to contradict her thoughts, he settled against the pillow and his eyes fell shut, revealing the length of his dark lashes. His breath came out on a sigh and the lines cut into his forehead eased as his fingers sought hers and wrapped tight.

Her presence did seem to offer some comfort after all.

Aubrey turned his head with barely a wince so he could look at her, and a smile graced his lips. "I thought I'd scared you into harm's way."

Despite herself, Barbara raised her free hand to brush the sweat-slicked hair from his face. "It's you who was harmed by my actions. I came through with nary a scratch."

His head shifted on the pillow as though he tried to shake her words away. "My injuries came from my own foolishness. I should have known you would have the woodcraft to fare well despite your upset."

She wanted to protest the assumption, but how could she with the truth hidden between them.

Aubrey must have seen the urge in her expression because he tightened his grip on her hand and pulled it closer. "This is not how I imagined our conversation, nor would I speak in such a state, but I cannot chance losing you again."

Barbara rose, suddenly nervous at his words, but his hold kept her close.

"I know not who stands for you as father, and once you tell me, I'll ask him proper, but I must know now. Will you do me the honor of accepting my hand, of becoming my lady wife?"

Forgetting everything but her need to escape, she tugged hard on her hand, but he wouldn't let go even though her movements clearly pained him. Barbara stopped only for fear of doing him greater injury.

She stood silent and tense, wishing she'd held firm in her intention to stay away.

"Please. Hear me out. I know the differences in our stations will cause difficulties. I know it sounds as unbalanced as the doctor thinks me with my injury. But this is not a sudden decision. My heart knew the truth long before my head would allow for it. In these short weeks, I've come to know you better than any woman I've ever known before."

"No!" The protest came from her lips before she could stop it, whether a denial of his claim or his request even she didn't know.

He gave a weak chuckle. "Yes. You're intelligent, quick, and curious. I know your nature and your strength. It won't be easy, but I will stand at your side the whole way. If you ask it of me, we can live here in the country, but if you're willing, in time, London will come to accept and love you as much as I do."

Tears gathered in her eyes at the words she had been longing to hear, only they meant nothing. "You claim to know me, but you do not," she said, tugging hard enough to free herself though she caused the lines to pinch his face once again. "You don't even know what the differences between us are, much less how to overcome them."

He reached for her, but she stepped back and out of the way, gathering her courage as she'd never had to before. The difference between them lay in his honesty and her falsehood. She could not let this continue any longer.

"Whatever it is," he said, his tone earnest, "we can work through it together. In everything that matters, we are a perfect match. Don't let some groundless concern stand between us. You have no idea how rare such a connection is."

His words, while meant to reassure, only stabbed Barbara to the quick. His perfect match had been built not on truth but on layer after layer of lies.

She stared down at him, the confession on the tip of her tongue, but the dreaded words would not come from between her lips. She could not do the deed that would rip both his heart and her own. Now more than ever, Daphne's warning rang in her ears, and she could not chance turning his recovery into a deadly spiral.

Emotions threatened to overwhelm Barbara, fear uppermost, and she could not stand here a moment longer.

Tears broke free to stream down her face as she twisted away from the bed, slammed the door open, and shoved through those waiting outside. She did not intend to stop running until she reached the farmyard and then her room, uncaring of all who saw her humiliation. She had destroyed her one chance at happiness, and took the man of her affection down with her.

Aubrey heard raised voices from outside the door but he paid them little attention as he focused on moving first one limb then another. His heart pounded out a rhythm demanding speed but he'd seen what rushing won him, and he needed to stand. He needed to catch her, to stop her, to get her to understand that nothing mattered more than the two of them together.

"Oh no you don't."

He'd been concentrating so carefully on achieving a seated position he'd failed to notice Daphne and the others flooding into the room until she spoke.

"Restrain him," demanded the doctor.

"Wait," he cried as their effort forced him down with a moan. Lights danced behind his eyes and pain stabbed him until his head spun, but none of that mattered with the love of his life getting further and further away.

Despite himself, Aubrey began to struggle. "Daphne, you have to listen to me. You have to stop her."

Liquid poured into his open mouth, choking him with the bitter burn of laudanum.

Worse even than the firm hands pressing him down, this would take away his ability to think. He locked gazes with Daphne, begging her to help him.

She put a hand on his arm and shook her head. "Aubrey, she's already gone. Whatever you did, she fled from here as though the hounds of hell were at her feet."

"I only asked her to marry me."

He sank into oblivion before knowing whether Daphne had heard his words or if they'd come out too slurred to be understood.

Chapter Thirty-One

By the time Barbara reached the farmhouse, her run had transformed into an exhausted stumble marked only by pauses to brush the tears from her cheeks.

"He didn't send you home on the wagon?" Georgiana called as the cousins gathered to greet her having caught sight of her approach.

"Oh hush," Charlotte said a moment later as her state must have become clear. "Barbara, are you all right?"

She didn't stop to answer as she pushed past them without a word on her way to her room. She'd only had the right to claim it for a few short weeks, but it felt like a lifetime, one she didn't deserve.

They gathered in the doorway, a silent witness to her efforts to pack up all her things.

Sarah came to help her without questioning, and they made short work of the task, easier than it should have been with most of her belongings still in the trunks because Charlotte declared them inappropriate for farm life.

"Talk to us," Marian demanded, blocking Barbara's path when she sought to find her uncle. "What happened?"

"I need to talk to your father. He'd been right from the start. I should never have spoken with Aubrey and should never have gone to the manor. I can stay here no longer."

Jane pressed a hand to her lips and tears glistened in Georgiana's eyes, but Charlotte tugged Marian and the others aside so Barbara could pass.

"He's in his office."

Barely aware of the procession behind her, Barbara made her way through the house to rap on the doorframe and announce her presence.

"Back so soon?" Uncle Ferrier said without even looking up, but when he did, he captured her in one of his long stares, taking in her dirt- and tear-stained state without comment.

A few weeks before, his silent regard would have unnerved her. Now, Barbara stood still under his assessment and waited for him to pass judgment on her as she had on herself.

This trip had succeeded admirably. It taught her humility and the cost of arrogance, but having learned the lesson, she needed to return home.

"Do I need to call on the manor?" he said at last, his tone such that she knew he'd defend her honor when she had none worth defending.

"No, Uncle. Please don't. The fault was mine. I only need to return home, and quickly."

His gaze narrowed. "The gent didn't die after all, did he?"

Barbara gave a strangled laugh. "No, he lives."

He gave a short nod and pushed to his feet. "I can't promise you a fancy carriage like you arrived in, but the farm wagon can get you to London if in less comfort." He paused at her side to examine her features. "Are you sure this is what you want?"

"Yes. I am sure. More sure than ever before."

Whether he'd asked only out of courtesy or her adamant answer decided him, her uncle delayed no further. He strode past her, calling for Thomas to bring the wagon around and pulling Charlotte aside for a quick consultation.

Barbara went to stand in the farmyard, remembering all the times she'd hauled milk drawn by her own hands, or when she'd searched the fields yonder for elusive delicacies. Her thoughts brought up pictures of Aubrey laughing, teasing her, and looking at her with such longing, but she crushed them down deep where they wouldn't plague her with her falsehoods.

Not one of those images meant a thing, their foundation a bed of lies rather than truth.

He said he knew her, but he knew only the mask she'd put on for his benefit, one she dearly wished she could call her own.

Charlotte appeared at her side to stand silent and watch with her for a moment before she said, "Can you not tell me why?"

Barbara gave a despairing sigh. "You know most of it already. You know how he saw me and that I said nothing to change his impression."

Her cousin let the silence grow between them until Barbara could suffer it no longer. She poured out a full confession, from her accidental eavesdropping to how she used that event to excuse her behavior ever since, even a plot for revenge he'd little earned. "If I'd only listened to your warning … But I did not, and now it's best I leave."

Though dreading a harsh scold, Barbara would have preferred it to her cousin's simple nod.

"I thought as much," was all Charlotte said before turning back into the house and leaving Barbara to her vigil.

The farmhands came from the house with trunk after trunk of worthless belongings, frivolous dresses, scarves, and slippers from her former life. Now she had calluses on her hands and on her heart where she knew more of real life than a dozen seasons would have given her.

The wagon drove up in a cloud of dust that settled on the worn, dirt-stained dress she still wore, having been unwilling to take the time to change. She'd have to wash and sew it before sending the dress back to Charlotte.

That thought drew forth a weak chuckle. Once she reached London, she would not be washing her own clothes, nor would she likely see to its repair. Sarah would once again take on the role of her maid more than her friend, and her life would revolve around events so much less important than the need to ease a cow's udder in the morning.

"I won't. You can't make me. Father, don't do this."

The cry from Georgiana startled Barbara out of her self-absorption to see her cousin struggling in her uncle's grasp, a solemn Charlotte following after with a small bundle.

"Uncle, I can fare without additional company," she protested, thinking Georgiana an odd choice in chaperone especially with Sarah about.

"She's going for her good, not yours," he said, lifting his daughter bodily onto the cloth sacks padding the wagon's interior. "She's grown too wild out here. My sister will have the taming of her where I have failed."

Georgiana made as if to climb down, but he stopped her with a stare. She sank to the wagon floor, a sullen look on her normally animated features.

Barbara glanced around to realize her baggage had already been placed in the wagon as well. Only she remained to be settled.

She moved to her uncle and threw her arms around him. "Thank you for taking me into your home, Uncle. I shall treasure this time more than you know."

He stepped back to take a look at her in silence. "You are much changed from the spoiled girl who arrived on my doorstep." He rubbed a thumb across her cheek. "I hope some of the change is to your betterment."

Her lips curved in a slight smile, the statement too complex to answer.

He only nodded, reading what he'd been looking for in her gaze. "See to it my youngest gets some culturing before she does something she'll regret, will you?"

Barbara glanced to where Georgiana scowled at her. "I will try. I do appreciate the company." She spoke not to her uncle but to her cousin.

The other girls rushed forward to hug her and say their goodbyes to Barbara and Sarah both. New tears sprouted in Barbara's eyes, but she blinked them away as her uncle lifted first Sarah then her into the wagon.

The driver called to his horses as soon as they were settled, and they started out, leaving behind a place of much happiness, both because of Aubrey and because she'd enjoyed the company of her cousins and even the tasks she'd had to perform.

No words came to her as she joined the other two in watching the farm retreat into the distance. Her pain grew no less for she carried it firmly rooted in her heart.

The farm wagon took them to London at a slow and plodding pace. Sarah attempted conversation a couple of times, but Barbara could not find the energy to respond, nor did Georgiana. Whatever sorrows plagued her youngest cousin, the end to an inappropriate dalliance could hardly weigh against almost killing the love of her life after betraying his trust in a misguided attempt to teach a lesson she had yet to learn.

"We'll soon reach the town house. At the very least, we need to figure out what to tell your parents," her friend said after a long silence.

Shaking off a fraction of her melancholy, Barbara glanced up to see Sarah had spoken only the truth. A sigh slipped from her.

"We shall tell them nothing for there is nothing to tell," she said in a tone that allowed for no protest even had there been time to make one.

"Here we are, Barbara," the driver said, pulling the horses up to her very doorstep.

The simple address seemed out of place here where it had felt welcome at her uncle's farm. Still, she held up a hand to prevent Sarah from taking the man to task.

"Thank you for driving us, Thomas. There's a stable four streets over where you can rest the horses, and I'm sure our cook can set something out for you to eat once you've seen to them."

Thomas laughed. "No fancy stables will suit for these. The master's sent me up to the city for supplies before, and he gave me what I need to secure lodging for the night. No need to worry about me."

The butler came down the steps then, his scowl warning of the charge he'd been about to lay.

"Simmons," Barbara called before he could begin. "Can you help Thomas get us down from here?"

The butler squinted up at her, his scowl softening to a look of horror, if she could call that softening. "Lady Barbara?"

She nodded. "We're back from the country. There are no steps to descend, and there's our trunks to be seen to before Thomas can take his wagon to more welcoming roadways."

"Certainly, mistress. Let me call the men."

In a surprisingly short time, most likely to remove the wagon from its position as an eyesore, Mr. Simmons marshaled the footmen and other servants to get their baggage. He caught Barbara lightly around the waist and lifted her down with little straining. Sarah and Georgiana had to wait on Thomas as the butler ushered Barbara up the steps and most likely to her father's study.

"Wait. Georgiana must come with me. She's my cousin."

He spun to stare at the only unknown female, his disgusted look a clear sign he'd thought her no more than a farm girl. But then, Georgiana wore a better dress than Barbara, if in a country style, and at least her cousin did not bear the signs of a long journey afoot as Barbara still did.

"Well? You heard Lady Barbara," Mr. Simmons snapped at one of the footmen. "Get the lady down. She can't be happy stuck in such a … rural … equipage."

Barbara let the title slip, a quirk of humor breaking through her sadness for a moment.

Georgiana had become a lady through association much as Barbara had taken on the guise of a country girl. And as Barbara's guest, she deserved the same consideration, her absence of noble blood of little consequence.

"Barbara? Is that you?"

At first, the sound of her name didn't provide any warning as she'd grown used to the familiarity, but then she recognized the voice though the tones were strained.

She climbed the steps once again, this time to hug her mother.

Lady Whitfeld let the hug stand for barely a moment before she held Barbara at arm's length, her brow furrowed. "We weren't expecting you back so soon. Had we but known, we'd have sent a proper carriage."

From the scowl her mother directed at the wagon, Barbara guessed it had taken the blow for her ragged appearance. "It was time to come home," she said simply.

Lady Whitfeld's gaze snapped to Barbara, and she stared at her daughter as though she hardly knew her.

Barbara could not tell what had attracted that particular brand of attention so stood still beneath it.

"You are different somehow," her mother said, her eyes narrowed. "I can't quite put my finger on it, but you are not the frivolous girl we sent forth."

Her tone shifted from confusion to satisfaction as she stated the transformation.

Barbara shrugged. "It's the clothing I suspect."

"No, it's more than that."

Georgiana could not have chosen a better moment to step up beside them in Barbara's opinion.

She had no intention of conveying the sordid details of her failure while at her uncle's farm. They had no need to know. It was enough she'd learned from the experience and would temper her behavior going forward.

Lady Whitfeld raised both eyebrows as she surveyed the intruder on their conversation. "And who is this then?"

Barbara put an arm around Georgiana's shoulders, grateful for the easy camaraderie she'd shared with her cousins. "This is your youngest niece, Mother. Georgiana."

"Little Georgie? Why it can't be. You're a woman grown now, and quite a beauty at that."

The distraction served its purpose as her mother tugged both girls up the stairs and into the town house, peppering Georgiana with questions about her father, her sisters, the farm, and any number of other things she could as easily have asked Barbara.

In the chaos of moving their things inside and arranging a room for their unexpected guest, the reason for their abrupt return, and for Georgiana's inclusion, seemed forgotten much to Barbara's relief.

She'd hoped coming home would ease the black emptiness where her heart had been, but the familiar walls only made the distance from Aubrey seem greater. It felt as though she'd slipped back into a time before she'd truly known him, returning to when she'd judged him on words overheard, her opinions no better than his for judging her on the experience with others in that season.

Her spoon drew patterns in the cream of her soup, the effort to consume it too great.

"So, Barbara, does that sound like a plan? Georgie needs a proper introduction before she can be included in anything regarding the season, but a quiet poetry reading would be just the thing to make others aware of her presence. She can borrow from your wardrobe." Lady Whitfeld paused. "Unless they are all in the same state as the rag you arrived in. I had it burned."

That brought Barbara's head up. "Mother, it was Charlotte's dress. I was planning to clean and repair it."

"All by yourself, I suppose. Of course my brother had you working like a maid. I should have expected as much." She paused, a thoughtful look crossing her expression. "Perhaps I did. You needed some reminding of the advantages you hold. But you're in London now. You'll be soaking your hands in cream before bed every night until they regain their beauty. You, too, Georgie. We can't have you showing at any less than your best."

Georgiana blushed and ducked her head, but she was wise enough to recognize a command when she heard one.

Barbara let her mother's strategies wash over her. They no more inspired a wish to engage than the soup had inspired her appetite. Though she planned to be the dutiful daughter, beyond that she could not promise while enthusiasm seemed too much of an effort.

Chapter Thirty-Two

"They're all so lovely." Georgiana stroked a hand down the third dress she'd pulled from Barbara's cabinet. "You really don't mind sharing? I know your mother said so, but these are your coming out dresses. It's just there's no time before the poetry reading Lady—Aunt Whitfeld arranged for us."

Barbara waved her permission, not even finding the heart to smile at how Georgiana continued to struggle with her mother's name. "Take whatever you need. I doubt I'll have much use for them." She turned back to the paper on her desk, though even a discussion of the latest London politics couldn't hold her attention for long.

Georgiana stopped her assessment to stare at Barbara, her intent look discomfiting. "For someone who was so eager to return, you don't seem any happier for being home."

Barbara shrugged. "You are happy enough for the two of us. From your scowl on our journey, I expected little joy. Yet not even a day later, and here you are admiring my dresses."

"And such wonderful dresses they are," Georgiana said, pressing a lovely cream satin to her as she spun in a circle. "Why shouldn't I make the most of it? I might not have had a choice in coming, but that's no reason to waste the opportunity. Besides, my Freddie will still be there when I return." Her eyes sparkled at the thought of her beau, something likely to upset both her father and Charlotte were they able to see.

"I doubt your family, or my mother for that matter, plan to have you return home to your farmhand. I'm sure they're hoping a young viscount or baron will turn your head until this Freddie is forgotten."

Georgiana laughed at some private joke, full of the supreme confidence of young love, then shook her head at Barbara's statement, her lips curling into a broad grin.

A flash of jealousy went through Barbara. Had she ever felt such simple knowledge about anyone? It seemed the moment she'd set her sights on finding love, every bit of confidence and surety were lost forever leaving her in a well of doubt and confusion.

After putting the dress over a chair, her cousin came to kneel next to Barbara. "We weren't talking about me," Georgiana said. "Why do you think you'll have no use for your dresses? There's time yet even in this season."

Barbara gave up all pretense of reading the paper to twist and face her cousin. "I already have offers to spare. I'll put their names on a letter, close my eyes, and jab with my finger. It doesn't matter which of them I choose, and this way I can't curse myself for choosing poorly if I don't come to love the man as my mother did."

"You love him that much?"

She rose to pace the room, fleeing from her cousin's knowing gaze. "I just told you I'd choose at random. Does that sound like love?"

"If it were my Freddie," Georgiana said as though Barbara had not spoken, "I would fight for him. It wouldn't matter what had happened. Besides, who is he to complain when he was right there in the fields with you? If propriety is at question, question his."

Barbara's path took her to her cousin once more, and she put a hand on Georgiana's shoulder in the hopes of ending this conversation. "If only it were that simple. No, what happened at the farm is over and done with. I must look to my future and you to yours." She forced a laugh past stiff lips. "If you don't have a dress chosen for the reading tonight, my mother will choose for you."

Georgiana watched Barbara for long enough she had to fight not to fidget under that penetrating gaze, but then her youngest cousin's nature reasserted itself as she swept up and back to the cabinet. "Well, then, I better be at it. So many to choose from. Do you have any you'd prefer I let be?"

"No. Choose whatever takes your fancy and get your enjoyment from them." She would not let her cousin's good spirits be dampened by her own. She'd proved to be a spoiled and foolish girl where she'd thought herself more than that, but at least she wasn't so horrible a person as to wish her cousin miserable just because she was.

Barbara moved to the window to stare blindly out on the busy street below. If she had only decided to prove to Aubrey that she could be steadfast rather than proving his falsehoods to be true, none of this would have happened. She had herself to blame for finding love and corrupting that very emotion.

She wished Georgiana a better road, though with her uncle set against this unknown Freddie, she doubted they had much chance especially now with her mother involved. Perhaps someday Barbara and her cousin could comfort each other in their grand houses with their well-positioned husbands, each having once known the simple freedoms of a love that sprang to life in the wild countryside.

Barbara turned to look on her cousin, grateful to find the other girl occupied in choosing which fancy, but not too fancy, dress to wear. She didn't want Georgiana to see the pity in her eyes, for all she couldn't help it being there. She might deserve the fate in store for her, but for Georgiana to lose faith in her love seemed needlessly cruel. Her cousin had done nothing to merit it beyond ignoring rules that held much less sway in the country, and less still for the daughter of a simple landholder regardless of what wealth he may have accrued.

Chapter Thirty-Three

Aubrey swam out of a laudanum-induced sleep to find a bitter taste on his tongue and the late afternoon sun filling his empty room. He had to find Barbara.

He braced his arm and rolled to one side, the expected groan unvoiced as his head, though aching, no longer threatened to split open wide. Emboldened by this success, he kept going, this time sliding both legs off the mattress and slowly rising until he sat on the edge.

A glance at the door, half-expecting to see the doctor charge in with another draught to force down his throat, revealed instead a small boy.

"You're awake," the boy said with eyes widening. "I'll tell the master."

Between one blink and the next, the boy disappeared like an apparition.

"Just how much opium did that blasted man give me?"

No one answered the question.

The very absence of watchers made Aubrey wonder if he wandered in a dream once again, the best explanation for his rapid recovery.

With one hand curled around the headboard, Aubrey heaved himself the rest of the way to his feet.

He swayed, grateful for the sturdy wood support, but upright at last.

A hand caught his other arm. "You're looking none too steady for all you're standing."

Aubrey turned to see Jasper had arrived, making the boy less ghost than guard.

"I'm steady enough. I have to find Barbara."

Jasper shook his head. "You have to let her go until you're fully healed. Another couple of days, and you'll be strong enough to go after her."

Aubrey stared at his friend, the words matching a little too comfortably with the way he felt. "Days? How long has it been?"

"Three if you count the first. The doctor thought you would refuse to rest otherwise, and his fears seem warranted," Jasper added with a nod to Aubrey's upright state.

Aubrey put a hand to his swimming head only to stagger against Jasper when he lost the headboard's support. "Three days is too long. I must find her."

Jasper raised an eyebrow as he steadied Aubrey. "She came to no harm in the forest. She'll have come to none on her walk home."

Aubrey only stared at his friend.

"I could send for the doctor."

"But you won't. I'm well enough, and I dare not delay any longer. It's not her physical state that concerns me now. Who knows what she will convince herself of in my absence?"

Jasper looked back in silence for a long moment, but then shrugged. "No, I won't. You supported me in the mess I made of my own courtship. What right have I to stand in the way of your own mistakes?"

Aubrey gave a feeble chuckle at that, recognizing the warning even though his friend used more subtlety than Daphne. Besides, the mistakes had already been made, and he had to repair them before the damage grew worse.

"Then show your willingness by bringing round a horse."

A bark of laughter escaped Jasper. "You can barely stand. There's no way I'm trusting you on even the most gentle of my stable. I'll call for the carriage, and you will drink the broth already on its way up. You'll do nothing to ease her fears if you swoon at her feet. An extra minute or five will make little difference when she doesn't know you're coming, and the time to regain your strength, at least in some measure, is time well spent."

Though every bone in his body demanded he hurry, Aubrey could hear the truth of his friend's statements. He made no protest as Jasper let go with a light push toward the bed, though this time only as a sitting surface.

"And here's your repast now."

The door swung open to reveal Willem carrying an aromatic tray.

The man glanced from Aubrey to Jasper before stepping inside, warning enough that the choice of servant had little to do with tradition and more with fear of another outburst.

"I'm done fighting, Willem, and Lord Pendleton has given in to my wishes already. There's no need for you to be on guard."

He'd meant the reassurance as a joke, but saw the truth to it when Willem relaxed enough to smile.

"You gave us a bit of a struggle, my lord. We're glad to see you better."

"Thank you." Though his words were meant for the well wishes, they would have sufficed for the food also as his stomach rumbled.

"It's not much to fill you after so long, but the doctor said to start small. No telling how your stomach has shrunk since your injury."

"From the feel of it, my stomach is as large as Hyde Park and as empty as same in the early morning hours."

"Prove yourself steady, and I'll have Cook make a heartier meal for you to feast upon."

Aubrey had not waited for Jasper's response so had to swallow before he said, "Once I've seen Barbara, your staff is welcome to do their best in stuffing me to full, but for now, don't you have a carriage to order up?"

Jasper laughed, his relief evident in the sound even as he turned for the door. "I do at that, and I best be about it. I have a sour feeling you'd set off afoot if it's not ready when you down the last sip. I should be grateful you're using a spoon."

He left before Aubrey could raise the bowl to his lips in teasing warning, a lucky fact from how the bowl trembled in his hands. Had he not been so hungered from the start, it would have had enough liquid to spill out.

After lowering his broth to the tray, Aubrey devoted his full attention to spooning the rich liquid into his mouth. He'd need every bit of strength he could muster if he were to succeed in convincing Barbara of his intentions.

Some hours later, after they'd gone down for tea and come back, Georgiana was still deciding on a dress for the poetry reading. She'd even pulled Sarah into the discussion.

"That one is much too formal for a simple reading," Barbara said of the gown her cousin had pressed to her front this time. "You should save it for a ball."

"But what if I never get invited to any? I'd have wasted the chance to wear it."

Barbara crossed the room to pluck the overly ornamented cloth from her cousin's hands. "That was never in question. You will be part of my mother's party, and my mother is always invited."

She'd never given it a thought before, but now it seemed as though she'd been trading on her father's blood and her mother's social standing her whole life. Certainly during this season.

All the men who sought her out, all of her suitors, and she had no way of knowing whether she herself had been the draw. The Whitfeld name held enough allure, even to those with higher-ranking titles than her father's, that securing her hand had more to do with securing the bloodline, and her inheritance.

"I'm no more than one of Uncle's mares."

"What was that?" Sarah asked as she took the ball gown from Barbara's hands.

Barbara shrugged the question off, not having meant to state it aloud in any case.

Only one man had come to her unaware of the titles she could offer his children, or the cushion marriage would mean to his coffers. One man had met her gaze and lingered even though her clothing had patches and her hair hung around her shoulders.

"Have you chosen a gown for her?"

Lady Whitfeld poked her head around the door, her gaze settling on Barbara despite the question being meant more for Georgiana or Sarah from the state of Barbara's empty hands.

"She's having some trouble deciding."

Her mother's gaze narrowed and tiny frown lines appeared in her forehead, a response not so much to the answer as the flat tone in which it had been spoken.

Barbara pushed aside her melancholy in an effort to assuage her mother's concerns. "Georgie's worried she won't have a chance to wear them all."

Lady Whitfeld choked on a laugh. "Oh, my dear, that is not a reason to hesitate. This will be your debut, if on a small scale. You're young and beautiful. The men will twist their mother's arms to make sure you get an invite and the mothers with daughters of their own will connive to keep you absent. Neither will matter, though. The Whitfelds are always welcome."

Stifling a laugh of her own at her mother's tone when making this pronouncement, Barbara arched an eyebrow at her cousin. Had she not said much the same?

"I'd be worried you'd outshine my very own daughter," Lady Whitfeld continued, "if she didn't have too many suitors to count as it was."

Barbara found herself trapped once again under her mother's piercing gaze, recognizing this to be something her mother shared with Uncle Ferrier.

"Word of your return has reached them already. You know how London has a way of spreading gossip faster than a plague. Two of your gentlemen have left cards this very day. I sent them invitations to the reading tonight."

Barbara turned away, pretending to look at the dress Georgiana now considered as she controlled her features.

She'd told her cousin of her plans to choose one of them at random, but she had no inclination to spend time in their presence beforehand. It would only be awkward, especially when her mother had invited not one but two.

Lady Whitfeld laid a hand on her shoulder and turned Barbara back to meet her gaze. "It does no good to delay. We'd hoped your trip to the country had restrained you, and it seems to have done so, but hiding from the men vying for your hand solves nothing. You must choose among them and set the rest free."

"I understand."

Though Barbara had meant to add more, Georgiana chose that moment to come over with a gown.

"Surely she could wait to choose a little longer. If they've stayed faithful to her cause all this time, they won't mind a few more days while my cousin guides me, will they?"

Lady Whitfeld gazed on Georgiana with twinkling eyes as she took in the gown now swirling around the girl's ankles. "No, it will not harm them any, you're right. And better not to cloud your introduction. A pity I didn't seek your counsel before I added them to the guest list. It seems you have a good understanding of these things for one straight from the country."

"I understand the strength of faith," Georgiana said with a pointed look to Barbara, "but I'm at a loss in choosing."

The shake she gave the gown in her arms showed her meaning, but Lady Whitfeld's murmur of, "You are not alone in that difficulty," had no object beyond her daughter.

"Don't worry, Mother. We'll have her appropriately dressed for the event even if it takes a blind choice to make it happen."

Her mother had no way of knowing just where that option had its roots, but she gave Barbara an intent look as though she understood all too well.

"I'll leave you young ones to the task then. Sarah, make sure they are both ready to shine by this evening. Though small, this gathering must quash any of the rumors began by Barbara's sudden departure. Cinch her gown tight in the latest fashion."

With that admonishment, Lady Whitfeld swept out of the room, leaving them no better off than they were before, and with an added complication for Barbara to address.

She'd thought to have a few days at least to contemplate her future, barren as it was without Aubrey in it, but it seemed she was to be thrust into the center as though she'd never been absent at all. Certainly not as though she'd spent a few short weeks running wild in the fields, finding — and losing — her one true match.

Chapter Thirty-Four

Aubrey refused to admit how exhausting the carriage ride out to the farm had been despite the strength offered by the broth. He couldn't hold back a relieved sigh when they reached the fence.

"You don't have to do this now," Jasper said, catching Aubrey's arm when he went to exit the carriage.

Aubrey shook him off. "I need to speak with her. You won't stop me, and I'd suggest you don't try."

His friend gave him an intent look, clearly seeing both his conviction and weakness. "Well, then, we might as well get it over with." He reached past Aubrey to swing the door open.

Whether they'd lingered a bit too long within or their arrival proved momentous, a small gathering had collected outside.

Aubrey stepped down and scanned those nearest. Charlotte stood among them, her solemn expression at odds with what he expected of her. Stern, yes, but not solemn.

"I need to speak to Barbara."

Her eyes widened, though she must have guessed at his reason for arriving there. Daphne told him how Charlotte had been in charge of his care before the doctor arrived. Surely the woman knew how he'd come to be there in the forest.

"Your father, then," he added when she showed no signs of taking him to the one he needed to see.

That earned him a stiff nod.

"Marian, get the gentlemen something to refresh themselves while I get Father."

Aubrey put up a hand to stop both from leaving. "That won't be necessary. I'll be coming with you."

She glanced beyond him and exchanged a silent communication with Jasper. "I'll take you to his study. Marian, get Father and bring him there."

As much as Aubrey wanted to argue, he could feel the weakness of too little food and too much rest in his knees. Standing in a field or stable would not be possible soon enough.

"Are you sure I can't get you some water at least," Marian said as he settled into one of the chairs and Jasper took another.

"Fetch him some vinegar juice if you have any," Jasper said.

Aubrey had no chance to protest before she left the room, not that he would reject something more to sustain him.

"You need to calm yourself or they'll think you came to lay charges. Something doesn't feel right here."

He couldn't reject the statement, not when he'd seen first Charlotte and now Marian acting both solemn and skittish, but the need to see Barbara was all that kept him upright. Calming himself might drain what little strength he had.

Mr. Ferrier entered just then, his daughter following with a tray of vinegars, bread, and cheese.

She placed the tray on her father's desk and left with unseemly haste.

Ferrier settled at the desk, his hands steepled in front of him. "You wanted to see me, my lord? Are you healing well? Last I saw you was to deliver you unconscious to the manor, so you seem much recovered."

Aubrey pushed to the edge of his seat, waving a hand to brush off the man's concern. "I'm well enough, thank you for that though it's not why we came. I need to see Barbara."

The farmer shifted so the wood of his seat creaked. "She is not here."

Aubrey leapt to his feet only to freeze as the room spun. He narrowed his focus to Ferrier. "Don't try to deny me. I know she's your servant. She has no other place to be."

Ferrier rose as well, coming round the desk to catch Aubrey's arm and offer a support Aubrey wished he didn't need. "You should sit. Have some of the treats Marian brought for you. Conserve your strength."

Though Aubrey sank onto the chair once again, he shook his head to deny the rest. "I'll be better when I've had my say to your servant girl. Bring her here promptly."

The farmer let out a heartfelt sigh and rubbed a hand along his jaw.

His response sent a jolt of fear through Aubrey. "Where is she? She's not fallen ill, has she? She came from the forest healthy. I saw her myself. Tell me nothing has happened to her since."

Ferrier's brow furrowed, and he rested against his desk for a moment before meeting Aubrey's gaze. "She's well. It's not that. This is much more complicated than you might think."

"Speak plainly, man. I have little patience."

Ferrier glanced to Jasper first as though looking for guidance, but his friend said nothing.

After what seemed an age, the farmer sighed again. "She's not a servant here. She never was."

"But I met her working in your fields with your daughters. What else could she be?"

"She's my niece."

Aubrey took a moment to digest that information, rewriting the family care between the women as bloodline rather than kindness. Her clothing meant she came from a poorer branch of the family, but that made no difference, or rather, it made what he planned that much easier.

He raised his eyebrows. "This changes nothing unless you're going to say she's already wed. I know her too well to think she'd trifle with a man when she has one waiting at home, though."

Ferrier shook his head. "That's just the problem. You know her not at all. My eldest gave me the whole story. How she let you think all sorts of things about her uncorrected, and how she had some plan for revenge after you cut her direct."

Anger uncoiled at the accusation and Aubrey's fists curled though he rarely chose physical violence as a first action. "I never gave her reason to believe I thought less of her. Your daughter tells tales to keep us apart."

Ferrier straightened at that. "My daughters are nothing but truthful. They are ashamed of their part in this, though you never saw fit to ask."

Aubrey jerked to his feet, unable to stay seated in the face of these accusations. "How do I know any of this to be truth?"

Jasper rose and caught his arm before he could advance on the farmer and beat the truth from him.

At the same moment, Charlotte slipped into the room to catch his other arm, having clearly been listening outside.

"Barbara," Ferrier continued, "Lady Barbara is not a simple country girl. Her father is a viscount. Her parents sent her down here after her season proved a little too frivolous for their tastes, a fact she credits to what you had to say of her."

Aubrey wanted to shake off his restraints, but a wave of weakness crashed over him, and he could only stand there between them, frustrated.

"Lord Aubrey, you are correct," Charlotte said from his side. "You never spoke to her before that day in the field."

He turned to face her. "Are you admitting now what you told your father was lies? Is there any truthful female in this family?"

She paled, and her father crowded forward, but Charlotte stopped him with a hand. "I suppose we deserve that, but you misunderstand me. You are as quick to judge now as you were in the fields, and the ballroom. You did not speak to her directly. She happened to be within hearing when you destroyed the character of almost every debutante at the event." Her tone sharpened as she continued, "But you singled out Lady Barbara Whitfeld with excessive care."

Aubrey opened his mouth to deliver a sound denial only to have a hint of memory trickle in to silence him.

He exchanged a pained look with Jasper, a moment of frustration with the frivolity of the season having consequences greater than he could ever have imagined.

He slumped into his chair, eyes closed on the vision of a white-clad girl with brightly colored ribbons who danced through the crowd of willing suitors. His only charge against her came from Jasper's mother attempting to create a connection where he saw none, but he'd let that control his tongue as he scorned her nature to Jasper.

Memory of his cutting remarks burned. Had he only given in to The Dowager Lady Pendleton's matchmaking, he would have spent the season squiring his Barbara around and securing her affections.

A groan slipped from him as he remembered his desperate search for Lady Barbara after their encounter in the park.

No wonder she cut him that day, not for an imagined offense but for one quite real, if unintended. Only arrogance made him bundled her in with the other debutantes who judged him by how they measured his purse or title. He'd had no cause to suspect her of being the same.

His head sank between his hands and he stared at the floor, cursing the time lost.

"Are you unwell?"

Aubrey looked up to find Ferrier, his daughter, and Jasper gathered close, their expressions matched in worry.

"It's not my injuries that pain me now but my past mistakes. I have much to apologize for. Charlotte, you called me out for jumping to conclusions, and you spoke the same truth you always had. If I'd seen fit to question, I have little doubt you'd have been direct whether Barbara — Lady Barbara — held to her plan. If I'd been willing to meet her before judging ... Can you now bring her forth? I swear I will not condemn her for her game. It's a fair enough return for my false commentary."

Charlotte stared into his eyes for a long moment, and Aubrey made no attempt to mask the desperate longing within, but then she shook her head as though finding him wanting.

"I need to see her," he burst out. "Don't deny me this."

"It's not that. She's not here anymore. My father spoke faithfully. She returned to her parents, unwilling to chance facing you once again after all the harm she'd caused you."

Aubrey gave a bitter laugh at that. "Any harm done was of my own doing." He pushed to his feet, finding them steadier than they had been with understanding to give him strength. "Jasper, it seems I'm off to London."

Chapter Thirty-Five

Discovering the truth about Barbara had taken most of the afternoon. Even if he'd convinced Jasper to lend him the fastest horse in the stables, his friend pointed out by the time he arrived, they would be off at some gathering or another, the Whitfelds lacking a reputation for staying home most evenings. He might as well have a good meal and take the carriage through the night, or so his friend declared.

As much as he heard the logic in Jasper's words, his continued weakness drove compliance more than his agreement, a fact that had him grumpy over dinner.

"Are you sure you're healed enough for the journey?" Daphne asked, her brow furrowed with a concern he knew he should appreciate. "I doubt your doctor would agree."

Aubrey gave a bark of laughter. "My doctor would hardly agree to me sitting at the table with you. If he had his way, I'd still be in a laudanum-induced stupor."

"It might be better if you were."

Jasper held up a hand to still his wife's words a bit too late, but Aubrey didn't want to argue.

"From what Ferrier told us, if I hesitate, she'll give in to her parents' wishes and marry one of a handful of offers she's received. I have to speak to her before all is lost."

He'd chosen the answer that trumped any protest she might think to make. She'd been the one to encourage him from the start. Surely she wouldn't hold him back with everything hanging in the balance.

"At least stay the night and set out well rested. You'll do no good showing up at Lord Whitfeld's doorstep mussed and raving at an hour when the household is still abed. Their butler would toss you out before you had the chance to make your case," Jasper said, perhaps seeing an opening to change their agreement. "I doubt they'll rush her decision what with her mysterious jaunt to the country. It would only cause gossip."

Aubrey's memory flashed back to when he'd first awoken and knew his friend suspected a similar event would occur when he reached London. "I promise you both, I will stay calm. Now that I know what was behind her tears, I cannot delay and chance her giving up on me. This all began because I saw fit to lay judgment on a slew of girls I hardly knew if at all. Why would she not presume the same when I learned of her mischief?"

Daphne pressed a hand to Jasper's arm before he could speak again. "Promise us this much. When the carriage reaches London, direct it to your lodgings. Lie down if you cannot sleep, at least until fashionable society recognizes the existence of the day. Remember you've been keeping country hours. Besides, after so long traveling, you'll need your rest. It won't help your case any to collapse on her doorstep. She might be moved, but her father would suspect you of being in your cups."

He nodded, seeing the wisdom in her words and knowing his other promise to stay calm had a greater chance when his energy wasn't at a low ebb.

The conversation turned to different subjects, much to Aubrey's relief, but his thoughts kept dwelling on what he'd learned.

He had no particular memory of how he'd condemned Barbara in specific, but that her name came from his lips stood crystal clear in his remembrances.

Perhaps Jasper's mother drove him, or maybe his heart recognized a connection before his mind could. Perhaps she'd been the focus of his thoughts not because he found her wanting but because he wanted her then as he did now.

He needed to make her see that even as he'd called her frivolous, he'd been the one too foolish to know what he'd cast aside. Her own actions paled next to that fact, and though extreme, he could see why she'd felt driven to seek recompense from him.

Daphne's hand on his shoulder brought Aubrey back to awareness only to discover the meal done and his friends already leaving the table.

"If she means this much to you, you're right to hurry. Fight for her. Don't let anything stand in your way even if she has accepted one of the others. If she feels a fraction of what you do, denying it will only make you both miserable for a lifetime, along with the poor fellow she's settled on."

He didn't know what to say in response, and she'd gone from the room before he could say a word anyway. In the distance, he could hear her calling her staff and assigning them tasks designed with one purpose in mind — to get him to London.

"Two better friends I could not have," Aubrey said, half under his breath.

"Two friends ready to be quit of your presence and the chaos you bring, you mean," Jasper said with a laugh. "Come on, old man. We need to gather your things and send you on your way to a respectable life. No more racing about the countryside like a rogue. You'll be an upstanding gentleman of politics sooner than any would have suspected."

Aubrey rose to join Jasper as they headed for his rooms. "You're describing yourself much more than me. You've adapted to the married life so well one would think you were born to it."

His friend gave a quick headshake. "Far from it as you know, but with the right partner my eyes were opened just as yours have been. Don't stress yourself. If she had nothing but friendly or revengeful feelings toward you, she'd have no reason to flee and every reason to linger so she could see your face when the truth came out. You have only to confront her, and her resistance will melt away."

"If I can get her to listen." The morose words were more for show as a certainty settled into his bones. Nothing would keep him from presenting his case even if he had to shout it up to her window as in many theatrical performances.

No matter what she might have thought of him, her laughter and smiles — how she'd teased him — showed her heart followed different instincts than her head. Just as he'd come to know Barbara beyond the shelter of her name, she'd seen deeper into him than he'd let anyone in a long while. She had to believe him, and he wouldn't rest until she did.

Chapter Thirty-Six

Georgiana thrust her hands through the hairstyle it had taken Sarah a good hour to perfect, sending a shower of pins across the room. "That was wonderful." She sighed and collapsed onto the bed. "How could you have given it all up to pluck berries?"

Barbara managed the first laugh since they'd gone down the stairs to greet her mother's guests. "It wasn't like I asked to leave."

Her cousin offered a level stare. "From what your mother told me over tea, you didn't protest that much either."

Turning so Sarah could help her with the last of her own pins, Barbara kept her expression hidden. She hadn't thought her parents so aware of how little their punishment had punished until now. Maybe they'd known it a kindness.

"And your suitors. I can see why you have so much trouble choosing between them. Handsome and witty too."

That brought a sigh from Barbara, and not one of delight. "If you like them so much, why don't you take them off my hands?"

Georgiana giggled. "From what your parents say, you have enough to spare, but no. My Freddie is the only one for me. I'm here to get a bit of culturing and enjoy myself before heading home. It's your job to choose a suitor since you've given up on the one you left behind."

"I never had him," Barbara said, her tone quashing any further conversation, for the moment at least.

She'd spent an uncomfortable evening between a marquess and a baron. Both of whom had sought her father's permission already only to be put off, and neither intended the other to get the slightest advantage. They'd exchanged biting remarks, ostensibly with her, about the readings, the latest politics, and whatever else they could come up with, challenging each other to provide a better topic or a wittier phrase.

Little had they known a different man all together held Barbara's attention, the reading only reminding her of the last one she'd attended. She'd wasted the event then, using it to condemn Aubrey when she would have lingered over every word and collected memories to sustain her had she only known. None of the readers tonight had his skill with the spoken tongue. Though he'd never consider such a thing, his talents would serve well on the stage of a public theater. She had no doubt he'd proven a favorite for more private dramatic parties a time or two.

While they'd captured Georgiana's attention, Barbara had been busy spinning fantasies all the more impossible for how they swirled around Aubrey. She pretended she could explain her behavior away once he returned to London, that Aubrey would see fit to forgive her and they could begin again.

Sarah tugged the brush through a snarl in Barbara's hair, startling her. She'd been caught up in her thoughts and hadn't noticed when the style fell.

"You'll find another," her friend murmured. "If not one of those two, then a different gentleman. Despite all that happened, your true nature is sound and pleasant as so many have recognized."

Barbara stood, ignoring the sharp pain as the brush tangled. "Why don't you help Georgie tonight? She's had quite the adventure in even such a simple gathering."

Sarah's lips pinched together, but she did not speak any rebuke as Barbara moved to the window that had held her presence more often of late than ever before. At least there no one could question how she looked into the distance, nor could they see the shadows in her eyes as she did so.

"Have you ever gone to a reading?" Georgiana asked Sarah from the same stool Barbara had vacated. "It was like when my mama read to us when we were little. Charlotte tries, and Father too, but neither have the knack for making the voices come alive like she did."

Tuning out Sarah's reply, Barbara wished she could go back to the time of innocence when she'd sat against the wall so she could see Aubrey without interference. She'd watched his lips form the voices, sometimes pinched together, sometimes wide and languid.

She'd known better then, seen the measure of the man in so much more than one remark not intended to be overheard.

With the maturity of experience though little time had passed, she recognized sharp words could be a release of frustration or other emotions kept hidden beneath a social mask. Rather than seeing through to the heart of him, she'd seen him at his worst, but at the same time at his best. He could have stood in the center of the dance floor and called out his cutting words to each debutante who circled him, ever hopeful of an interested look from someone who had station, finances, and a fine figure. Had he spoken then, his intent would have been to damage. Though his remarks had not been far from the truth, they were hardly what one wanted bandied about.

Instead, he'd chosen a secluded corner and had spoken to a trusted friend.

Fate and bad luck had her near enough to overhear, but it had been her own willfulness that took his words not just to heart but to the point of revenge. Her uncharitable nature had almost cost him his life, and for what crime? A moment of irritation at the marriage mart? Could she stand tall against such a happening?

"You'll have the curtains down on the floorboards and the bright sun to wake the two of you much too early if you don't leave off your moping."

At Sarah's words, Barbara became aware of how she'd taken hold of the curtains in her fist and now tugged them far too taut. She let go, the fabric still wrinkled from her attack as it swung into place.

Georgiana came up on her other side and pulled Barbara over to the bed. "The standard you hold for yourself is too firm by far, Cousin. And you measure him too low."

Barbara tried to protest, but a callused finger against her lips forced silence.

"We all know who held your thoughts as you stood by the window, fists clenched and shoulders slumped, don't we, Sarah? You let thoughts of him take all the joy out of life and yet won't give him the chance to bring it back."

Barbara shook off her cousin's hold. "You don't understand. There is no chance. I need to accept my path and put him behind me. All this lingering is the cause of my sorrow, and it's a further sign of my foolishness. What I've done is unforgivable, and I know it."

Georgiana burst out with laughter sharp enough to bring the blood rushing to her features. "You think playing on his own arrogance the worst a girl could do? Freddie has forgiven me that more times than I could count and me the same for him." She shook her head. "There is a chance if only you give it. You have to stop running away before he can catch you, and until he does, he cannot forgive because he knows not what makes you run."

The wisdom coming from a girl she'd thought truly frivolous where Barbara had only pretended stunned Barbara to silence for a moment.

When she found her tongue though, she didn't bother to explain the difference between a simple farm boy and a nobleman when it came to playing the fool. Instead, she said only, "You are a very lucky girl, Georgie. I hope your Freddie proves as steadfast, and my uncle sees the good in seeking happiness over the chance at a rise in station."

Chapter Thirty-Seven

Aubrey had reason to appreciate Daphne's advice as he stepped down from the carriage and mounted the stairs to Barbara's home.

His mother had been stunned to see him home again with no warning, but when he asked for a certain address from her, she'd forgiven him entering her bedroom so early in the morning. Somehow, he didn't think Barbara's neighbors would have felt the same should he have banged doors up and down the street when the carriage first rumbled into London. He'd known the location of the Whitfeld town house generally, but not well enough to arrive here without assistance.

The knocker thudded against a solid door twice before Aubrey stood back, not wanting to appear rushed for all his blood sang with urgency. He'd rested both in the carriage and at his home, regaining more of his natural energy than he'd believed possible, or perhaps thoughts of Barbara gave him strength.

"Your card," the butler said, holding out a silver tray on which lay two others.

Aubrey patted down his pockets in the vague hope his valet had tucked one into his waistcoat, but he came up empty handed. "I have none on me, but I didn't intend to leave a card anyway. I'd like to speak to Lord Whitfeld."

The butler's eyebrows rose. "Lord Whitfeld is not receiving visitors yet." He shook the plate as though to suggest Aubrey's claim not to have a card on him a prevarication.

He'd come too far to turn away now, and no butler would block his path. Aubrey thought about pushing past the man, but remembered his lessons from the country. His first proposal had been to a farm girl. No matter that she turned out to be of high standing, he could not act the superior here and would not unless he had to.

"I understand the hour is early for London," he said, "but I've come of late from the country where the sun seems to rise much earlier."

A smile threatened to undercut the man's severe expression, which Aubrey took as a good sign.

"It's a matter of some urgency. It's about his daughter."

The butler frowned. "It's always about Lady Barbara when they come calling so early," he muttered as though talking to himself. "I guess you better come in then. His lordship is in his study."

Aubrey offered his thanks with a smile even as he suppressed a sigh of relief that at least he wouldn't be rousting her father from his rest. If Lord Whitfeld had discovered any portion of Barbara's experience in the country, he'd need all the help he could get. Turning her father's favor would be a big step toward that.

"My lord, you have a caller. It's about Lady Barbara."

Aubrey had not realized how his lack of card would make introductions awkward, but the butler acted as though lacking a name meant nothing.

"Aubrey St. Vincent," he announced himself as he stepped through the opened door. "I've come to speak to you about your daughter."

"You and half of society, the male half," Lord Whitfeld said, pinching the bridge of his nose. "Have your say and be done with it. I have work to do."

"I wish to ask permission to marry Lady Barbara." He carefully used proper address to prevent the appearance of impropriety. And they'd been well chaperoned on every encounter except the last.

Her father sighed, not quite the response he'd been expecting. "You are aware, I'm sure, of the number of suitors already declared for her. There's little point in adding to the list, especially as she shows no inclination toward choosing a favorite." His hands slapped the desk in front of him. "I pray you do not end up with daughters, but if you do, never give them their heads. Like barely broken stallions, they'd prefer to toss you off than carry you forward."

Aubrey didn't know what to say in response, though he understood the sentiment all too well from helping raise his two younger sisters.

Lord Whitfeld bit off a laugh. "Here I am speaking disparagingly of my very own flesh and blood though it be poorly done. And like the others, nothing I could say would dissuade you short of denying my permission."

"With all due respect, Lord Whitfeld, I have a feeling Barbara would not let your permission stand in her way."

The man's eyebrows rose almost to his hairline. "Barbara?"

Aubrey swallowed a curse at his mistake. "My apologies. When I met your daughter, the circumstances were a little less formal than here in London."

Lord Whitfeld straightened and fixed Aubrey with an intent stare. "When you met her she wasn't in London, and you come to me now." He paused and his eyes narrowed. "You, sir, may just be the cause of my daughter's change and not the change I'd been hoping for. She's lost the frivolity, but returned disinterested in most everything. Not even her cousin can keep her spirits up for long."

"I swear to you I did nothing to harm your daughter on purpose."

Lord Whitfeld laughed. "I don't suppose you'd be here if you had, young man. She mopes as though of a broken heart, and yet here you are, steadfast in your regard."

"The situation is a bit more complicated than you might suppose," Aubrey offered.

"With my Barbara, it usually is." He looked about to chuckle then Lord Whitfeld froze and shoved to his feet to level a glare on Aubrey. "Have you compromised my daughter in these less formal circumstances?"

"Never." The confidence in his tone stayed strong through the one word, but his thoughts wavered. Had she not broken away from him that last day, he might just have given in to his desires, thinking her no more than a country girl who had therefore not been as sheltered. Or more likely, thinking not at all. It burned him her station would have determined his behavior. No matter her willingness, he should have shown more restraint.

"Well, then what is it?" Lord Whitfeld demanded, drawing Aubrey back to the present and her impatient father.

"When I met your daughter, she was wearing worn clothing and working in the fields," he began.

"I should have suspected Ferrier would do such a thing," Lord Whitfeld interjected with no sign of distress.

"I mistook her for a country girl," Aubrey continued, spilling out the whole story. He spared himself not one bit, recounting his ill-thought-out comments that unwittingly brought about a complicated scheme for revenge which rebounded on both of them.

Lord Whitfeld shook his head, but a smile played about his lips. "With the two of you having suffered so much in this affair already, and her mother and I as well, I should punish you both by denying you, but I will not be the one to hold you back." He held up a hand when Aubrey went to rise. "You'll have the devil of a time convincing Barbara all is well if I know my daughter, and from what you said of your injuries, you'll need all the strength you can muster."

He crossed to the bell, and the butler responded much too quickly to its ring. Aubrey wondered if curiosity made the man linger or if he'd expected to show Aubrey out bodily.

"Send word to my daughter her presence is wanted in my study at once. And have a tray sent here as well."

Though too full of nerves to enjoy his breakfast, Aubrey had made sure to eat before coming to the town house. Still, he did not protest. Having something to do with his hands might be wise. From her father's telling, the urge to shake some sense into her might overcome him.

When Lord Whitfeld turned to face him, Aubrey sought some form of conversation to pass the time, but his mind seemed blank.

Her father offered a stiff bow that ended with a wink. "It seems to me you'd do well with some time to gather your thoughts, and you have no need for further witnesses to this mess. You've likely given her cousins gossip fodder for some time to come. I'll leave you to your speech planning, but remember while she may be headstrong, her heart's a delicate instrument."

With this warning, Lord Whitfeld quit the room.

Chapter Thirty-Eight

Summoned to her father's study this early in the day, Barbara had little doubt as to the cause. Her mother must have lodged some complaint about the poetry reading. As much as she knew she needed to choose among her suitors, Barbara had the hardest time imagining them willing to wander at her side picking berries and talking of important things like politics, or less so like theater.

It all seemed so permanent. A lifetime spent with the wrong person when she'd lost all hope of the right one.

Perhaps the time had come to confess her sins so her parents could understand why she'd behaved the way she did then and now.

Aubrey consumed her thoughts as she rapped on her father's study door, not that he'd ever been far from them. From the moment she'd first set eyes on him, she'd either craved his attention or hated him. Never had she found his presence as innocuous as the men on either side of her the previous night.

Her mind was so caught up in Aubrey that even her father's voice sounded like his as he bid her enter. She had no idea how to purge the man from her very being so she could move on with her life. Perhaps her father could give her some much needed advice.

The door swung wide, and Barbara froze at the sight before her.

The man who rose not from the desk but one of the companion chairs was none other than the same one to consume her thoughts.

She stared at him, propriety forgotten as she cataloged his handsome features, noting where mottled browns and greens showed still-healing bruises, but also that he looked much more lively than when she'd seen him last. No one would suspect him of lingering at death's door now.

Barbara took a step toward him, drawn against her will by the need to touch, to reassure herself that he actually stood there and was not an apparition.

Then she sank against the doorframe as her scattered mind put together the clues to realize what his presence here had to mean.

"So you know," she murmured, her gaze now pinned to her father's carpet. He'd come to accuse her of falsehood, wanting to measure out his punishment in person.

He must have revealed all to her father before she could.

She'd been prepared for a lecture, and she'd earned one from his lips more than any about her behavior.

Despite this knowledge, her heart ached at the thought of hearing his condemnation a second time for now she knew it was deserved.

Warm fingers brushed her chin.

She jerked her head up to meet his gaze, drowning in the emotions there. His eyes held nothing of anger or condemnation while that beloved mouth quirked to one side in a sad smile.

"I've come here to learn exactly why we cannot be married, and I'm not leaving until you satisfy me even if it takes a lifetime."

Her breath caught in her throat, the slight sound all she could offer him. She could not have heard him rightly. Her mind had cracked and now daydreams crossed over with the waking moments.

Aubrey placed his hands on her shoulders and held her fast. "When I proposed, I thought you simply a country girl without the culturing necessary to survive London. I needed you at my side even so and would have stood by you until you found your bearings. How much better we suit than I knew, and yet you still ran from me."

She wanted to smooth his wrinkled brow, to wash away the confusion lingering in his eyes, but could only stare back at him.

"I cannot believe you find me repulsive."

Barbara's hand crept to the lips he'd kissed only once, a moment she'd relived more than any other. She shook her head.

"I'm no good for you, Aubrey," she whispered. "You deserve better than my lies, and better than the disaster that seems to follow in my wake."

Unable to help herself, she reached out to brush the back of one hand against the shadowed bruise marking his cheek. "You barely escaped with your life the last time you chased after me. Next time, you might not be so lucky."

He turned into her touch to lay a kiss on her hand before she could withdraw. "If you do not run, I'll have no cause to chase."

She jerked free and moved behind one of the chairs, her face turned from him because she could not bear to see him as she did what needed to be done. "I cannot have you on my conscience."

Aubrey stretched out an arm and pulled her forth, shifting her until she stood pressed to his body. "Your conscience will only be satisfied if you accept what beats in your heart is the same as what has hold of mine. I've gotten exactly what I deserve in you and more just as you deserve the whole of me, flaws and all."

She leaned away once again, but only so far as to see his face. "You have no flaws, Aubrey, except those I imagined in my anger. You deserve better than a foolish, deceitful, betraying girl who didn't have the sense to recognize the hazards in her path."

His chuckle rumbled through every point they were still connected, its humor warming Barbara against her will.

"No flaws? Am I some paragon to be set atop a pedestal only to be admired from afar? You forgot how all this came about. Had I not been so arrogant as to dismiss you out of hand, we might yet have come to a more traditional courting. I believe we would have as our souls are drawn to one another."

"You spoke in confidence. It's not a flaw to vent frustration, or if it is, the measure of such a flaw would require a jeweler's glass."

He stroked a thumb across her lips, causing shivers to work their way under her skin in a pleasant manner.

"You were not meant to overhear. No one was. But I gave no thought to the possibility, no more thought to the consequences than you with your scheming. It seems to me we make a perfect imperfect set."

Every bone in her body wanted to give in to his urging, to wash away all the wrongdoings as though they had never been, but conscience wouldn't let her.

Once again, Barbara pulled free, thrusting a hand into the air to stop him when he would follow. "You speak pretty words, and I want to believe them, but they're not the truth. You said yourself you meant no harm to come from your cutting remarks. How does that measure against my actions? I set my cap not for you but for revenge against a slight so small it had passed beneath your notice. I'm everything you said to your friend and worse. I was willing to play with your heart, your very life, as though I had any cause to stand above you."

She choked on a sob, but held firm, loving him too much to burden him with a wife who held rot at her core.

Aubrey laced his fingers through her outstretched hand, bringing it to lie against his chest. "You may have started with a vengeful heart, but you never carried out that plan."

Her eyes narrowed. "I was waiting for the moment it would have the most impact."

A laugh burst from him at the return of the Barbara he'd come to love, not this chastened, mournful lady, but the one with passion in her face and tone.

"Why should I question that lesson any more than when you held forth an opinion about a play I thought you'd never seen, or taught me how to pick the best of berries and mushrooms?"

She tugged her hand, but he refused to release it.

"Don't you see? Every word we shared was laced with falsehood. You thought I had never seen the plays we spoke of when at least with one of them, I could observe you in your box not far from mine. And I know little more about nature than you do, my teachings stolen from what Charlotte had shown me only moments before."

Aubrey brought her hand to his lips, pressing a kiss on her fingers before breathing his words over them, "It matters not the source, but the offering. Had you nothing but my destruction in your heart, why would you think to share your newly won knowledge or your opinions?"

That brought a reluctant smile to her lips. "Sarah would say I'm never slow to share an opinion."

"There. Yet another way we are alike. Arrogant, quick to judge, and opinionated, whether or not we have the right of it." Aubrey recognized the irony in winning her favor by telling of his faults and hers rather than promoting his virtues, but he could see her softening.

"I had lessons to learn," he continued in a gentler tone, "Of the dangers in judging others as wanting, and the risk in using my wit to denigrate instead of praise. Only you recognized my flaws and chose to guide me in them. All others were blinded by affection or my social standing."

He stepped closer, her arm bending to narrow the gap between them until he stood right before her.

"Every moment you spent scheming brought me nearer to the one person who caught my attention, who plagued me long before your plan came into effect. I escaped London when I couldn't find the Lady Barbara Whitfeld who had cut me in the park. I needed to know what I had done to offend her, but even then I focused more on myself than on her. So much so I couldn't recognize the very one I sought when she appeared before me. Sure, I noticed your hair and name held in common, but I never imagined you could be she."

"A vision of patchwork and brambles," Barbara cut in, the undertone of amusement giving him hope.

"A vision despite the smudge of dirt across her cheek." He stroked that very same skin as though to rub away imaginary smudges.

Aubrey thought she hesitated a moment before pulling away from his touch, and he realized the one argument she could not deny. Much as he had in the field, he slowly lowered his lips to settle against hers. If she could reject his kiss as easily as she had his words, he had no hope left to speak of.

Chapter Thirty-Nine

All words fled as his warm lips brushed against hers, bringing back a moment in the hot sun with the scent of rich soil and sun-warmed rocks filling the air. Barbara knew she should pull away, should reject him for his own good, but she couldn't hold fast any longer.

Her hand came up to catch on his waistcoat as she leaned in to the touch.

This had been her fantasy. She'd had too little faith in believing it could come true, and yet he'd come to fight for her instead of with her.

Nothing else mattered. She loved him too much and didn't have the strength to give him up a second time.

Even as she found that understanding, he pulled away to look down at her with laughter sparkling in his beautiful eyes.

"Please say you'll marry me and you'll stay by my side. I fear for my safety should I spend a lifetime chasing you down. Especially if you lay claim to a horse. I've seen your skill."

"You seek to win me with humor when you couldn't by argument?" Though her words might have seemed harsh, her laughing tone showed him she would not fight their connection any longer.

Aubrey dropped to his knees and caught her hand between both of his. "Had I known I need only make you laugh, I'd have pursued that method from the start. Ease my concerns, my love. Tell me plainly."

Barbara gazed down at him, her whole body aglow with the knowledge she had not lost him. She had only to speak the words and her future would hold not desolation but love.

Confidence made her cocky, and after all, it was this aspect of her nature that had captured his interest from the start, not her ability to conform to the rules he'd been so quick to scorn.

"I'm afraid, my good man, that there is a list, a good number to consider before you. I must assess each and every one for their suitability."

He rose to catch her in his arms and spin her around only to lower her so he could give her a kiss deeper than any other.

When she came up for air, she could only gaze at him with clouds in her eyes. "I have not said yes," she murmured.

Aubrey shook his head. "If I were to wait for a simple agreement from you, I'd grow old and grey."

"But what of my suitors? There is a duke among them even."

"Had you interest in your duke, or any other on that list, you would have decided already. You wouldn't have been sent off to the country to learn your faults. No, my love, you were meant only for me, and it's about time you realized it."

Barbara slapped his chest where her fingers had been pressed before. "There's the arrogance that got you into this trouble in the first place — your fatal flaw," she said, more humor than rancor in her tone.

Aubrey laced his fingers with hers and pulled her ever closer until Barbara had to tip her head back to see him. "This trouble is exactly where I want to be, now and forever, so if arrogance won me the place, it's less a flaw than a virtue."

"With virtues like that, it's no wonder you remain unmarried."

His expression took on a mournful cast, broken only by the dancing in his eyes. "I had to search high and low to find a woman with virtues to match my own."

She laughed then. "Is this your courting speech? You tell a woman her flaws so she is brought down and considers herself lucky to receive only you? You forget the others who have made their case in this very room."

"They matter not at all, not to me or to you. Give me your answer,

Barbara. Put me out of this misery. Do you have any affection for me at all?"

She felt the heat of a blush sweep her features and leaned into his chest to mask the response. "Do you think I'd have been so quick to condemn if I had none? Or so quick to cast aside your offer for fear of your safety?"

"As you've mentioned a time or two, my offer is but one of many, and claims for my safety could have been naught but excuses to let me down gently."

She jerked away. "Gently? Since when do you match that word to my behavior?"

"You are all that is gentle, and fierce, and strong. What you are not is forthright."

Barbara felt her brows come together as confusion broke through their repartee.

As though he were capable of reading her very thoughts, Aubrey's voice dropped to a low rumble as he said, "You still withhold your answer, and your feelings."

Barbara threw her head back to laugh. "Yes, I love you, Aubrey St. Vincent. I think I have from the start, though it was nothing but an infatuation in a girl fresh from the schoolroom then." Her voice softened. "And yes, I will marry you."

A grin cut dimples into his cheeks as he said, "Good. I was worried I'll have to confess our kisses to your father so he'd force your hand."

He bent to repeat the offense, swallowing her joking protest. Their lips came together unerringly as they sealed a bargain to last a lifetime.

Chapter Forty

A cough sounded from the corridor, intruding on their moment. Barbara pulled away from Aubrey to see her father come to check on them, having forgotten until this moment how she'd never closed the door.

Lord Whitfeld raised both eyebrows. "I returned to make sure St. Vincent had not come to greater injury at your hand, Barbara, but I assume instead he's won his case. The banns need to be posted or license secured. The sooner the better from the looks of what I interrupted."

Aubrey gave her a pointed look, and Barbara laughed as her father proved the secondary plan would have been successful regardless of her stance.

"You're not surprised?" Barbara asked her father after a moment. His easy acceptance startled her when she'd put her poor parents through so much.

Lord Whitfeld gave her both a smile and a wink. "Whatever your lips said, or refused to say, your heart had chosen before you left your uncle's dwelling. We are neither so blind nor ignorant not to see it. And you are not so foolish as to deny the truth when face to face with the man in question."

She glanced at Aubrey, and meeting his gaze, lingered there for a moment. Her father had understood what she'd been too mixed up to admit. "You have no objection then?"

"Your lord has already sought my permission, which was gladly given once I learned where he'd chanced upon you. And might I say, I appreciated your determination." The last was to Aubrey, who only shook his head in response.

"However, you do need to inform the others before we make any announcements."

"It is only fair," Barbara said, not looking forward to the meetings she'd be facing.

"Perhaps I should sit in on these meetings. After all, I wouldn't want sight of your duke to change your mind." Aubrey struggled to maintain a somber expression, but his eyes gave him away as they always would.

Barbara put a hand on his arm as though to restrain him. "I think the meetings will be awkward enough without the victor lurking in the room, but you have nothing to worry about. These others only understood how to appreciate a frivolous girl."

Aubrey barked a laugh and snaked his arm around her waist to pull her firmly against his side. "Whereas it takes a true fool to lay claim to her once the frivolity has been stripped away."

"Your virtues are showing again," Barbara told him with a chuckle.

Her father shook his head. "I'll expect both of you at the breakfast table shortly, but I know when three is too many, and I think you deserve a moment to celebrate having captured a wild heart, St. Vincent."

"You might as well call me by my first name. I plan to be part of your family for a long while." Though Aubrey spoke to her father, his gaze stayed linked with hers.

The door closed with a solid thump as her father left, given them privacy. Barbara hardly noticed as Aubrey bent to claim her lips once more. Georgiana had been right after all. Kisses were wonderful things, and she planned to enjoy her full share.

A Note to Readers

Thank you for reading *A Country Masquerade*. I hope you have enjoyed the story and spending time with the characters old and new to the *Uncommon Lords and Ladies* series. Many will find themselves starring in later works, beginning with Barbara's cousin Georgiana.

Would you like to know when my next book is available? You can sign up for my newsletter at http://margaretmcgaffeyfisk.com to be kept up to date with my publishing.

Can I enlist your help in spreading the word about *A Country Masquerade*? The best way to do so is through writing a short book review and posting it on online retailers, reader sites, and/or on your blog. I appreciate all reviews, positive or negative. All I ask is you give your honest opinion.

If you'd like to read an excerpt from *Beneath the Mask* (the first book in *Uncommon Lords and Ladies*), or one of *Safe Haven*, a steampunk sweet romance, please continue reading.

Beneath the Mask

Excerpt from

Uncommon Lords and Ladies, Book One

(Available in Print, eBook, and Audiobook)

In the flash and glitter of the Regency Era, a young noblewoman craves to dance not in the ballroom but on stage, blending music, movement, and soul. Will these scandalous dreams destroy her family, or gain her a loving patron?

"So? Which one is it?"

Jasper turned toward his friend and shot Aubrey a heated look. "I think Baker's boy has the best whip hand I've seen for a while. Thatcher, though, can take corners with no regard for the innocent traffic. That alone will shave minutes from his time."

Aubrey jerked the monocle out of Jasper's hand. "You know full well that's not what I'm talking about. Your mother gave you a month to choose a bride, and today's your last day. Who have you chosen?"

Pushing to his feet, Jasper tossed down enough to cover their light lunch, suddenly having lost interest in seeing the end of the cart race. "What does it matter? They're all much the same. Not a single real thought to spare among them. The same teachers, the same dressmakers … they are block prints on the fabric of my life."

Aubrey wisely kept silent as they strode through the streets of London, passing the places frequented by their mothers and heading for those where they'd best not be identified by any of the female persuasion.

Finally, Jasper stopped outside a pub catering mostly to sailors fresh off the naval boats. "I couldn't choose," he said, the irritation clear in his voice. "I couldn't debase myself further by actually considering any of them."

"You're letting your mother choose a wife?" Aubrey asked, horrified. "This is the woman you'll spend the rest of your life with. Can't you find the slightest interest?"

Jasper reached out to clasp his friend's shoulder. "If I do this to please my mother, let her be pleased. If I chose one of them and she turned out to be a hag, I'd have no one to blame but myself."

A surprised laugh burst from Aubrey as he shook his head. "You're an original, Jasper. Never would have thought it out that way, but you're right. She turns out horrible, and you'll be able to wind your mother around your little pinkie. I can see you now, 'I did it all for you, Mother, and see what I'm left with?'"

Pivoting Aubrey so he could push his friend through the door, Jasper grinned. "It's not like I'll see much of her anyway. I'll just whelp a child or two on her and spend my days here in London while she lords over one of my grand properties. We may not have the fancy titles, but my family is loaded."

"A caution, my friend. Your mother's like as not to choose some impoverished earl or duke to bind to the family. I can see her now, going over huge lists to find the candidates who have more title than coin. Oh, and don't forget, those without male line entitlements. If she can't raise her own standing or yours, she'll be sure to raise that of your get. Just imagine when your lady's father passes away and your oldest son outranks you."

Jasper signaled the barkeep. "Two porter, my good man," he called before answering Aubrey. "Does it matter? Her title means nothing once she's my wife. I will have charge of her and all her doings. She'll stay in the country as I will it, and the children with her."

Aubrey looked dubious, but said nothing further as their tankards arrived.

"Just think," Jasper added, laughter gleaming in his eyes, "You're next for the marriage bed. I'm sure your mum could happily find some chit to slip between your sheets."

Choking on his stout, Aubrey glared at Jasper. "I'll do the choosing," he finally gasped out. "I'm not leaving my future to chance as you seem willing to do."

Jasper took a long draw of his beer then wiped the foam from his upper lip. "At least you have a year or two before your mission is proved foolhardy. I tell you, there are no women among that gaggle of girls. Enjoy what time you have of freedom."

The door slammed open and a group of seamen staggered through the entrance, this obviously not the first stop in their day's revelry.

"Come, let's go find a more hospitable location to take our rest." Jasper strolled to the bar to pay his bill, unwilling to keep a tab at every place he went like most of his class. The smell of sea salt only brought back memories of what he could have been had either of his brothers survived to sire an heir. He'd been promised the Royal Navy since he wore short pants, but fate had a way of changing things.

"There's a dance troupe not far from here," Aubrey offered. "I've heard they're solid if not exciting."

Jasper forced his mouth to smile. "Solid describes much of my sorry life now. I might as well add another to the mix. It'll give us something to pass the time until we head to White's to check the results and collect my winnings."

Aubrey punched Jasper in the shoulder. "You're so sure of winning?"

"I always do."

A wave of his hand and a hackney pulled up next to them. "Give him the directions, Aubrey, and we'll go see these solid dancers of yours."

"**H**e's from a good family with a title even if you'll bring in a stronger one. Lord Pendleton is a baron, not some tradesman buying his way into nobility."

Daphne slipped into the sitting room, wondering how to ask her mother to let her dance. She'd waited for the best moment to raise it, but Monsieur Henre was due back this very day, and she wanted to be able to tell him so. At least they seemed happy now with the question of Grace's marriage resolved.

"And money, dear, don't forget his family properties are exceedingly well managed. The boy goes wherever he likes just so the men can badger him about husbandry and farming. I'll be taking him around our properties myself."

Their mother laughed, gently stroking Grace's arm. "She doesn't care about husbandry, my love. She cares about the husband she'll spend the rest of her life with."

"And titles make the man?" their father asked in a gruff voice.

Rising from the settee, Lady Scarborough wrapped her arm through his. "Of course, my love. Titles are the icing on a delicious snack cake. If you hadn't a title to speak of, my parents would never have let me meet you, much less marry, and see how that turned out."

He patted her on the cheek, his smile so full of love, Daphne almost envied them, but she had more important things to do with her life than marry well.

"Exactly my point, dearest. We have to make sure the boy meets our criteria and then love will come in time."

"He's a man, not a boy," Grace muttered, her gaze modestly entangled with her twisting fingers.

Both parents turned to stare at their eldest daughter, surprise painted on their faces.

"How would you know?" her mother asked.

Grace looked up, her smile a fragile thing to see. "I've seen him at the Mackeley's ball. He didn't seem all that interested in any of us. I wonder that he wants to marry at all."

"Oh posh, no young man wants to be married. They don't understand just how wonderful it is until they experience the bliss themselves. Don't give it a second thought." Mother came to sit next to Grace again, pulling her eldest daughter's hands into her lap. "They see all they'll lose and none of what comes to them. Even my Thomas was reluctant at first, and see what we've become." She sent their father a look.

Daphne felt the tension between them as easily as she'd felt the love. Grace worried them. So much depended on her sister marrying well, but they wanted her to be happy.

Her request no longer seemed favored, so Daphne rose, trying to slip out of the room while they hadn't yet noticed her.

"Daphne?"

She froze as her father called her name.

"I hadn't seen you there. Do you have something to tell us?" Her father tugged out his gold pocket watch and checked the time before looking toward her again.

Daphne squirmed a little, trying to come up with something else she could say instead of begging to be allowed to dance professionally.

Father laughed. "Out with it, my girl. Ask any boon you want on this day. With Grace's future secure, there's little I'd withhold."

She moved to her father's side, pulling him into a hug. "You are the best father in the world," she whispered, meaning every word.

He put his hands on her shoulders and pushed her far enough away so he could meet her gaze. "Now I know something important is dancing around in your little head. Come on and tell your dear father. I never did like to wait on surprises."

Daphne took a deep breath before speaking, dragging her courage about her. "Dancing is right. Monsieur Henre says I'm really good. I'm better than any of his other pupils." The words burst out of her in a rush, then she paused, waiting to see their effect.

Her father mussed her hair and smiled. "As it should be when you do something you love. I'm glad you enjoy dancing so much, but you have to remember there's more to life than just that."

"Not for me," she said, shaking her head. "I want to dance for always." She twirled in a circle, showing them a bit of the routine she'd been practicing.

Catching her outstretched hand, her father moved her through the complicated steps of a line dance until they both sank into chairs, exhausted.

"She definitely gets the dancing from you, Thomas. I've never had quite the balance to pull it off."

Too tired to move, he waved to Mother with a limp hand. "You have grace in other ways that make up for the dancing."

"I had Grace some nineteen years ago. And now I'm planning to let her grow up."

They all laughed at the wordplay as Grace rose to ring the servant's bell for drinks.

Only when they'd sipped lemon tea and nibbled on cucumber sandwiches did Daphne remember her purpose in coming to this room. "Father," she said, catching his attention. "I really am a fine dancer."

He smiled. "I'm sure you are. As your mother said, you come by it honestly."

"I could do so much more than be graceful at my sister's wedding," Daphne said, unsure how to ask.

"Oh, dear." Lady Scarborough put down her cup and rushed across the room. "You don't think we won't take care of you as well, do you? I know it's all been about Grace this season, but you're growing up as well. Don't think we haven't noticed. Once Grace is settled, she and I will give you the best coming out ever seen. Won't we, Grace?"

Her sister nodded, fingers tense around the handle of her teacup. "I'll do whatever I can," she murmured.

"There. You see? Nothing to worry about. You just keep up with your lessons, and we'll find a man worthy of your love as soon as Grace is settled."

Daphne clenched her fists, angry at their preoccupation. "I don't want to marry," she declared. "I want to perform."

The room fell silent. Even Grace seemed stunned by her pronouncement.

Daphne wished the words unsaid, ashamed not of their content but of how she'd offered them. "Monsieur Henre says I'm good enough. He says I'm as good if not better than the dancers in his troupe."

She leapt out of her chair and went down on her knees before her father. "If you would just give your blessing, I could dance for real. I could become famous."

"Get up off the floor," her mother demanded. "More like infamous. What do you think the ton would say if my daughter joined the performers?" The way she said the last word made it sound dirty.

Daphne got up, but only to round on her mother. "They're nothing more than hardworking artists. You wouldn't condemn a poet for living for his art. Why keep me from mine?"

"Daphne Louise, you will respect your mother and honor her word. You are not to make a spectacle of yourself in front of strangers. It's not fitting."

She quailed a bit under her father's firm stare, but tried to stand her ground.

"I had no idea what foolish ideas that Frenchman instilled in her, Thomas. I'll not have him in this house again."

Daphne turned to face her mother, horrified. "You can't," she wailed. "I'll do anything."

Her father took hold of Daphne's shoulders and turned her back to face him. "You're a young woman now. Another year and your mind will be filled with thoughts of a husband and children. I take full responsibility for letting it go this far, but with delaying your coming out for Grace, and your mother being so busy, it seemed a fair exchange at the time. I should have paid more attention when I knew you mastered the formal dances, along with your other studies, long ago." He sighed and shook his head. "It's time to grow up, my dear. To take on adult interests. I know it seems harsh now, but you'll come to understand once you're out in society. Some things are just never done."

She raised trembling fingers to her mouth, water gathering in her eyes as her world tore apart. "I'll never understand," she cried. "Never."

Daphne pulled free of her father's hold and raced through their townhouse until she reached the nursery that had been her home every time they'd come up to London. She threw herself down onto her bed and stared blind-eyed at the ceiling. Never before had she felt so angry, so lost.

Purchase a copy at your local bookstore or preferred online vendor.

Safe Haven
Excerpt from
A Victorian Steampunk Sweet Romance
Prequel to *The Steamship Chronicles*
(Available in Print and eBook)

Sworn to protect her sister from unjust laws in steam-driven Victorian England, Lily's wayward heart settles on the one man she cannot have: a police officer.

"So, Madam, can you describe the mechanical?"

Henry Stapleton tapped his charcoal stick against a piece of paper, keeping the notebook angled away from the housekeeper. He'd learned, when he first joined the police force, where his uniform might not win him answers, the appearance of writing would.

After all, the staff had been trained for generations to bow before nobility, and only the upper class could write.

The housekeeper wrung her hands so strongly he feared she'd strip the flesh from her bones. "He'll blame us, Sir. I swear none of the staff put a hand on the cursed thing. Only brings the attention of Naturals, it does, having those contraptions in the house."

She leaned in close to add, "He thinks it makes 'im big. Important like. He goes showing it off to everyone. No wonder it's gone missing." She glanced around, features pinched as though worried she'd been overheard.

Henry swallowed a sigh. He'd joined the police force to help people in need, not track down rich men's toys. Some family legacy he followed. Though if it took the edge of fear from this woman and the rest of her staff, at least he'd have accomplished something.

Their master should be whipped for how he clearly treated those in his employ, but it wouldn't happen. The laws had yet to catch up to this new world where blacksmiths could put out steam-driven mechanicals and the new industry raised country merchants to the big houses. His father would have rejoiced to see this come about in his lifetime, if he'd lived to see it, without noticing the troubles it brought.

"Don't you worry, Madam. We'll find your master's mechanical, and who's behind this rash of thefts."

"Thank you, Officer Henry. Thank you." She grabbed his hand and clutched it between her pillow breasts. "I can't tell you how much safer we feel with you about."

"Just doing my job." Henry extracted the hand and touched the rim of his top hat in a half salute. "I'd best get back to my team."

He'd gained a reputation as the voice for the small folk despite his bloodline, but hearing her, a soul would think he did so much more than take their word as evidence. His grandfather had hidden political fugitives. His father helped bring about laws to protect the weak. Just listening seemed too little an action to win such approval.

He turned away before his frustration caused him to lash out at the one who didn't deserve it, but she caught hold of his arm and pulled him back.

"You said a rash of thefts, Officer Henry. You don't think …" Her fingers tightened even more as she failed to bring forth the rest of the question.

A short laugh escaped before Henry could corral it. "Mum, we haven't seen a Natural on the loose in over a year, and never down here in these parts. Mechanical contraptions are expensive. Those that have them tend to wave the devices about just asking for them to be lifted. You said so yourself. More like some enterprising fellow is taking them up on the challenge and reselling the mechanicals for a steep profit."

She released him with a laugh of her own, one hand pressed to her bosom. "Oh, Officer Henry, I'm sure you have the right of it. The stories one hears are enough to send terror through the stoutest of hearts, but not yours. No sir, not Officer Henry. I'll keep you no longer. You'll find the fellow and bring him to justice for all of us."

"My team and I will have this wrapped up in no time," he said, squashing the inappropriate hope that this time it would be something more than just a common thief. He strode down the steps to join the other officers where they'd gathered in the street.

Catching a Natural would make a difference to more than just the wealthy. Naturals posed a real danger to the people with their wild contraptions running about harming folks. He'd seen them in the asylum — all new officers were required to do a stint there. Pale, wraith-like beings only vaguely showing their human beginnings.

That stint was the first time he'd left his grandfather's pocket watch behind since he inherited it. No metal objects of any kind were allowed within, but one of the attendants had been kind — or cruel — enough to demonstrate the reason behind the rule. Memory of those grasping hands and mewling cries haunted his dreams for weeks afterward.

"So, Sergeant, what you think it is this time?" Fitz asked, his words thick with the Irish brogue he'd shown no signs of losing.

Henry shrugged. "What else? A bunch of wealthy men showing off their contraptions to any comer." He glanced from one to the other of his five men, settling at last on Parson, a Scot from upcountry. "Tell me any of you found something more interesting."

They each waved their own notebooks, filled with random marks because none could read or write beyond their names, but those they interviewed never knew the difference.

"You know I can no more read those scratches than tea leaves." Henry said with a laugh. "Ken, what do your instincts tell you?"

Nicknamed for his ability to sense the truth behind almost anything, the skinny man looked nothing like a police officer, but Ken had better instincts than any other Henry had seen. Other officers had tried to pull him to their teams, but he'd refused each time, something that brought Henry a measure of relief.

Tugging on his forelock as though the night-dark strands held the meaning of the universe, Ken stared at the ground while his mind churned through the possibilities.

The others waited patiently despite the chill of late fall. Better patience now than wasting time Ken could have saved them.

Henry stamped his feet and wound his scarf tighter around his neck.

"Sergeant, it doesn't make sense. Not so many. What thief is so skilled, and yet so foolish, as to keep coming back to the same place?"

Ken's words brought a tension to every one of the six of them, the implications what an officer longed for — and dreaded.

Henry's heart beat faster. Here he could make a difference on par at least in part with that of his ancestry. Only a matter of time before the Natural started building mechanical monsters to terrorize everyone regardless of social position. The monsters got their name from a natural affinity to all things mechanical while their nature could not have been further from the meaning of that word.

Lily smoothed away the wrinkles from where her fingers had clenched on her best skirt.

The solicitor continued his list of her father's debts, unaware of how his words condemned her, and condemned her sister Samantha most of all.

Mister Cooper, Lily's employer and a friend of the family, shot her a concerned look, but she forced a smile on her face and tried to listen.

The solicitor paused to draw in a breath, his sunken eyes blinking at her and Mister Cooper as though just becoming aware of their presence. "Now it's not as bad as all that," he said, rubbing his temple with one hand. "You have a good job and a place to stay thanks to Mister Cooper here. I know it's not what you'd hoped, especially with having to sell your family home, but it's not like you'll be sent to debtors' prison."

Lily just sat frozen with her hands once again tangled in the rich fabric she'd never be able to replace, not here nor on the Continent where they'd been planning to go.

"Lily, you're a hard worker, don't think I haven't noticed in all these years you've been working at my bakery." Mister Cooper sent her a kindly smile, a fatherly one when she had no father left. "I should have done this sooner, but there was the age to consider what with you being younger than some, and I didn't know what you'd planned once your inheritance cleared."

He paused, and the solicitor waved a hand as though to encourage him to go on.

They thought they had it all figured out. That the promotion Mister Cooper had hinted at for a year now, even when her father still breathed, would solve all her problems.

"It's about time I spend less of the day at the bakery anyway, or so my housekeeper, Edna, tells me. I'll put you in charge of the place, with a reasonable increase in your pay, of course."

The solicitor clasped his hands together and grinned a little too enthusiastically, showing he hadn't been as immune to the impact of his accounting as she'd thought. "So it's all settled then. And a pretty girl like you from a respectable background, and with a good job, well, you should soon find a husband to care for you so you're not out on your own."

Lily rose, yards of cloth falling into place to hide her trembling knees. "Thank you, both of you. I'm sure I'll do just fine. I'd best get back to the bakery."

She was happy to hear the firm tone she used on the youngest of bakery girls issue from her lips. They meant well, but she could not take their kindness any more, not when they knew nothing of her sister, or rather both thought Sam had died at a young age. It had been the only way to protect her, but Lily never expected to face this alone. Her father had been healthy and strong despite all the troubles life sent his way.

Mister Cooper laughed once. "As you see, she's already been in charge, and we all know it. I should have promoted you long ago, but never expected ..."

His face turned the color it did when pulling hot bread from the oven, and his words stopped.

Lily put out a hand to brush his arm lightly. "I know you didn't, Mister Cooper. None of us did. But you've been such a help in these past six months since Father died, even before that truth be told. He couldn't have chosen a better friend."

She swallowed hard against the threat of tears. She couldn't afford to give in to her grief, not now, and not ever. All their plans to take Sam to the Continent, to one of the few places she would be safe, destroyed in a single, horrifying moment. If only her father hadn't gone to Dover on business that morning. If only the carriage had held true. If only he'd been more frugal.

None of that could be changed now, so it didn't matter. She had to be strong for her sister. She had to figure out some way to fix this. They'd been counting on the inheritance, especially once it became clear hiding Sam at her lodgings was too risky. The abandoned stables Lily had found would not be comfortable once the winter's grip took hold, but now it would have to serve until the passenger ships started running again in the spring.

"He was a good man," Mister Cooper said, clearly not for the first time. "We shall all miss him."

Lily stifled a bark of laughter, knowing it would take her too close to hysteria and be something she could never explain to these two gentlemen. A good man for sure, and a better father than any others knew. These two would have had him clapped in chains for the choices he'd made, her along with him.

"Come, Lily. Let's not dwell on what we can't change. There's baked goods to be tending." Mister Cooper tucked her hand around his arm and turned to the door, his determined cheerfulness one of the things she'd always liked about her father's friend, a bright light in the gloom that threatened to swallow her family whole.

"Wait," the solicitor cried, "there's more."

Lily shivered, her body unable to mask the upset a moment longer.

"No, no." The solicitor rounded his desk, arms waving as though to wipe her fear away. "Don't you worry. Nothing bad. The debts are paid."

She focused on that fact with all her might, pushing aside the awareness that besides the single trunk of clothes she'd been allowed to take, everything else was gone. Every memento of her mother, every bit of inheritance from her father, the paintings, carpets, and statuettes that had decorated their home, all sold at auction. Even the toys she and Sam used to play with were gone, vanished just like both parents: one in childbirth and the other to a carriage accident.

"It's just I almost forgot what with all the bad news today. Your father had a single request about his belongings in the unlikely event of his early death. He asked that his journals be saved for you. They have only sentimental value I'm sure, not that I pried into his personal thoughts mind you, but they would have fetched nothing at auction."

He kept on about how little value the journals had, but his words became a blur as she tried to comprehend what he was saying.

Not until he placed the seven leather-bound diaries into her hands did she accept what he gave her. Tears sprung unbidden to fall on the top edges as she clutched this tangible piece of her beloved father to her. A sharp image of her father bent over these very books to record his thoughts came to her, a vision she'd seen every night as far back as she could remember. Within these pages, she'd find her father's voice restored to her and to Sam so they could keep his memory fresh and know him better even than when he still lived.

"There now, no need to fall to pieces."

The solicitor, when she raised watery eyes to look upon him, seemed flustered and actually backed away from her.

This time Lily did laugh, a small hiccup of sound as her lips spread into the first genuine smile since entering his tidy office. "Thank you for these. It means so much to have something to remember him by."

The man nodded twice, enthusiasm replacing a fearful expression. "Glad I could give you something. Sorry it couldn't be more, but what with his debts ..."

Lily waved off further words with just her fingers, unwilling to chance dropping her father's journals. "No need. I understand better than you know. Thank you again for his words."

She spun for the door once again, but now her steps had more eagerness than weight. For the first time since her father's death, she felt close to him instead of abandoned.

Purchase a copy at your local bookstore or preferred online vendor.

About the Author

Margaret McGaffey Fisk is a storyteller whose tales often cross genres and worlds to bring events and characters to life. She currently writes romance, science fiction, and fantasy but will go wherever the story takes her. Foreign Service brat, data entry clerk, veterinary tech, editor, manager, and freelance programmer are among the roles she's lived, giving depth to the cultures and people that form the heart of her works. As her website is titled, she offers tales to tide you over.

She'd love to hear from you through any of the contact points listed on her website (http://margaretmcgaffeyfisk.com/), or you can subscribe to her newsletter for release announcements, snippets, and other news:

http://margaretmcgaffeyfisk.com/subscribe-to-my-newsletter/

Other Places You Can Find Her:
Twitter: http://twitter.com/Marfisk
Facebook: https://www.facebook.com/MargaretMcGaffeyFisk
Google Plus: https://plus.google.com/+Margaretmcgaffeyfiskauthor

Other Works by Margaret McGaffey Fisk

Shafter – Seeds Among the Stars: Spacers, Book One (science fiction)

Living hand-to-mouth in the tunnels below the colony of Ceric, most shafters fear the open sky, but nothing can bind Trina to the darkness once she sees the stars.

Secrets – The Steamship Chronicles, Book One (steampunk)

A Victorian adventure with steam, sail, and troublemaking sentient machines. When a sheltered girl with an extraordinary, if wild, gift is cast into the world, her self-control is all that stands between the dreams of a ship engine and the lives cradled in the wooden hull.

Forged (fantasy)

A swordsmith's unappreciated apprentice puts her career, and even her life, on the line to confront a knight with a deadly secret.

Visit http://margaretmcgaffeyfisk.com for more information about these and other titles.

Acknowledgements

The first thanks must go out to my loyal readers who fell in love with *Beneath the Mask* and asked for more. Thank you for taking the chance on my debut novel and for conveying your wishes to me. I hope Aubrey and Barbara lived up to your expectations despite being very different people from Daphne and Jasper.

My husband again offered his encouragement, proofing, and general support to make this book happen, as did several other members of my family and friends. I appreciate the time and energy each of them gave whether it was listening to me work through plot points or helping refine the back cover text to entice you to pick up *A Country Masquerade*, helping me with the final steps before I could put the story into your hands.

Last but not least, thank you Patrick Lynn Smith for the beautiful cover gracing this book.

Welcome to A Conspiracy of Authors

What is the conspiracy?

We are a group of authors conspiring to bring readers excellent material by making our work accessible to as many people as possible. We feature fiction and nonfiction and both short and long publications, mostly in electronic format.

http://aconspiracyofauthors.com/

www.ingramcontent.com/pod-product-compliance
Lightning Source LLC
Chambersburg PA
CBHW030611120726
47904CB00006B/1858